I0547731

Although born in New York, Tara has called Florida, home for over 30 years. Whether journaling or creating stories, writing has always been her outlet. Her home is her sanctuary and she is most complete when surrounded by family.

Dedication

I would like to dedicate this book to my husband, David, daughter, Natalie, and mother-in-law, Carolyn, who bring me great joy. Without your support, this book would still be sitting in my nightstand drawer.

Tara Johnson

MORAL INVENTORY

AUSTIN MACAULEY PUBLISHERS™

London • Cambridge • New York • Sharjah

Ordering Information:
Quantity sales: special discounts are available on quantity purchases by corporations, associations, and others. For details, contact the publisher at the address below.

Publishers cataloging in publishing data
Johnson, Tara.
Moral Inventory

ISBN 9781641820240 (Paperback)
ISBN 9781641820257 (Hardback)
ISBN 9781641820233 (E-Book)

The main category of the book—Fiction / General

www.austinmacauley.com

First Published (2018)
Austin Macauley Publishers Ltd™
40 Wall Street, 28th Floor
New York, NY 10005
USA

mail-usa@austinmacauley.com
+1 (646) 512-5767

Acknowledgment

I would like to give God the credit for giving me the courage to share this story with others. A story which parallels with my own life.

Chapter 1

This was ridiculous. Elizabeth had plans to go see her boyfriend, and now her mom was trying to screw it up by saying she wanted to go to some family counselor. She knew her mom did not approve of her 23-year-old boyfriend, Marcus. Sure, she was only 17, but they had been together a year, and there was nothing she could do to stop them from seeing each other.

"I don't want to go see a friggin' shrink mom!" she yelled. Usually if she got aggressive, her mom would back down. Today, however, she stuck to her guns.

"She is not a shrink, Elizabeth; she is a family counselor. Our home has been a war zone, and I think this counselor can help us to set household rules that we can both live with. Our appointment is in an hour, and then you can have the rest of the day to do what you want."

The desperation in her mom's eyes caused Elizabeth to waver. She figured she could get this over quickly and then head over to see Marcus. He would probably just be waking up when she got there because they had thrown another big party at his apartment last night. She felt cool being a part of that scene. Marcus dealt weed and coke, so as his girl, she never had to pay for it.

"Fine, let's go," she said.

The drive there was quiet, and Elizabeth had begun to think of how she could get the counselor to see things her way. She was quite manipulative when she wanted to be but knew she wouldn't mention her mom's drinking as a bargaining chip. The only time she had the guts to throw that in her face was when she herself was drunk, and then all the anger and rage just spewed out. They had been driving for over a half hour and Elizabeth didn't even recognize where they were. It was somewhere in Cape Coral, which was the city over from where they lived. It was very rural with only a house here and there.

They pulled into a driveway that led to what looked like a residence. She walked in brooding and barely acknowledged the woman who greeted her. She dug her hands in the pockets of her denim jacket and followed them into the room she was led to. Inside, there were chairs formed into a big circle and Elizabeth became outraged at the thought that this would be some kind of group session. She snapped her head up to accuse her mom of trickery when she finally realized that each window had a painted board blocking it.

What the hell is going on? thought Elizabeth.

"Did you bring her luggage, Ms. Grant?" asked the bitch who seemed to be running the show.

"Yes, it is in the car," Elizabeth's mom murmured.

They began to lead Helen to the door when Elizabeth found her voice and began yelling, "Where are you going, mom?" There was no mistaking the fear in her voice and now it was her mom's turn to almost give in.

Blocking her line of sight, the intrusive bitch said, "Elizabeth, I am Mrs. Stein and this is Helping Hands Rehab Center. Your mother brought you here because she really loves you and fears for your safety. You will be staying in our program now, where we will be able to treat you. Did you smoke pot this morning?"

"No," sneered Elizabeth.

"Your jacket smells of marijuana."

"Whatever," replied Elizabeth.

As her mother turned to leave, she told Elizabeth that she loved her and that was why she was doing this.

"Fuck you, I never want to see you again!" screamed Elizabeth.

When her mom had left, two teenagers who were part of the staff escorted her to the bathroom. They told her that they had to be sure that she was not carrying any drugs on her and asked her to remove her clothing. She was trying so hard to not act scared, but the tears that ran down her face betrayed her. Luckily, she had not brought anything illegal with her and she was promptly brought to another room filled with kids of her age. The room was barren except for rows of church pews and a few taller stools up front. There was an older man speaking as Elizabeth was led to the front row. Within minutes, she realized that he was some kind of psychologist, and although she was still shell shocked as to what was going on, she could not help but keep eye contact when he looked her way. There was nothing good looking about him with his receding hairline and glasses, but he seemed to command attention and got it. He was addressing peer pressure and what causes us to give in to it. He spoke to the group as if he really understood what even our parents couldn't. Our day to day problems and how turning to drugs and alcohol was not the solution.

Elizabeth's mind began to wander throughout the rest of the day about how she had wound up here. Not that actual day, but where her life had gone astray. Before she met Marcus, she was teaching at a local modeling school and beginning to get some acting jobs. Within weeks of meeting him, she was not only fired from the school for showing up late too often but had quit high school as well. She was brought back to reality as the group leader announced who would be going home with who. It had been explained to her that she would be placed with a family who lived a minimum of 15 miles from her home to ensure that she would not try to run. The homes had alarms set as well that would detect a door or window opening. She was assigned to a girl named Marie who was on "Stage three" of the program.

Stage one meant you had to stay with other families. Stage two allowed you to go back home, but then you would have other girls from the facility stay with you a couple of days per week. Stage three meant you could sign back up to go to the school that was closest to the rehab center. Stage six was the highest, and then you could even become a youth counselor.

Marie and her family seemed nice enough, but Elizabeth couldn't help wanting to be with her mom. If she had been honest with herself, she would have had to admit that it was only because she was trapped. She hadn't spent more than three days per week at her mom's house for the past six months.

It was obvious that Marie's family had money the minute they entered a large gated community in Naples; the city just south of Fort Myers. Of course, the Mercedes she had been riding in for the last hour hinted at their wealth as well. Upon entering the house, Elizabeth met Marie's younger brother Eric. He seemed kind of

10

shy as they sat down to dinner, but Elizabeth had him giggling in no time as she shared the story of how she and her brother had tried parachuting off their roof armed with a sheet when they were about seven-years-old. With wide eyes, he asked, "Did it work?"

"We fell like rocks," she said, and the whole family laughed. Elizabeth felt very warm inside and, peering at the four of them, could not understand how Marie could have gotten herself so mixed up when she had what seemed like the perfect family. Her own case, she could understand and, to her surprise, was asked to talk about it the next day at the center.

Chapter 2

Mrs. Stein was standing in the front room that held all the kids for group discussion. "We have all met Elizabeth Tartaglia who joined us at Helping Hands yesterday." She glanced at Elizabeth and said, "Today marks a very important day for you Elizabeth. A day where honesty will be rewarded with trust and dishonesty with a prolonged stay at Stage one." Elizabeth swallowed hard. "As angry as you may be with your mom right now, I trust that you will want to be joined with her again in the near future. I won't lie to you by saying that it will be easy, painless, or fast. No one has ever made it to Stage two in less than ten weeks."

"Ten weeks!" Elizabeth screamed in her head. "That's a lifetime." She was a pro at hiding her feelings and the passive look she gave Mrs. Stein was hopefully sending the message "big deal."

"I would first like you to tell us all of the drugs you have ever taken. You will then share this with your mother and other parents at the visitation dinner tonight." Mrs. Stein said.

"I have smoked pot and taken speed" said Elizabeth quickly. Too quickly, by the raised eyebrows of Mrs. Stein who replied with a curt "I will give you five minutes to write down <u>all</u> of the drugs you have ever taken."

When the five minutes were up, Elizabeth walked to the front of the room and handed her paper to Mrs. Stein who handed it back and asked her to read it aloud. With hands shaking, she read "I have used pot, speed, hash, cocaine, crack, acid, mushrooms, and valium." The shame and embarrassment she felt as all eyes were on her was unbearable. To hear herself say out loud, the drugs that had such an impact on her. Had she been in a room full of her party buddies she would have stated them almost braggingly but in this group, it made her realize how sick it sounded. There were no longer any drugs in her system to help numb her, to help her feel in control. What started as a few sobs soon escalated to full blown wails. All of her failures were floating in her brain along with broken promises and regret. She suddenly felt an arm wrap around her and then another. Before she knew it, the whole group had surrounded her murmuring their understanding.

"Can you try and tell us why you are crying Elizabeth?" asked Mrs. Stein.

"Well," sniffed Elizabeth "as I was listing the drugs I have used I kept seeing flashes of the things that I have lost because of them.

"Like what?" Mrs. Stein asked

"I won this modeling contest in town and got to go to the modeling school for free. They offered me a teaching job right after I graduated; I was the only student they asked. I had a class of my own and a few months later I met Marcus. I showed up late a couple of mornings because I was up late partying with him and I know I didn't show up looking professional. Some of the parents reported me and I was

12

fired. My class graduated a couple of weeks later but I wasn't even allowed to attend."

Shaking her head slowly, Mrs. Stein said, "That is disappointing, but do you see how with every action there is a reaction?"

"Of course, I don't blame the school at all. I just wish I could get it all back." The tears had returned and Elizabeth felt like she was on an emotional roller coaster.

As she got herself together, a youth leader named Paul spoke about that night's "Moral Inventory." It was a type of journal that was kept by each person and different topics were given each night. "Tonight, we are going to do something a little different. We usually write about events that took place as we were using drugs, but tonight I want you to think back on a memory of yourself when you were much younger. We are trying to go back to see what took place way back when, that may have contributed to our future need of drugs."

Although she was pleased with her little breakthrough today, Elizabeth wasn't so sure about how much she was going to tell the group in the future. She has spent so many years not wanting to appear weak and now these people just wanted her to share everything. She wanted to reach Stage two though, and this might help her get there quicker. Maybe she could just scratch the surface with them, tell just what she wanted to. They wouldn't know the difference, would they?

Chapter 3

Dinner turned out to be a pot luck affair. Each parent brought a dish they had prepared.

Elizabeth could smell her mom's spaghetti and meatballs before she even lifted the lid off the pot. Whenever mom would make a batch at home, she was sure to skewer the first two piping hot meatballs with a fork and hand them to her and her brother, Nicholas. Mom knew her meatballs were fabulous but would still look at them in anticipation of their reactions. It brought her happiness to hear their words of satisfaction. Their mother's happiness would only make a guest appearance and would be gone in no time but the kids were always hopeful that one day it just might take up residence.

Unfortunately, the only thing Elizabeth could concentrate on was how her mom was going to react to her confession tonight. Mrs. Stein had told her that she would speak before the dinner would be served. This was a huge relief because she was sure she would have thrown up had things been reversed.

Here we go, she thought to herself when she heard Mrs. Stein making her introduction on the microphone.

As Elizabeth approached the microphone, she caught her mom's eye, smiled sheepishly and took a deep breath.

"Hello, my name is Elizabeth Tartaglia and the drugs I have used in the past are: pot, speed, hash, cocaine, crack, acid, mushrooms and valium." There, she said it. Now to look at her mom again.

Helen was sitting up straight looking at her daughter; not in disbelief but rather like her worst fears had finally been confirmed. A small tear escaped, which she quickly blotted away with a tissue. She nodded to Elizabeth as if to say she understood her struggle.

"You may greet your mother now, if you wish Elizabeth," said Mrs. Stein.

Forgetting all the cruel words she had so recently said to her mother, Elizabeth raced to where her mother was seated and embraced her. She just wanted to go home with her right now. Leave this place and start all over again. She knew it was too late for that. There had been too many broken promises, too many lies on both their parts. If they had any chance of a real relationship again, they both had to work this program.

She made a promise to herself in that moment that she would begin tonight with the Moral Inventory assignment.

Chapter 4

Elizabeth was excited when she heard that she would be at Marie's house again tonight. As they sat in the car, she started talking about bands and music.

Marie quickly said, "We aren't allowed to talk about that."

"What do you mean?" Elizabeth replied.

"We aren't allowed to talk about songs and stuff from our past."

"Not even the Beatles?" she asked in astonishment. It wasn't like she had brought up Metallica or anything.

Marie giggled a little nervously, "No, now stop or I will have to report you in the morning." she said.

"Whatever," Elizabeth exclaimed. This school seemed determined to take everything away from them. They were not allowed to use makeup or hairspray. It was explained that it was all meant to humble them. The clothes that Elizabeth's mom had packed for her were atrocious. Something you would get at Goodwill, not the usual rock gear Elizabeth wore. Gone were the leopard pants, high heels and short skirts she was so accustomed to.

Journal writing time came way too fast. She tried to think of the first time she smoked pot and what made her try it. It didn't really seem like peer pressure, nobody had teased her into doing it. She had heard about how good it made you feel. She had liked the sound of that. Okay, so that meant she hadn't felt so good at the time and wanted something to fill the void. *What was her life like at that point?* she asked herself. She knew she had not felt comfortable in her own skin. She wore the flashy clothes but shrunk from the attention it brought to her from onlookers. She was left alone a lot with mom working and drinking and her brother running the streets. She guessed that was it; she had wanted something that would make her feel all right when she was alone. Her mind went to the past too often and she wanted to live in the now. So that is what she wrote.

With a sigh of relief, she closed the book and her eyes slowly followed suit. That night, Elizabeth dreamt about her childhood. Images flashed through her mind at a speed that barely allowed her to comprehend one memory before another came. It was her childhood where it all began.

Chapter 5
Winter, 1978

It was three weeks before Christmas and eight-year-old Elizabeth was trudging through the snow, trying to make her way home from school. One day, she could regale this "trudging home from school" story to her own children who would roll their eyes and say "Yeah, yeah, we know how much harder you had it growing up than we do."

Her brother, Nicholas, was nowhere to be found. *What else is new*, she thought. Her face lit up as the three-story apartment building came into view. Elizabeth's mom, Helen, had recently moved them to Hartford, Connecticut to be closer to her side of the family. Their dad was back in Florida, where they used to live together. Her eight-year-old mind couldn't grasp the whole situation and she felt split between both missing her dad and a sense of relief that he and mom weren't together anymore.

She climbed the stairs to the third floor and tried to turn the knob but the door was locked. She tried knocking lightly so as not to alert the floor below that she was locked out again. Too cold to hang out in the hall waiting for her mom to wake up, she headed to the landlord's first floor apartment. "My mom fell asleep and locked me out by accident," she told the landlord. The woman's eyes told her how little she believed the story but nonetheless returned a moment later with the key.

Elizabeth opened the door slowly, not knowing what to expect. Days like this could find mom sleeping soundly on the bed with nothing out of place. Other times, a spilled purse and messy path would lead her to wherever her mom had fallen and decided to stay. Today was the "nothing out of place" day and Elizabeth could head straight to the bathtub to get the feeling back in her toes. She ran just the hot water at first and the numbness turned to painful prickles. Slowly this led to the heavenly feeling of warmth enveloping her whole body. She was little for eight, weighing less than 50 pounds, so this winter business really took a toll on her. After her tub, she wrapped herself in her fuzzy bathrobe and proceeded down the hall to check on her mom. Helen was lying on top of her blankets and was still wearing her shoes. Elizabeth watched for signs of breathing and when she saw her mom's chest rise and fall she could then breathe easier herself. It was a sad kind of funny when she thought of how she held her own breath as she watched to see if her mom was breathing. She removed her mom's shoes and then began walking through the apartment.

The new apartment was the biggest place she could ever remember living in. It took up the entire third floor with each of them having their own large bedroom. She loved her room with its princess bed and pretend kitchen. Her imagination could go wild, pretending her room was her own apartment or restaurant. The front room was great too. Its big bay windows overlooked the street below, sometimes to a scene she would rather have not witnessed. There were a few bullies in the neighborhood and she shivered with the memory of her brother screaming one day as they initiated him by rubbing his knuckles on a light pole until they bled. "Jerks," she said, shaking her head and retreating to the eight track player that would transport her to another world. She could spend hours listening to Barry Manilow, Dionne Warwick and Barbra Streisand. Music was very powerful to her even then. Some songs, while enchantingly beautiful, still left Elizabeth feeling incredibly lonely while others like "Do You Know the Way to San Jose" had her digging through her mom's shoe boxes in the hall, strapping on some high heels and dancing to the beat.

These are the highs and lows that Elizabeth would feel throughout her childhood and teenage years. This is how she coped with how her parents' decisions affected her life. They say, no one gives a new parent a "how to" book, well they don't give kids one either. If they did in Elizabeth's case, Chapter One would begin with:

What to Do When Your Dad Hits Your Mom.
Five Easy Ways to Pick Your Mom off the Floor When She Passes Out.
What to Tell the Daycare Workers When They Have Been Closed for over an Hour and Your Mom Still Hasn't Picked You Up.

She was already forming a wry sense of humor. These kinds of thoughts just helped her laugh rather than cry. She knew her mom loved her but couldn't understand why the beer or wine seemed more important to her than she and her brother did.

The next day began with an overeager mom busying herself with breakfast. It was her way of making up for the day before. The kids were pros at pretending things were normal so no words of apology were necessary. Elizabeth had to admit her mom made wonderful breakfasts. This morning was biscuits and sausage gravy. Mom equated food with love, the result of marrying two Italian men. Unfortunately, she jumped out of the frying pan with the first one and into the fire with the second, Elizabeth's dad. Her first one, Frank, left mental scars; the second, physical ones.

"I want to talk to you kids about something" said mom between bites. "Your dad is coming here for Christmas and we are hoping to reconcile." She saw their puzzled faces at her last word and added "Daddy would like to be together again as a family."

"Does that mean we will go back to Florida?" asked Nicholas.

"We haven't gotten that far yet honey. Let's take it one day at a time" said mom. This was one of mom's new phrases she picked up from the AA meetings she infrequently attended. It seemed like they would sit through more meetings when she had gotten herself into some kind of trouble and then, when the coast was clear, she would stop.

Elizabeth was glad to have school as a diversion. She got her backpack ready and headed out, "coming Nicholas?" she asked.

"Yeah, hold on," he said. "Love ya, mom."

"I love you too kids. I'll see you after school," she said.

Elizabeth's school was a bit intimidating. It housed students from kindergarten through high school. She would be walking through the halls passing students that looked like giants to her. The cafeteria was in a basement which was something else she wasn't used to. Being underground made her feel a little trapped.

17

Throughout the day, she found herself thinking about what mom had told her at breakfast. *Why would mom want to be with dad again?* she thought. She remembered mornings after the separation when her mom would wake up to flat tires and missing license plates, courtesy of her father. Bouts of drinking, yelling, and crying were how her mom had dealt with things.

On the walk home from school, Elizabeth tried talking to her brother about things. "Do you think mom and dad could be happy together?"

Nicholas shrugged his shoulders to appear disinterested. "How should I know?" he said.

Keeping things bottled up was his way of coping and Elizabeth felt like there was no one to share her problems with. No one she could trust.

When they got back to the apartment, two huge boxes were waiting for them. "Christmas presents from dad," Elizabeth yelled when she saw the Florida return address.

"Can we open them now, mom?" asked Nicholas

Always the indulgent parent, mom said, "go ahead." She was beaming at their excitement. It had been awhile since she had seen them truly happy about anything. If she could bottle this moment, she would.

Elizabeth struggled with her large box and revealed a brand new organ. Her mom played the piano by ear. That meant she could not read sheet music but could listen to a song a few times and pick out the tune on the piano. Mom had shared the story about when she was little and her mom tried to have a piano instructor teach her how to read music. After several lessons, the instructor announced "She has a music block and will never learn how to read it." That was the end of mom's lessons. Elizabeth thought that her mom played beautifully and hoped to, one day, learn to play too.

"Cool," Nicholas yelled as he pulled a brand new bicycle out of his ginormous box. It was supposed to look like a chopper style motorcycle. It had a banana seat which was all the rage. Within minutes, he was outside tearing up the block.

These were the biggest presents they had ever received. Elizabeth wondered how her dad could afford them. She was too young to realize that there was the possibility that these were gifts bought out of guilt. That these were a form of apology on her dad's part.

"I know what I am going to make dad for Christmas," she said to her mom. "I am going to make a hand puppet." Her mom helped her get all of the materials together that she would need. She decided on a duck and took her time making it as perfect as possible. As she put the finishing touches on it, she wrote 'quak' inside its mouth (not realizing she had misspelled the word). She thought that her dad would think that was funny. She placed the puppet under the Christmas tree. The tree was one of the prettiest ones they had ever had. They had actually gone into the woods with one of mom's friends and chopped it down. Both she and Nicholas saw it at the same time and agreed, for once in their lives, that it was "the one." Elizabeth was convinced that this would be the best Christmas ever. It was Friday, so she had the whole weekend to finish decorating the apartment and go Christmas shopping.

18

Chapter 6

It was Saturday morning and something was up. Elizabeth could sense a change in the air. She was pretty sure mom had been crying in the night. When mom was like this, Elizabeth would work extra hard to be helpful and would do just about anything to get her mom to smile. There was a slight slur to her mom's speech. Not a good sign since they hadn't even sat down to breakfast yet.

"Don't worry about breakfast today, Mom. I have it covered." She ran to the cupboards and grabbed some bowls. Putting them on the table, she realized that she should forewarn her brother about mom's mood. As she skidded into his room, she found him already awake in bed, reading one of his many comic books.

Nicholas could feel the tension the minute his sister flew in his room. He loved Elizabeth but didn't like how she came to him all the time looking for help. What was he supposed to do about everything that was happening to them? He was just a kid. She was always trying to fix things that he would rather ignore.

"Nicholas, something is wrong with Mom" she said. "She's been crying. Let's make a special breakfast to cheer her up."

"I'm just going to grab some cereal and go to my friend's house."

"You can't leave us Nicholas!"

Just then, a crash of something breaking was heard. Both children ran to the kitchen to find their mom on her hands and knees simultaneously cleaning up glass and crying. She was getting nowhere with it for with each wracking sob, the dust pan would drop the glass particles back on the floor.

"Get dressed," mom said, "you're going to your Uncle Nate's house."

"What?" said Elizabeth, "But I thought we were going Christmas shopping today?"

This only triggered more crying before she screamed "I said get dressed!"

The kids knew this was not the mom to argue with so they did as they were told. The anxiety began to build for Elizabeth as they rode in the car. She tried to stop her imagination from going wild. Tried and failed. "Mom doesn't want us to live with Uncle Nate, does she? Maybe she doesn't want us anymore. Dad should have us before him, right?" and on and on her mind went. Mom's driving was not helping to calm her nerves either. *How the heck can she see with all that crying,* thought Elizabeth. She shut her eyes and wished to be out of the car.

19

Chapter 7

As they screeched into Nate's driveway, they could see he was already outside waiting for them. Helen did not get out of the car and sped away as soon as the children had shut their doors. Uncle Nate suggested they go for a walk to the corner store that was in his neighborhood. He wasn't sure how to proceed with these children that were obviously confused and frightened. The boy was trying hard to act untroubled but the girl's eyes were as big as saucers and she looked on the verge of tears.

What must be going through their heads? he thought to himself.

The corner store was small and the tinkling of a bell rang when they opened the door. The clerk knew Nate by name and asked who the kids were. After the introductions were made, the kids found comfort near the comic book section. Right now, Elizabeth was into the "Archie" comics while Nicholas preferred X-Men. To their surprise, Uncle Nate let them pick out two comics each and they still got to buy a Coke.

On the walk back, a chilly breeze struck them. Elizabeth tried to huddle closer to Nicholas, but in times like these he wanted no contact with anyone. He moved quickly away from her.

Uncle Nate finally spoke "You kids know that your mom seems very sad today, right?"

Duh," thought Nicholas in his head.

"Your mom just found out that your father has died. He is in Heaven now."

Silence…complete and utter silence. No crying, no screaming, no questions.

Uncle Nate continued, "Your dad had a heart attack and is in a better place right now." Man, he was botching this big time. How the hell could his sister throw this in his lap? Not only tell them their dad was dead but to lie about how he died. She was out trying to forget and he had the responsibility of these two young kids. He thought that for sure, Elizabeth would have cried and he had planned exactly how to hug her and tell her everything was going to be okay but he never got the chance. The child just walked like a zombie, no, more like someone completely numb. She was in shock. Helen would be back for them tomorrow and God only knew what they would do then.

Elizabeth whispered to Nicholas, "I think we are supposed to cry."

Nicholas just shrugged.

The walk back seemed to drag on forever. When they finally reached Uncle Nate's circular driveway, they were all physically and emotionally drained. Uncle Nate's house felt safe and warm to Elizabeth. He was a diabetic but still loved his sweets and could only have the sugar free variety. Elizabeth had grown to like them from her last couple of visits here.

Elizabeth thought that Uncle Nate must be rich. His house was spotless and every inch of it seemed to be decorated. She saw her school picture in a frame near the television. It was from her school they left in Florida. She remembered how hard it had been to smile that day for the picture. The night before she was awakened by the sounds of her parents arguing. Her dad's voice was slurring and she knew he had been drinking again. She had snuck out of her room and witnessed her dad choking her mom in the living room. She was too frightened to scream. Her dad had pushed her mom against the wall and began kissing her roughly. Her mom had tried to turn her face away but her father's hands kept her face pinned. She had been so confused because she thought that you kissed someone when you loved them, she had never seen it done in anger. How could looking at one picture bring back such strong memories? She never wanted to look at that picture again.

That evening, Uncle Nate set them up in a guest room with a huge bed. Elizabeth had to use a tiny step stool at the foot of the bed to climb up. The comforter was super fluffy and she lifted it over her head and pretended she was in a tent. She wanted to pray but did not quite know what to ask for, "Just bring mom back," she finally whispered.

"Quit hogging the covers," hissed Nicholas.

Poking her head out of the covers she asked, "Does dead mean we will never see daddy again?"

"Yeah," he replied and she heard the catch in his throat.

She felt the need to rescue again, oblivious to the fact that she was clinging to the same life preserver in the same stormy sea.

"Mom will know what to do. She just needed today to plan everything and Santa will be here soon too," she said.

No reply.

She closed her eyes and tried to escape into her own little world. She pictured a perfect Christmas, the smell of turkey filled the room, Christmas carols played, and the whole family giggled as they opened their presents. She was twirling around the room like a ballerina and had reached for her dad's present. As she turned to give it to him, the fantasy faltered. He was missing from the scene. She squeezed her eyes tighter trying to will him back. "Take your present, dad," she kept saying.

"I can't," he replied in her head. "I'm dead."

Without warning, the tears ran down her cheeks and onto the comforter she had just been admiring. Her chest was heaving as she gulped for air in between sobs. She curled into a fetal position and held her own hand clasping one with the other. That is when she felt Nicholas gently wrap his arms around her. He still did not speak but that was okay; she knew she wasn't alone.

They awoke to the sounds of cooking downstairs and the smell of frying bacon and fresh coffee. Elizabeth's mom allowed them to drink coffee and she preferred hers with both cream and sugar. She had stayed the night at a friend's house one time and asked for coffee the next morning. Her friend's mom smiled and jokingly asked, "How do you take your coffee?"

To which she had responded, "Cream and sugar please." The smile cracked as she realized Elizabeth was not joking and promptly gave her a coffee mug. It didn't end there because then her friend wanted coffee too which put the mother in a tough

21

position of saying 'no' to her own daughter while trying to justify why it was okay for Elizabeth. Needless to say, she was never invited to a future sleepover.

A knock on the door interrupted Elizabeth's reverie. Mom entered the kitchen with a look of defeat. She seemed to have aged overnight. Not that her mom was super young to begin with. Helen had Elizabeth when she was 40-years-old against the advice of her doctors.

The adults adjourned to another room to whisper about God only knew what. It wasn't long before mom came back into the room telling the children to give their Aunt and Uncle hugs and kisses goodbye.

Back in the car, Helen felt safe enough to talk to the kids because she didn't have to look them in the eye. Pretending to concentrate harder on the road than was necessary, she began her speech.

"I'm sorry for the way I left you yesterday. I needed time to think about what we should do next. Daddy will be buried back in New York because that is where his family is. We take a train tomorrow to attend the memorial service."

The kids remained quiet.

"How are you kids doing?" she asked.

"OK," they mumbled.

"Daddy's sister, Aunt Rosie, would like us to stay the night with her. She has been the only one in that damn family that has shown us any respect."

"What is a memorial service?" asked Elizabeth.

"It is where all the people who loved daddy can go to say goodbye." After a slight hesitation she added, "It will be an open casket so you will be able to see daddy. He will look like he is sleeping so there is no need to be frightened."

Reaching to the back seat, Helen opened her hand for Elizabeth to take. Feeling the warmth of the little hand gave Helen the strength to go on.

22

Chapter 8

Four weeks had gone by and Elizabeth was ready to petition her right to go to Level Two in the program. She had done everything they asked of her from cutting off six inches of hair to confiding intimate details of her life. She had shared her love of the theater and how acting played a huge role in her success in middle school. Her dreams of becoming a movie star and model seemed like they could be a reality again.

Seated in front of her was a panel of both her peers and staff members: Jason, Christy, Paul, and Teresa. She felt pretty comfortable with all but one, Paul. He just seemed to hate her from the start. Combatting every issue she tried to discuss. Well, she wasn't about to let him get in the way of her finally getting to go home.

"Can you share with us the reasons you feel you are ready to move on to Level two?" asked Christy.

"Well, I have never gone against anything or anyone in the program since I have been here," Elizabeth began, "I have participated in all the group classes. I know that doing drugs and drinking is wrong and I am ready to see my mom again."

"Bullshit," said Paul, "you have already admitted to being an actress and that is what I think you have been doing all of this time…acting. Nobody learns or changes as quickly as you claim to have. Nobody has reached Level Two in less than ten weeks and you waltz in here after four expecting some sort of favor."

"I'm not asking for any favors. I have earned the right to Level Two!" Aware that she was raising her voice she quickly calmed down. "I don't want my old life back; I have been living in a fog for the past two years and am looking forward to starting over. I have told you things that nobody else knows about. What more do you want?"

Christy's eyes had begun to tear as she listened to Elizabeth's plea. "You make some convincing points Elizabeth and believe me no one wants you to succeed more than I do." Wiping a tear away she added, "You remind me so much of myself when I started treatment. It took me 12 weeks to get to Level Two and to be honest, I still wasn't ready for it. Within the first two weeks of Level Two, I tried to run away and find my boyfriend. A boyfriend that was very much like yours: abusive, demanding, and a liar. I found him all right; at my best friend's house. Her bedroom to be exact. I was tossed back to Level One and had to start all over again. I don't want to see that happen to you."

"I appreciate what you have said," replied Elizabeth "but that was you. We are two different people. I don't care where my EX boyfriend is (lie), I never want to see him again (lie), I have never felt better than I do right now (lie). Don't you get it? I never stood a chance before." She had begun to yell but didn't care. She began to look at each of her peers letting them think they were gaining entrance into her very soul. This program had cleared her thinking as far as the drugs. She really did not want to go back to them, but still thought there may be a way to clean up her life but keep the same people in it. She was warmed up now, feeling the adrenaline surge through her body. Elizabeth wanted to win this game and Paul wasn't about to rob her of her victory. "My dad was murdered when I was eight. My mom got drunk all the time and I was put in two foster homes. One of the foster parent's sons tried to abuse me. I have been taken advantage of when I drank. My boyfriend beat me up. Nobody gave a shit about me until now, that is why I have excelled in this program. I want to go home," she began to cry, "I want to see my mom." Unaware that she had even stood up, Elizabeth dropped back into her chair continuing to whisper, "I want to see my mom."

The room was completely silent. As Elizabeth looked up, she saw that Mrs. Stein had entered the room without her knowledge. How long she had been standing there, she did not know. Mrs. Stein took a few steps towards Elizabeth, raised both her hands and began a slow clap. Before Elizabeth realized what was happening, the room erupted in applause. Mrs. Stein hugged Elizabeth and whispered, "You did good honey."

Elizabeth did not allow a smile to escape because this proved nothing. She would not smile until the decision was read at the end of the day. The applause was still ringing in her ears as she caught sight of Paul. He was the only one who had not stood up, the only one who did not applaud. He was peering at her with such directness that she was sure he could read her thoughts. She quickly looked away as the room began to settle down.

"I would like the staff to join me in the meeting room. We have much to discuss," said Mrs. Stein. She spun on her heel and exited the room. The others looked like little soldiers as they filed out. Each with a sense of purpose, each feeling the power they held regarding other people's lives.

It was 4 p.m. Elizabeth would know her fate in the next couple of hours. She was startled when Mrs. Stein reentered the room 30 minutes later. With a grim tone, she asked everyone to gather around her. "As you know, our staff votes unanimously or not at all. We have had a very heated conversation in the next room and some things have been brought to my attention, therefore we will dismiss you for the day and have a final answer first thing tomorrow morning. Elizabeth, I know you were expecting an answer tonight but what you are experiencing right now is real life."

"I understand," said Elizabeth "I can wait another day."

"Very well, class is dismissed. Elizabeth you will be staying with Trina tonight."

Shit, thought Elizabeth, Trina was the weird one. Now that was a family Elizabeth could understand wanting to use drugs to escape from. Trina's mom drove a long Lincoln but lived in a crappy part of town in a crappy house. The father seemed like the root of the problem. Although Trina had never mentioned it in class, Elizabeth saw the dad as a pervert. It was all in the eyes. She shivered at the thought of having to stay the night there but figured she had lived through worse. Talking herself through things was one of her strengths. "Let's do this," she said out loud.

Chapter 9

Upon entering the main therapy room the next morning, Elizabeth could pick up nothing in anyone's body language. Well, Paul had his usual scowl going so that meant nothing to her. She could hear her peers murmuring to each other of what they thought the final decision would be. She heard "no way" more than once.

Mrs. Stein called everyone to order and asked Elizabeth to stand in front of the staff as their decision was announced. Elizabeth had dressed with care that morning. She was not allowed makeup or hair care products but still pulled off what she hoped would appear to be a helpless young girl who had changed her ways look. Her short hair was tucked behind her ears, she had worn a simple dress that went just past her knees with a pair of black flats and she kept her eyes downcast.

"Elizabeth, I will not lie to you," Mrs. Stein began "not everyone wants to see you at Level Two this early in the game. They believe they would be setting you up to fail. I have been told that I am being made a fool of by you. I tend to disagree. I will not prolong the suspense any longer. You, young lady, are going home. You are officially on Level Two."

The tears were real this time, not rehearsed or forced. The relief that swept through Elizabeth's body could not be put into words. Never had the word "home" sounded so wonderful. "Can I call my mom?" asked Elizabeth.

"She has already been notified" Mrs. Stein answered. "Your mom is so very proud of you but more importantly you should be proud of yourself."

"I am. Thank you all. You won't regret it," Elizabeth said.

The rest of the day was a blur. Elizabeth sang during their chorus time louder and prouder than she ever had before. She led exercise class and had everyone begging for mercy but her energy did not wane. The thought of going home that night and sleeping in her own room was more than she could handle. How many times had she complained about their house that was built in the early 1900's? Now, she was so grateful to call it "home." The old saying "you don't know what you got, till it's gone" was really ringing true. Just as Elizabeth had the class begin to cool down from their grueling workout, the door opened and another student told her she was wanted in Mrs. Stein's office. Elizabeth turned to her friends and smiled. "This is it," she said.

As Elizabeth approached Mrs. Stein's office, she noticed the door was ajar and could hear mumbled voices inside. She knocked lightly before opening it further. Mrs. Stein rose to greet her and she noticed her mom sitting down. Her excited smile was met with downcast eyes from her mom and a faltering smile from Mrs. Stein. "Have a seat Elizabeth," said Mrs. Stein and her hand absently patted the seat across from her desk.

Elizabeth sat, suddenly aware of the tension in the room. *What the hell is going on?* she thought. She reached across to hold her mom's hand and that is when she heard her mom say "I am so sorry." *Oh, no*, thought Elizabeth, *oh no, oh no, oh no!*

Mrs. Stein cleared her throat and began. "In preparation of you returning home Elizabeth, we are required to do a random house check. In addition to your brother Nicholas having marijuana in his possession, there was alcohol present in the home which your mother has admitted as being hers. Therefore, I regret to inform you that you are no longer eligible to return home. It is obvious that this is not a healthy atmosphere to be in as a recovering addict. Until your brother has been removed from the home and your mother has attended several AA meetings to show she can be trusted, you will remain in the care of other families. Elizabeth was unaware of when the tears had started. *What a ruse,* she thought then repeated out loud. "What a ruse. Why mom?" she asked "I have been held against my will by your orders, to get me off of drugs and alcohol. I have been working the system and you couldn't stop drinking in order for me to come home? I thought you loved me."

"I do," said Helen, "I am so sorry."

Elizabeth was beginning to see their pattern of behavior more clearly now that her body had detoxed. Her mom played the classic victim while Elizabeth was left to reassure her while suppressing her own feelings. *Well not anymore*," she thought and wiped her face dry with her sleeve. "I deserve to come home, mom. Get it together so that I can." Nothing in life seemed fair. Nothing was in her control and it felt terrible. Dealing with this kind of pain was nearly unbearable without something to help numb it. Having to face her friends in the other room was the next hurdle. She asked if she could be excused and even though she felt like she hated her mom, the desire to hug her goodbye won out. They hugged each other tightly and with the worst sore throat she ever had, she returned to the main room where everyone was waiting to congratulate her again.

Chapter 10

As she opened the door to the main room, all eyes were on her. She hadn't expected to feel like such a spectacle. As she glanced around the room, Elizabeth noticed something, or more accurately, someone…Paul was peering at her but very much unlike the others were. His look was all knowing. He knew about her mom and he was waiting for her to crack. The worst part of it all was that it appeared he was enjoying himself.

OK, you son of a bitch, she thought, *this is how you want to play? Let's play. Watch this, pecker head.* It was as if his desire to ruin her fueled her instead. She smirked as she realized that Helping Hands had, indeed, helped with her drug and alcohol use but seemed to have failed in the cursing department. She said aloud, "Hey guys, I just got some bad news regarding my going home today. My mom has some stuff she has to work out and then I can go."

Marie was the first one to speak, "I'm so sorry Elizabeth. If you want, I can ask Mrs. Stein if you can stay with me and my family until everything is worked out; that way you don't have to bounce around to different houses."

"That sounds great" said Elizabeth. She looked around and saw that everyone, Paul excluded, seemed genuinely upset about her situation. It was amazing how quickly she had grown to care about these kids. They were like some band of misfits that had been following different paths that somehow ended up here. "Let's look on the bright side," she said. "Stage two will now allow me to sign up for a tutor to come here so that I can make up my school credits and I can now take a shower and pee without being accompanied by someone." Laughter echoed through the room and if that wasn't enough to cheer Elizabeth, the look on Paul's face was.

Jason walked into the room at that point and with much persuasion, got everyone back in their seats. "Listen up, everyone. I know that the majority of you came from households that had drug or alcohol users in them; whether it was your mom, dad, brother, whoever. Tonight's Moral Inventory topic is how someone else's drug or alcohol use affected you. You can talk about a specific incident or just general feelings. This exercise is for you to start seeing a pattern of how your own drug use began. I can venture a guess that many of you started using due to a feeling of helplessness. Raise your hands if you hated seeing a loved one drink or use drugs." Without a pause, every hand went up. "How many of you ever thought you would do the same thing that they were doing?" Not a single hand raised. "Interesting, isn't it? Well, my friends this is where your journey continues. Check the roster on the door to see what homes you are going to tonight and I look forward to reading your inventories."

Elizabeth had been impressed with Jason from day one. The fact that he was pretty cute didn't hurt. Christy, the other counselor, was his sister. She assumed they were twins but never asked. He had dark hair, dark eyes, and had almost a Hawaiian look to him. Christy, on the other hand, was blonde and had light eyes. But aside from the cute factor, he didn't judge her like Paul did. It was like Paul forgot that he had once been a patient, inmate, or whatever the kids were called that were there for treatment. *Boy, I would love to know his story,* she thought, *I bet he had held the record for quickest one to Stage two and that is why he hates me so much. I bet I broke the sucker's record.*

The tiny sound of a bell ringing marked the end of another day at Helping Hands.

Chapter 11

To Elizabeth's relief, the housing chart showed that she would be remaining at Marie's house until everything with her mom had been cleared. She thought that she wouldn't be in the mood to talk on the long drive to Naples but surprised herself by bringing up the subject to Marie's parents.

"I was supposed to go home today," Elizabeth said. "But my mom got caught with alcohol and I guess the school found out that my brother has been smoking pot."

Marie's mom's name was Claire. She was very soft spoken with short chestnut colored hair. Her eyes were a hazel color and when she looked at you, you could always tell she was really listening, not pretending like most adults did.

"You know Elizabeth," Claire said. "I grew up in a family where my dad was the one who drank. There were many times that he wouldn't even show up at home after he got off from work. He would just stumble in the house the next morning all bleary eyed and full of remorse. My mom didn't work so we really counted on his paycheck to see us through. As I grew up, I always had to come up with different stories as to why I couldn't go on certain trips that my other friends went on or why I couldn't have sleepovers. I resented my dad for a long time but as I got older, I was able to understand him more when I learned about how he had grown up. Sometimes, we just keep repeating bad behavior."

Marie spoke up, "That's what Jason was talking about today, before we left. How most of us never thought we would do the same things we hated but wound up doing them anyway."

"As I grew up," Claire continued, "I did not find it too hard to decline invitations to go to bars or parties because I was so determined in my school work but I can't help but wonder if Marie's addiction is a direct result of my family background. I have struggled with guilt over the fact that my daughter could have been spared all of this suffering if I had somehow shared with her sooner how I had grown up instead of trying to hide our family's past."

"Mom, I never knew you felt guilty," said Marie after a pause, "Please don't. I knew what I was doing when I tried smoking pot the first time. Our school showed us what could happen to kids that do drugs. I just wanted people to think I was cool."

Claire smiled and said, "I bet you didn't know you would be helping this family out today, Elizabeth. See, there was a reason you didn't go home today. We needed you to open the door to this discussion."

Elizabeth smiled. It felt good to help, for a change. She felt that she had done nothing but hurt others for the past year.

That evening, it was time to start on the Moral Inventory. Elizabeth was nervous because even though she was telling the truth when she shared her stories, there was still a sense of betrayal when she did. When she began to write, the first few

29

sentences were strained but before she knew it, she was staring at a complete detail of one of the worst holidays of her life.

Moral Inventory

It is amazing how much can happen to someone in a short period of time. Right after my dad died, my mom returned to work. One night, she was late picking my brother and I up from the daycare that was watching us since we were on holiday break from school. All of the other kids had already gone home and it was beginning to get dark.

The daycare workers began questioning me and Nicholas, asking if we knew where our mom could be. I still didn't know what you called what mom did; I just remember thinking "she's doing it again" while nodding my head "no" to the workers. At that moment, a loud crash came from outside. It was the sound of my mom's car crashing through the gate of the playground.

The police were called and mom got taken away. I remember the daycare worker bending down to me and asking if I wanted a piece of gum. "No, I don't want a piece of gum," I screamed in my head. Not out loud though, never out loud.

The rest of that night is a blur. It was now about a week until Christmas. Nicholas and I were put in a foster home. I know now that we were very lucky to have been kept together but the situation still sucked.

The foster 'mom,' and I use the term loosely, was this fat woman who had cribs lined up against a wall which each held a foster baby. She also had her own son who was 17-years-old. I don't recall his name so I will refer to him as "bastard" as I tell my story.

Bastard didn't waste any time entering the room that was given to me and Nicholas. He shut the lights off and in the dark I felt him grab me and press his mouth against mine. He was trying to force my mouth open when I screamed for Nicholas. As I pulled away, Nicholas had found the light switch and turned them back on. He then put himself in front of Bastard in an attempt to defend me. Nicholas was only nine and was no match for him. His arm was twisted behind his back and when he screamed, I thought for sure that Bastard had broken it.

We thought we were saved when his mom came in the room screaming but quickly realized it was us she was blaming. Come dinner time, she placed a bowl of split pea soup in front of us. Now how many eight-year-olds like split pea soup? When she saw that I did not dig right in, she said, "You either eat that soup or go back to your room with no dinner." A choice, right? As I began to excuse myself from the table, she went ballistic, yelling "you better eat that damn soup!" I was so confused. One thing I can say about my mom is that she always spoke to us like we were equals. She never talked with the fake voice so many adults use. I had honestly thought this woman was giving me a choice, yet when I acted on my decision, she flipped out. At this point, I was beginning to think that all grownups were nuts and the kids were the only ones that knew what was going on.

Later that evening, Nicholas and I were in their backyard trying to come up with a plan on how we could jump the fence and run away. But run where? We didn't have to think about it for long because the fat wench and her Bastard son had called child services and had us removed from the house.

The second foster home was much more pleasant with stockings hung up and a pretty tree. There was a husband and wife that had a son who was about four-years-old. Nicholas got to sleep in the room with the little boy and I was put on a cot at the top landing of the stairs. I remember crying myself to sleep because the rails from the stairs cast a shadow on the wall that looked like bars from a jail cell. I didn't care how sick my mom was from her drinking. She was all we had and I would give anything to be back home with her.

Within a couple of days, my prayers were answered and we were able to return home just days before Christmas.

Whew, Elizabeth thought, *I'm glad that is over with.* She had begun to notice a recurring sentence not only in her journal but in her talks at group therapy. The words "I remember." It wasn't that she had ever forgotten, not for lack of trying anyway, but rather did everything in her power not to think about things. Although reliving past events caused quite a bit of pain, she was proud to say "I remember" now because she was finally beginning to believe that was how she could finally heal. She closed the journal and then her eyes.

Chapter 12

The next few weeks flew by because Elizabeth had begun working with a school tutor a few hours a day. She used to hate homework but now dove right in. She had been a voracious reader before the drugs had taken over and could again lose herself in a novel for hours.

She was currently reading "Little Women" by Louisa May Alcott for her literature class and was moved by the bond the March sisters had, not only with each other but with their mother as well. The hardships the family faced only strengthened that bond.

Elizabeth felt a kinship with Jo when she sold her hair in the story. Touching the nape of her neck, Elizabeth twirled the short hair around her finger. Although they both had loved their long hair, they willingly sacrificed it; Jo to help her family and Elizabeth to move ahead in the program.

She was still a bit confused by how the program justified what they did as a way of "humbling" you. She guessed that they wanted you to like yourself from within, not being defined by your clothes, makeup, or hairstyles. To take those things away from a girl growing up in the glam age of the 80's, was very difficult. Even the boys were known to wear black nail polish and eyeliner.

Although the days went by quickly, the monotony was beginning to take its toll. The same mundane routine, the same cold lunch, the same 20 or so faces she saw each day. The same, the same, the same.

Elizabeth glanced at her arm and was grossed out by how pasty white she had become. She really missed being able to go to the beach. The first thoughts of leaving the program began to creep into her mind but were quickly replaced by recent events.

A boy named Jessie had tried to leave and got caught. He had been on Stage five and was now back to Stage one. Pulled from his own home only to be babysat by other people again. The scariest part of all was that he had trusted his parents and they were the ones that told Mrs. Stein of his plans.

It was all a bit of a mystery because you weren't allowed to talk about it. Everyone was curious but had become so suspicious of each other they didn't dare try to talk in confidence.

When other kids had actually escaped in the past, you were told to never mention them again in class. Elizabeth thought that it was a bit ironic how the program always wanted you to share and be honest but the staff never wanted to share or be honest with them about students who were there one day and gone the next. They spent so much time warning you that there was no chance of getting away and were probably embarrassed by the fact that some kids did escape. *To share how the kids managed to do it, would surely give us the courage to try as well,* Elizabeth thought. *If you can't trust your own parents, who can you trust?*

Speaking of parents, Elizabeth's mom and brother were coming for a visit that day. She wasn't going to get her hopes up about returning home. She was just going to enjoy the time she got to spend with her family. She glanced at the clock and realized they might already be in the building. Her thoughts were confirmed by the entrance of Mrs. Stein.

"Elizabeth, if you are done with your reading, I would like to see you in my office." said Mrs. Stein.

Smiling, Elizabeth closed her book and said, "All done." She stood up and her grin became a grimace as she caught sight of her "high water" pants. She was embarrassed to have her brother see her like this. They had both made fun of kids in the past who dressed exactly the way she looked right now.

A conference room had been set up to give them some privacy. Nicholas sat fidgeting in his seat; obviously uncomfortable. He didn't like dealing with things on an emotional level. His being here meant a lot to Elizabeth. It proved how much he cared about her.

They all hugged and immediately started talking at the same time. They all stopped to allow each other to speak and only silence followed. After a few beats they all started laughing.

Sitting down Elizabeth asked "Wow, when did we all start acting like strangers?"

"You look like a stranger," quipped her brother.

Smiling, she knew they were back to being the siblings they had always been. Teasing, fighting siblings.

"I think we are just a little nervous, honey," Helen replied. "You're looking healthier, Elizabeth, like you gained a couple of pounds."

"Thanks," said Elizabeth. Turning to her brother she said, "Thanks for coming Nicholas."

With a shrug of his shoulders, Nicholas said, "No problem. Hey, you don't think they are like, recording us or anything, do you?"

Elizabeth glanced around the bare room, "I don't think so. I can't see where they would hide something."

"I feel bad that you have to be here" he said. "I mean I am glad you're away from Marcus but man, Elizabeth, you don't look like yourself. Did they have to cut your hair that short?"

"I guess they wanted to get most of the black dye out." Elizabeth responded.

"Speaking of Marcus," Nicholas continued "He keeps calling the house at all hours, sounding like he's drunk. One night he called bawling because someone told him you moved to New York and were in a car accident and died. I actually felt kind of bad for the jerk so I reassured him you were alive but wouldn't tell him anymore."

Helen looked at Nicholas with a scowl and said, "Nicholas, I told you that you were not allowed to mention anyone from Elizabeth's past while she is here."

Nicholas snorted, "Her past, mom? She's only been here for a few months."

"You know exactly what I mean," she replied.

"It just came out; besides if the guy would stop calling the house and driving by at all hours, he wouldn't even occupy space in my brain."

Elizabeth realized she had not let go of her mom's hand the entire time she had been in the room. The mere mention of Marcus had caused her heart to palpitate. She hoped she hadn't given herself away by squeezing her mom's hand or anything.

Elizabeth knew not to say anything out loud just in case they were being recorded. A foolish slip like that would see her right back to Stage one.

Things had been pretty bad with her and Marcus at the time she had been taken away. One of the last times she had gone to see him, she was greeted outside of his apartment by another girl that she knew, named Jennifer. You could hear music blaring from inside and as she had approached the door, Jennifer grabbed her wrist and told her that she might not want to go in just then. After a few pleas to be more specific the girl told her that Marcus was inside with another girl. They sat on the hood of her mom's car that she had snuck out with. As Elizabeth was trying to decide what to do, she remained facing the front window of the apartment that was covered by a sheet. In an instant, the moment turned surreal when the sheet fell from the window as if on cue and Elizabeth was staring at her best friend Kristy, sitting on the lap of her very own boyfriend, Marcus. At that point, the decision had been made for her and she climbed back in her mom's 69' Rambler and drove home.

That memory helped Elizabeth get her mind refocused on the present. Kicking herself for even entertaining the thought that Marcus really cared about her. That incident was only one of many in the whirlwind relationship they had. She was embarrassed to think that she had still stayed with him even after that event; trying to blame her friend for crossing the line. *Why was it that girls always want to blame the other girl and overlook the guy's involvement?* she thought.

Elizabeth's train of thought was broken as she realized her mom was giving her own hand a squeeze. As their eyes met, she could tell right away that her mom knew exactly what had been going through her head.

Getting back to their meeting, Elizabeth said, "Mom, you look good too."

"I've been attending my AA meetings again," Helen proudly replied. "I would do anything to get you back home. I sure made a pig's behind of things."

"Have you heard anything about that? Do you know when I get to come home?"

"Would tonight be soon enough for you?" asked her mom.

Elizabeth's hands covered her mouth in disbelief. "But what about you, Nicholas? I thought you couldn't stay in the house?"

"My friend Robby and I got an apartment together. It's close to work." Nicholas said.

With a big smile, Helen said, "Mrs. Stein would like you to pick a friend to come home with you tonight, not as a babysitter, as a friend. She has also said that you will not have the responsibility of a newcomer until next week so that we can have time to catch up."

When Elizabeth could finally gather her thoughts, she said, "Marie, I want Marie to come home with me."

34

Chapter 13

Later that evening, as they pulled into the driveway of her home, Elizabeth felt a contentment she hadn't felt in years. Marie was oohing and aahing over everything once they were inside. She was intrigued by the skeleton key locks on the doors and said the wood floors and tall ceilings reminded her of when she had lived up north. Elizabeth couldn't believe that this little rich girl that lived in a huge, brand new house in Naples and drove in a Mercedes Benz car thought she, Elizabeth, had it made.

"Do you know what's the first thing I am going to do?" asked Elizabeth. "I am going to take a long, hot bath in the claw foot tub." Giggling, she ran to the bathroom and began running hot water. She could remember her first few weeks in the program when you were only given three minutes to shower. The water had actually been turned off on her once when she hadn't finished in time; leaving conditioner still in her hair. *There is no going back,* she thought to herself.

Marie began talking through the door. "Your mom wants to know if you want a breakfast dinner, whatever that is."

"What do you mean, 'whatever that is,' do you mean to tell me you have never had a breakfast dinner?"

Marie replied, "Well I am assuming by the name that you have eggs and such."

Elizabeth laughed, "and such indeed." *Marie would just have to see for herself,* thought Elizabeth.

Sitting at the dinner table, Marie's eyes said it all. There were pancakes stacked high with a plate of bacon and sausage on the side. The kitchen smelled of fresh coffee and cinnamon rolls. A covered dish revealed biscuits and sausage gravy. All of Elizabeth's favorites served at once.

"Thanks so much, mom," she managed to say in between bites.

"You're very welcome," replied Helen.

It was nice to see how quickly Marie just fit in with everyone. It was like she was part of the family, some long lost relative they had stumbled upon in the most unlikely of places. Rehab.

This feeling is what gave Elizabeth the courage to bring up a topic that up until now she had been leery of. "Marie, I have something I have been wanting to get your opinion on."

Marie held up a finger to her mouth indicating she couldn't talk just then. Taking a large gulp of orange juice, she finally said, "What's up?"

"I wanted to know how you would feel if I put in for Stage three at Friday's group meeting?"

"What's the big rush, Elizabeth? Just because you lived most of your life at full speed ahead, doesn't mean you have to do the same in rehab. You already broke the record for Stage two."

35

"I know, I know and I appreciate my tutor and all that but Stage three would allow me to enroll at the same high school you attend. I could be a real student again."

Marie had begun to scowl, "You know, it took me eight months to get to Stage three. Granted, I was a real pain in the ass in the beginning but still. I guess what I am trying to say is, if I am your friend and I feel a tiny bit of resentment at how quickly you are climbing, imagine how people like Paul are going to feel."

Bristling at the mere mention of her nemesis, Elizabeth said, "Why should I care how Paul feels? If he is going to sit in that counselor stool, then he is supposed to be unbiased. He seems to have decided that there is some sort of vendetta between us."

"Well, I can't stop you from trying; I just hope you know what you will be up against. When I asked to be put on Stage three, the counselors read from my journal and questioned me about personal things. I wound up breaking down and crying and my request was denied. After another month, I tried again and luckily had a one on one meeting with Mrs. Stein who granted my request."

"I appreciate your concern Marie. I know you wouldn't try to discourage me for any other reason than that you care. I am almost as shocked as you, considering I couldn't wait to quit school and now here I am begging to go back."

Helen, who had been watching the exchange between both girls began to laugh at Elizabeth's last comment which caused a ripple effect. The tension had been broken and the rest of the evening consisted of stories, reading, and a tour of the house including the attic, which Marie had been dying to take a look at.

Chapter 14

The next morning was a Thursday, which gave Elizabeth one more day to gather her thoughts and strength to face the group meeting and ask to be bumped up to Stage three. She looked at herself in the mirror and actually liked what she saw. Her hair had grown past her ears and her natural waves formed into what Italians called "bologna curls." Her face had finally adjusted to being under fluorescent lights all day, every day and the breakouts had stopped.

She had thought about everything that Marie had said the night before. She was glad that Marie was now on Stage four so that they weren't stuck in some weird competition. Although she liked everyone in her group, Marie was her best friend and she did not want to jeopardize that friendship.

Elizabeth had questioned her own motives as to her decision to ask to be promoted to the next level. Was it really about school or the added freedom it would give her? She knew the temptation to run away would be very strong once she entered into school and was away from the Helping Hands building. She had never seen Mariner High School but was told it was a beautiful two story building and was brand new and that the kids could eat lunch outside in the courtyard if they wanted to. Elizabeth could enjoy hot lunches again. *Yes,* she thought to herself, *this will definitely be worth it. The worst they can do is say no.* With that thought, she gathered her things and was ready for the new day.

Unfortunately, as the day progressed, her confidence was replaced with a melancholy feeling. She felt like she was going into battle with this request as if she had to constantly prove that she was worthy. Some of the kids seemed content to stay at a certain stage for six months which made her stand out even more. The staff were beginning to look at her as if to say "What's the rush? Where do you want to run off to?"

The day was winding down and with it being Thursday, Elizabeth knew that final announcements would include asking the kids who would be planning on petitioning the right to go up a stage. It was hard to tell if any of the others had intentions to request a bump up the old ladder, so to speak. Elizabeth glanced at each face, trying to read them. Lisa, a girl who had been there for almost a year and was still at Stage three, was looking a little nervous. She had her hands at her sides but Elizabeth noticed her fingers kept fidgeting with a loose thread on her pants. *She's definitely going to ask,* thought Elizabeth.

Someone cleared their throat and Elizabeth looked up to see that Jason had entered the room holding a "Moral Inventory" journal. "Before I ask who plans on requesting a promotion for tomorrow, I want to discuss the topic of our Moral Inventory lesson for tonight." he began. "Each staff member has been assigned a certain number of students. We have each gone over the moral inventories of the students we have been given. Whatever we feel has not been touched on or has been

37

avoided by the student, we will be asking that they finally face it at this time. As you know, we only ask you to do things for your own good whether it feels good or not."

Elizabeth prayed in her head, "please, please don't let Paul be the staff member assigned to me." She had been so intent on her chanting that she missed the entire reading of the list. As she looked around, she noticed the students breaking up into groups.

Off to her right she heard a voice say, "Off in La La Land again?" It was Paul. He beckoned her over with his hand and then pointed to an empty chair. As she began to sit, he said, "On second thought, I'll do you first. I've decided to meet one on one with each of you. The rest of you can talk quietly while I am in the other room."

Elizabeth tucked her journal under her arm and began to follow Paul. They entered a room she had never been in before. It was dimly lit with a rich cranberry colored leather couch against the wall, two plush armchairs facing each other and a small desk placed in the corner. The water colors that hung on the wall reminded her of Norman Rockwell drawings. She smirked and thought, *I bet these are meant to evoke hope in the poor saps that meet with Mrs. Stein.* She could picture Mrs. Stein reassuring distraught parents that they could get their innocent little darlings back if they just invested a mere $8,000. Elizabeth had overheard her mother on the telephone one night speaking with a friend about how she was struggling financially with the cost.

After this brief evaluation of the room, Elizabeth turned to face Paul. "Where would you like me to sit?" she asked in a tremulous voice. She was getting a bit nervous being in a room alone with him. It was the first time she was alone with a guy in almost five months. Even during their co-ed lessons, the boys sat on one side of the room and the girls on the other.

"Wherever you would like," he said pleasantly. This new tone of voice threw Elizabeth for a second.

Is this some kind of trap? she thought. She chose one of the arm chairs so they could face each other. The couch was out of the question since she felt a stirring in herself that could only be described as attraction.

Paul asked to see her Moral Inventory and as he perused its pages, Elizabeth was able to observe him further. He was wearing a short-sleeved polo shirt which allowed a peek at his biceps. He had a chiseled jawline, which reminded Elizabeth a little of Marcus. He looked up at her quickly and she was clearly busted. He smiled and she felt herself blush. *Thank God this room is dimly lit,* she thought.

Paul cleared his throat and said, "I know what you are up to."

How do you respond to a statement like that? thought Elizabeth, but said aloud, "What are you talking about?" Her voice came out sharper than she had intended.

"There is no need to get defensive," he said while flashing that smile again. "I just meant that I know you are about to ask to go up to Level Three tomorrow, that's all."

"How could you possibly know that?" she asked.

He began laughing and shaking his head from side to side. "You give yourself so much credit for your past acting skills but I swear you give yourself away when it comes to stuff like this. You have been inattentive in the last couple of group sessions and you tend to jump when your name is mentioned. It is either that or you're planning on running."

Startled by his last sentence and knowing what even a mere suspicion of running could get you, she blurted out, "No, no, you're right, I do plan on asking tomorrow and I also expect that you will again be giving a million reasons why I am not worthy."

It was like they went right back to the old relationship in a split second. She on the defensive and he acting like the "know it all." Who had she been kidding at the thought that they might actually be on the same side. His smile had been meant to disarm her, boy had her street skills abandoned her since she had come to this place.

"Whoa, hang on a minute," said Paul. "Believe it or not, there is a part of me that thinks you are ready for Level Three. That is to say, if we can get through this conference without cursing each other out." His laugh came out clear and hearty.

Elizabeth felt a flutter in her stomach. *I must be hearing things,* she thought.

"You have been very frank in your Moral Inventory, sharing experiences that some people with years of counseling would still not be able to face. Because I believe your childhood is what opened the door to your later drug abuse; this is the area I would like to discuss with you today."

"Okay," responded Elizabeth, "shoot."

"There seems to be a gap in your timeline of childhood events; you left off by telling us of the dream you had a couple of months back about the day you found out your father had died. Although you were misled into thinking it was a heart attack, there had to come a time that you found out the truth. This is what I want you to write about tonight in your Moral Inventory."

Elizabeth swallowed back the lump in her throat and said, "Well, no one could ever accuse you of beating around the bush."

"I know what I am asking is tough but I know you can do it Elizabeth."

Before she could even respond Paul stood up and opened his arms as if waiting for an embrace. Elizabeth did not want to make a fool of herself if she had misread his actions so as she stood she began to straighten her blouse and turn toward the door. Paul slowly turned her shoulders toward him and hugged her. Just a soft, gentle hug.

"Good luck tomorrow," he whispered and just as quickly, released her.

"Thanks," murmured Elizabeth. She looked in Paul's eyes but was not sure what she read in them. She left the room more puzzled than when she had entered.

Chapter 15

Sitting at a small vanity table that faced her bedroom window, Elizabeth stared at the blank page of her Moral Inventory journal. She had been forced to take this new girl, Marcy, home with her, who hadn't stopped crying since they arrived. So much for getting the week off without getting a newcomer. She had been told that the whole family was sick at the house Marcy was supposed to go to.

Elizabeth was seething because this kid shouldn't be here. She had tried pot once and her family freaked. Elizabeth had spent many nights with hardcore partiers and this girl just did not fit the bill. The reason Elizabeth was so angry was because she was beginning to think that the program was a ruse; just a way to get money from families using scare tactics. *I bet Mrs. Stein told Marcy's family that by her using pot once, she was on a road to destruction with heroin not far away,* Elizabeth thought.

She had spent the last hour reassuring Marcy that it wasn't that bad and trying to give her pointers on how to get through it without giving too many of her trade secrets away. Marcy had been impressed with Elizabeth's quick climb in the program and that had calmed her down a bit until she began missing her toy poodle, Twinkie. That is when the floodgates really opened up.

Just then, a thought came to her. "Why hadn't I thought of this sooner?" Elizabeth said aloud. She had almost taken a step through her door when she remembered that newcomers were never to be left alone. "Mom!" she called out.

Helen came rushing to the door looking wildly around ready to be told of some drama with the newcomer. The program had caused a sense of paranoia in everyone. "What, what happened?" asked Helen.

Shaking her head, Elizabeth said, "No mom, everything is okay. I was thinking that Cali might help calm Marcy down. Is she in the house?"

"I think so, let me go look."

A few minutes later, Helen returned with the family cat, Cali, short for Calico. As Elizabeth placed the cat in Marcy's lap, the transformation was instantaneous. Marcy began to "ooh" and "aahh" over the beautiful cat and before long, with Cali snuggled in her lap, Marcy fell asleep.

No more excuses, thought Elizabeth. She bent over the journal and began to write.

By the time I was nine, we had moved from Connecticut back to Florida. We were living in Fort Lauderdale in a trailer park. It was pretty decent as far as trailer parks went. It had a big pool and playground and this rec type center with a juke box. I loved to listen to Joan Jett's song "I Love Rock and Roll."

I was a pretty quiet kid and spent most of my time observing people. One of these people happened to be a teenaged boy, whose name I can't remember. He had

40

shoulder length hair and wore those tan suede shoes called Wallabees that were so popular in the 70's.

One day I was sitting on the swings and he walked right up to me and asked if I wanted him to push me. I couldn't find my voice but shook my head "yes." It is all a blur, but in a nutshell, he was very nice, asked me simple questions which I finally began to answer. I don't know how we said goodbye or ended the conversation but I do know I sat on that swing a good long time after he left, wondering what had caused him to notice me. I was flattered without even knowing what flattered was; this is the hindsight kicking in. Anyway, that was that, don't remember ever talking to him again.

I mentioned all of that because that is what marked the day that my mom confessed to me how my father really died.

I had returned home to the smell of burning pot pies. Sign number one that mom had been drinking. I turned off the stove and pulled the pies out of the oven. Mom used a fork to poke our initials in the pot pie's crust so we knew which was ours. Nicholas liked the chicken pot pies while I liked the turkey.

Mom was sitting at the kitchen table with her face buried in her hands. She was crying and after a few minutes of persuading, she began to talk. She had just received a call from my Uncle Victor, who was my dad's brother in New York. He had told her that my Uncle Nicki had just died. Uncle Nicki was also my dad's brother. He came from a family of 16 children. Crazy, huh? Anyway, Nicki was one of the only relatives from my dad's side that still talked to my mom. The minute my dad died, they just wrote us off. My grandmother blamed my mom for some reason. I was confused at the time because how could you blame someone for another person's heart attack.

Nicki loved my mom because she accepted the fact that he was gay. He was one of the handsomest men I can recall ever knowing. He always reminded me of Jesus because he had some length to his hair and a beautifully shaped beard with soft brown eyes.

I was so sad to know that another member of our family was gone so soon after my dad. Mom must have been thinking the same thing because the next thing I knew, she began cursing the owner of the restaurant my father had been working at, at the time of his death. It was called Mario's in Fort Lauderdale. My dad rented a duplex from him as well that was only across the parking lot of the restaurant.

"That son of a bitch," my mom said. "I wish I could kill him. It is his fault your father is dead."

I know this is going to sound melodramatic, but I am dead serious when I say that before my mom uttered another word, I thought to myself, "My father was murdered."

Mom opened her wallet that had been lying on the table and unfolded two small pieces of newspaper. One had my dad's obituary written on it, the other was an article about my father's murder. It appears that one night while he was leaving the restaurant to go home, someone came up behind him and stabbed him six times in the back. He was found in his living room where it appeared that he had tried to stop the bleeding on his own because the police found a towel that had been wrapped up and placed behind him. It did not look like he had even tried to go to the phone to call for help.

41

I don't know what came over me, but I ran to my bedroom and began writing on sheets of paper with my crayons. I wrote "my dad is not dead" over and over and hung them on my walls with tape. My mom stumbled in my room and began to hug me. We both sat crying on my small twin bed.

I am sure my mom regretted telling me that way but I can't imagine there being any less painful way in the end.

I was still mulling over my mom's comment about it being Mario's fault. How could a robbery (that is what the police were calling it, although my dad was still wearing his watch and gold necklace at the scene) be Mario's fault?

I remembered a night that Nicholas and I had stayed with my dad right before we knew that mom was moving us back to Connecticut. Dad was working at the restaurant and Nicholas and I were home alone. It was pretty late. We were watching TV when my dad's back door began to open quietly. It had one of those inside chain locks up top and we saw a hand appear and begin to reach for the chain.

For some idiotic reason, I thought about going into the kitchen to get a pan to hit the hand with but before I could take action Nicholas bolted through the front door and I was hot on his heels. We were dressed in our pajamas when we flew into the restaurant and began screaming for our father. My dad calmed us down long enough to get the gist of what was going on. By this time, the owner Mario came up to us and my dad grabbed him by the shirt and yelled, "If this ever fucking happens again when my kids are there, I will fucking kill you."

We were in such shock that nothing registered with us about that comment but as I got older I pieced together the timeline of that incident and my father's death. Over the next several years, I learned that Mario's restaurant was a front for the mob and my dad was a numbers' runner for Mario. You see stereotypes in the movies about Italian mobsters but some stereotypes are true. My dad loved his black Cadillac, the horses, and women. He also had a terrible temper when he had been drinking.

To this day, there are several theories as to what happened to my dad, but in my heart, I know it will remain a mystery. I think whoever tried to get in my dad's house the night Nicholas and I were there, was there to kill him. With him working in a restaurant, I am sure his hours changed last minute and the person screwed up by not knowing dad wasn't home. Some family members even think that the police were involved in a cover up. I have been tempted to contact the "cold case" department in Lauderdale to see if there have ever been more developments but sometimes, not knowing is better.

Chapter 16

Friday morning greeted Elizabeth with pounding rain that matched her pounding head. She was feeling grumpy as she and Marcy shuffled into the kitchen.

"I know that face," her mom said as she glanced up from the table, "What's wrong?"

"I am going to ask to be bumped up today and I know that the staff has been trying to figure out my strategy so they can refuse."

Helen smiled. She was very proud of how far Elizabeth had come with the program but knew her mouth could be her downfall. "You know I support whatever you decide to do honey." She stroked Elizabeth's hair before leaving the room.

As Elizabeth sipped her coffee, her mood seemed to reflect the weather outside. As the sky got darker, her mind did too. *How dare they tell me what to write in my journal?* she thought. *They already control everything else. I haven't even been allowed to watch stinking TV since I have been here. Gotta wait till the fifth Stage for that. Enough is enough; they want the truth so I will give it to them today when I tell them what I really think. It is time someone stood up to them. Hell, the counselors are kids just like us. We'll see who is in charge today.* She felt adrenaline surge through her body giving her an almost natural high.

"I'll be ready in 20 minutes," she called to her mom.

A beautiful rainbow appeared as Elizabeth stepped from her mom's car into the entrance of Helping Hands. She took it as a sign that things were going to go her way that day. She had never been very spiritual but today she sensed that she was not alone.

Her first order of business was to hand in her Moral Inventory and place her name in the 'requests' box. She knew she had a couple of hours to kill before her royal highness, Mrs. Stein, would call her up. She watched as each counselor pored over everyone's journals, sometimes commenting, sometimes laughing but mostly whispering amongst themselves. They sat in tall directors' chairs and it struck Elizabeth for the first time how apropos that was because they had been directing her since day one. Where to sit, when to eat, when to pee and giving permission for each and every little thing. Elizabeth was seething by the time everyone was asked to form a circle and group therapy began.

The requests box was brought to the center and Jason randomly picked a piece of paper from inside. "It looks like Elizabeth would like to go up to Level Three" he said. There was an audible gasp from the group which immediately stopped as Mrs. Stein cleared her throat.

Mrs. Stein turned her gaze to Elizabeth and said, "The staff and I have read your journal from last night and are most impressed with what you shared with us."

"About that," said Elizabeth as she rose from her sitting position and looked from one counselor to the next. "I am feeling very resentful right now."

43

"Well, this is the perfect time for you to express your feelings Elizabeth." Mrs. Stein drew up a chair and sat.

Aware that all eyes were on her, Elizabeth couldn't help but feel like she was an actor on stage performing in one of those theaters in the round. Her audience was not strictly in front of her but facing from every angle.

"Although I have known most of you for some time now, I have had to share my experiences with you from the time you were strangers to me. You refuse to allow me to keep some of my private memories on the shelf. In order for me to move up in the program, I have been forced to dust these memories off one by one and relive them." Turning to Mrs. Stein she continued, "Mrs. Stein likes to say, 'where there is pain today, there is healing tomorrow'." My question to you is…when will my tomorrow come? I am in more pain now than when I began. I know that Stage three will help to alleviate some of this pain by allowing me to go back to school. School can be my new reality, not this redundant schedule I have had for months. Getting in a car, coming here, sitting in a pew for seven hours only to go back in the car and go home. Day after day after day." Elizabeth realized that she had turned in a complete circle as she spoke and had tried to make eye contact with everyone.

Mrs. Stein rose from her chair and said, "That was quite a little monologue but need I remind you that before you came here you were content with getting high, sometimes going to work and waking up in time to be sick and witness the destruction you had caused in your home. Day after day after day."

Feeling as though she had been sucker punched, Elizabeth wrapped her arms around herself. It was as if all of the air had been let out of her lungs while she had to contend with the fact that Mrs. Stein was completely right. In her past, she would wake up to find new injuries to her body, broken glass and mirrors on the floor with a vague memory as to what had caused it all.

With her head hanging down, she stared at the floor and whispered to the group, "The shame has become unbearable. Even though the drugs only helped me to forget for a little while; they still helped me to forget.

"Yes," said Mrs. Stein in a calm voice, "but then the next day you had more shame than the night before. Don't you see the vicious cycle you were in?"

Elizabeth began to cry. It sucked feeling like a kid but in reality, that is what she was. She had spent so many years trying to act like an adult and was beginning to realize that she had failed miserably due to the lack of examples she had been given.

"All I have ever wanted was to be loved." She wiped her nose on her sleeve and didn't care. Continuing she said, "I mean I know my mom loves me but not as much as she loves her alcohol. I know she can't help it but it still hurts." Trying to turn her pain into a joke she shrugged her shoulders with her palms facing up and said, "How do you compete with a liquid beverage?" The groans in the room brought her back to the gravity of the situation and she said, "Marcus seemed like a father figure since he was so much older than me but I guess that is twisted too because what kind of father sleeps with his daughter?"

Mrs. Stein broke in saying, "That is where your innocence was led astray, Elizabeth. You sought protection and love from Marcus but he was a predator. There is no other way to say it. He knew exactly what your vulnerabilities were the minute he met you." It was her turn to go in a circle as she said, "I am speaking to all of you now when I say that all that time you thought you were so "hard" and tried to portray this rough exterior, it was a dead giveaway for people who are takers and abusers."

Sitting back down Mrs. Stein said, "Now getting back to your journal, Elizabeth. It is one thing to read someone's thoughts and quite another to hear them directly from them. I thought you did a great job of letting us in on the night you found out about your father's death but you kind of left us hanging. I know there is a lot of pain in this memory but how did you and your mom end things that night?"

Elizabeth scrunched up her forehead in an attempt to recall what had happened after she had written all those notes and hung them on her wall. That is usually where she stopped herself when her mind wandered back there. That was always the point where her chest began to hurt and she would quickly change her line of thinking. But now, as she concentrated, she remembered her mom coming in to the room to comfort her.

"Well, at first my mom was caught in her own self-pity. I had left her in the kitchen when I ran to my room. She eventually came into my room as I was screaming, but being intoxicated, she was very sloppy in trying to comfort me. She was off balance and seemed confused as to why I was crying and acting hysterical.

The moment I saw her distress I went right back into "fix it" mode. I shut off my pain and led mom back to the kitchen. Once I had her seated, I tried to make a pot of coffee because that is what I had seen people do in movies to help someone who was drunk. I was able to persuade her to take a few sips and she passed out at the table. I had to leave her there because she was dead weight and I couldn't move her. I have felt guilty over the years for my inability to move her. My common sense knows I was just a weak little kid but something else in me, condemns me for it.

Elizabeth glanced at the half of the circle that was the boys' side and said, "I also began to really resent my brother because he wasn't there to help me. It wasn't long after that incident that mom moved us to a trailer in the boonies because she thought that whoever had killed my dad may come after us. We lived on three and a half acres of land in a place called Pioneer Plantation and let me tell you, the name of that place says it all. Nicholas and I used to have to walk in the dark on this unpaved road to get to our bus stop and one day on our way back home, we heard an alligator croak in the bushes that ran alongside the canal. My brother ran and left me there. When I started running, I could hear the bushes rustling like it was right beside me. I have never been so scared in my life."

Elizabeth curtsied to the group and said, "Well, that's all folks." Looking out into the group, her final words had seemed to bring everyone back from a trance. Her stories, no matter how short or long, always seemed to captivate the group. It was as if by her sharing her story, she had allowed them to experience it too and they almost seemed to become her as well during the telling.

It was Paul's turn to speak and when he stood and looked at Elizabeth, his eyes betrayed nothing of their talk the day before. He began by saying, "Let us break for lunch before we launch further into your request to go to Stage three. With this being such an important stage, considering the fact that it would allow you to leave the premises of Helping Hands, I encourage all of you," he pointed to everyone in the group and continued, "as Elizabeth's peers to add your thoughts or concerns regarding this request. Whether you are for or against, it does not matter. We will resume in one hour." He parted the circle by walking directly through the middle and everyone watched his back disappear from the room.

And he says that I am dramatic, thought Elizabeth. She had to admit he had an authoritative air about him that she had always resented but now that there was a trace of him being on her side, she began to respect him for it.

Chapter 17

Lunch was a drab affair of bologna and cheese. There were no cooking facilities at Helping Hands so lunch was always bagged. The sandwich kept getting stuck in her throat because there was no mayo or mustard on it. Elizabeth began to daydream about the school's hot lunch and chuckled to herself because never in a million years would she have thought that a school lunch could bring her such joy. She was struck again by the saying of "you don't know what you've got till it's gone."

Elizabeth leaned over to whisper to Marie, "So did you put in for Stage five?" Without making eye contact, Marie just nodded her head up and down. It was then that Elizabeth noticed that Marie had not touched her lunch. She could only imagine the uneasiness that Marie was feeling. Stage five was a big deal. If Marie was allowed to bump up, she could then begin to blow dry her hair, go to outside places like the mall with her parents and watch one hour a day of television. Suddenly, Stage three seemed so boring but in the same token, reassured Elizabeth that what she was asking for wasn't so much after all.

Usually before a group meeting, Elizabeth would rehearse what she wanted to convey to the group but today was different. Elizabeth was going to do what actors call Ad Libbing. It would either be her saving grace or her downfall.

With just enough time to brush her teeth and catch a glimpse of her appearance, Elizabeth ran to the bathroom. She took a moment to just stare at herself in the mirror. This was something she had done for years when she was searching herself. She had been startled at times to see in her eyes, the younger version of herself and it was so painful when she did that she would quickly look away to break the connection to the past. Today, however, she saw strength for the first time in a long time. She took a deep breath of air through her nose and released it out of her mouth. *Let's do this*, she thought and exited the bathroom.

As she reentered the room, the old system of boys on one side girls on the other had resumed. Elizabeth liked this and thought it would be easier to have everyone facing forward as she pled her case. She made eye contact with Paul who made a slight nod to let her know she could begin.

"Before I get into everything," began Elizabeth, "I just want to say, thank you. Not to anyone in particular just you all as a whole. I know I acted like a wench when I first came and I didn't trust anyone who breathed." There was a slight giggle from the group. "It didn't take you long to see I was just a scared little girl. You never judged me whether I was sharing about my sexual escapades or law breaking behavior, so again, thanks."

Elizabeth took a long pause looking down at the floor, trying to regain control as her emotions began to build again. "Although I wake up each morning to a new day, I feel like someone pressed the "pause" button on my life. It has been good and bad. Good because it stopped me from doing any more damage to myself and others;

bad because I am stunted and not becoming who I was meant to be. The ultimate to Stage three for me would be returning to school. I realize I would be entering in halfway through the school year which will be difficult academically as well as socially but it is time. My time. My tutor can tell you how hard I have been working and how I have maintained an A/B average in my subjects."

"I won't be alone though, there are a dozen of you that attend Mariner as well. I have heard that most of you like to be incognito at the school because there have been whispers about this place and stories of how we are all held captive." The stern look on Mrs. Stein's face alerted Elizabeth to the fact that she was beginning to stray and she quickly got back on point.

"Anyway," she continued "It will be reassuring to know that I am not alone but at the same time, I will have to stand on my own and get through my insecurities without drugs or alcohol. Quite a challenge but one I am ready for."

Mrs. Stein thanked Elizabeth for her comments and then addressed the group, "Is there anyone that would like to render an opinion on whether Elizabeth should be granted her request or not?"

Marie raised her hand. "Yes, Marie," said Mrs. Stein

"Well, I have known Elizabeth since her first day here and she has stayed at my house several times, so I have really watched the changes in her. In the beginning, I thought she was a scammer because she seemed to latch right on to the ways of the program and I thought it was a ploy for her to manipulate us. Even though I liked her personality, there was always a part of me watching to see if she would try to sneak out of my house or something." Glancing at Elizabeth, she added "Sorry Elizabeth."

"It's OK," her friend reassured her.

"But it didn't take long to see that Elizabeth was just as shocked with the ease of her transition as we were. It was like the real Elizabeth who had lain dormant those few years had awoken. I began to see that she was a girl who could accomplish anything if she set her mind to it. I find myself struggling with jealousy sometimes because she makes it look so easy. I didn't mean to ramble and I guess what I am trying to get at is this; Elizabeth definitely deserves to be given the chance to go back to high school and fix some of her past mistakes. She can be trusted not to run." Marie sat back down a little red in the face due to the emotion she showed in her speech.

"Thank you, Marie." said Mrs. Stein, "Anybody else?"

Trina raised her hand and stood up. Her glasses were slipping down her nose and she quickly pushed them up with her hand. Something she did at least a dozen times per day. She would not make eye contact with Elizabeth but would stare at the floor and make brief passing glances to the staff. Elizabeth was taken aback by Trina's desire to speak. They had not shared a friendship and the few times that Elizabeth had been forced to go home with her, she had felt very uncomfortable. Her whole family was weird. When Elizabeth had walked into a room that they occupied, there was this underlying tension that she could not figure out the cause of. None of them seemed to love each other, they were just co existing.

Trina's voice had a sniveling quality to it. A mixture of whining with a touch of know-it-all. She had recently cut her hair into a bob and wore a samurai type of ponytail on top that caused everyone to laugh behind her back. "I have been watching

Elizabeth lately and I think she will run the first chance she gets. She thinks she is better than us. She has spent the night at my house before and refused to bond with my family."

Elizabeth couldn't believe what she was hearing. Knowing this had nothing to do with Elizabeth's request and more to do with an incident that had happened a couple of months earlier, Elizabeth couldn't help but smirk a little. Elizabeth had been asked to stay at Trina's house to help with a new arrival. When Elizabeth had been introduced, she recognized the girl from a party she had attended in her past but gave no indication of it. Her first name, Karen, had never been known to Elizabeth so she felt justified in not informing the staff that they had partied together. Elizabeth had known her as "Ozzy" because she resembled a female version of a heavy metal singer named Ozzy Osbourne. On the morning of the incident, they were headed back to Helping Hands and Trina assigned herself to the middle while Elizabeth was told to sit on the right passenger side with Karen behind the driver. Elizabeth found the seating arrangement odd; she herself would have had the newcomer sit in the middle. Protocol was that if someone tried to escape you were to do everything you could to stop them. At the time, Elizabeth just figured it was a jealousy thing due to the fact that she and Karen had virtually ignored Trina in her own house the night before. Elizabeth was, by nature, kind at heart but could still find herself sporting a mean streak sometimes.

The car had been stopped at a red light in front of this run-down neighborhood called Pine Manor. The neighborhood was also aptly nicknamed Crime Manor due to the number of drug dealers that inhabited it. Karen took that moment to simply unlock her car door and bolt right out. Timid little Trina had done nothing to stop her. She always appeared stiff as a statue when she was sitting and Elizabeth had noticed no difference on that morning.

Mrs. Stein had questioned both she and Trina when they arrived at the facility empty handed. Trina and her mom spluttered through the interrogation contradicting each other the whole time. Feeling no loyalty to either of them, Elizabeth told the truth. That was when Trina began to hate Elizabeth. It wasn't because what Elizabeth had said may have caused Trina to be held at her Stage four any longer. Trina was a classic example of someone who was institutionalized. She wouldn't know what to do if she were released. Elizabeth had been shocked when she found out that Trina had been there for over a year and a half and never once requested to be moved up to another stage. She had been forced to move up by the staff.

Her thoughts returning to the present, Elizabeth was quick with a rebuttal to Trina's comment. "Are you talking from experience Trina?" she asked. It was an inside joke because nobody ever knew what had happened that morning due to the rules of the program to never mention an escape to anyone. Trina got the message loud and clear and looked back down at the ground.

Moving in for the kill, Elizabeth decided that she had held back her experiences at Trina's house with everyone at the rehab long enough. "Now getting back to what you said about your family. Would this be the same family that wouldn't allow me to flush the toilet if I had only peed in it? I fail to see how that would draw me closer to you, not to mention the way your father leers across the dinner table."

There was a gasp from the group, some by people who were shocked by the accusation and others because they could relate to what Elizabeth had just said.

49

Elizabeth continued, "As far as bonding with your family, shouldn't that begin with you, your mom and your dad before an outsider? You three barely say anything to one another. Don't try to throw some spotlight on me Trina. I'm cool with the fact that you don't think I should go to Stage three but you better have solid reasons for it, not this crap you're trying to fling."

Trina's face had turned beet red during the altercation and Mrs. Stein felt the need to step in. "It was not my intention to start a feud or use this as a platform to air personal feelings. Let us all stick to the facts, okay?"

A random voice called out, "You mean like how she is crushing on a counselor?"

Elizabeth was startled to see how visibly shaken Mrs. Stein appeared. She had always remained stoic through any crisis Elizabeth had seen her face. What made tonight so different? Had she found out about the hug that Paul had given her? Would she hold Elizabeth back for fear of showing favoritism or looking the other way regarding one of her counselors?

All of this happened in a flash but the room had turned chaotic. Everyone was talking aloud which was unheard of during evaluation time. The staff members were out of their seats, some leaving the room only to return a moment later.

Before she knew what was happening, Paul had taken her by the arm and steered her out of the room. Elizabeth's anger had not had a moment to simmer so she whirled around on Paul and hissed through her teeth, "What are you trying to do? Ruin everything for me? You know the boys are not to touch the opposite sex, what do you mean by taking me by the arm like that? And what the hell is going on?"

"You're right," Paul replied. "I should have had a female counselor chaperone us during our last meeting. I forgot how catty everyone can get due to the boredom of this place. How quickly gossip can form. I was selfish because I wanted that time with you. I will grab Christy in just a second but I just wanted to tell you that I will do everything in my power to get things back on track for you. I lost focus and it won't happen again."

Before his words could even register in Elizabeth's brain he had turned and walked back into the main room; a few seconds later he reappeared with Christy in tow. Christy was actually smiling as though she were getting a kick out of the whole situation.

"I haven't seen this much action since that day Mrs. Stein tackled the kid who tried to run last year. You should see the room right now, it is split into two groups…those who want you to fail and those who want you to succeed. Girl, you are a superstar." She began to laugh to the point that tears were running down her face. "Damn, my mascara." She began to wipe her eyes with the bottom of her shirt.

Paul had tried to appear nonchalant during this exchange. Christy looked him up and down and said, "You can cut the act in front of me Paul, I have known you too long. You have always been calm and cool until Elizabeth arrived. The way she got under your skin from the moment she arrived, was a dead giveaway. You were able to keep it from Mrs. Stein until the idiot in the group just shouted it out."

Paul's jaw was clenched and Elizabeth could see the muscles in his face. She would never have taken a second look at him had she ever crossed paths with him in her past. He looked like a jock and she had always gone for the rockers. But having that body walk by her every day for the last several months had taken its toll. Having been removed from her normal environment gave her a new appreciation for all types of men. It was nice to be attracted to someone closer to her own age too. Paul had to be about 19, she guessed.

"I'll take care of Mrs. Stein, we all know I am her favorite." Paul said. "Thanks for everything Christy. Do you mind bringing Elizabeth back into the room and I will follow in a minute?"

"You sure you two don't want a minute without all those prying eyes watching you?" Christy asked. "Look, I will even turn my back to you," she giggled again. "I love being part of a conspiracy. Old Helping Hands thought they killed the rebel in me but there is still a bit of it left and man it feels good."

Paul gently stroked Elizabeth's face with his thumb and whispered, "I know I have been very cryptic in my attempt at letting you know how I felt towards you and I probably caused more confusion than anything else. Hell, I don't even know how you feel about me, but let's get you to Stage three and go from there, okay?"

Elizabeth grabbed hold of the hand that was against her cheek and brought it to her lips. She was speechless but her smile and the nod of her head let him know that the feeling was mutual.

Chapter 18

By the time Christy brought her back to the group, it appeared that order had resumed. Mrs. Stein looked at Elizabeth and said, "I have decided to stop this town hall type of meeting and will not be allowing others to speak regarding your request. Therefore, it will be up to me and my staff to sort through matters and make our decision."

"You have always been fair to me Mrs. Stein, so I will await your decision and will respect whatever it will be."

It was Marie's turn to talk about why she felt she should move up and Elizabeth felt bad for her because it was very anticlimactic compared to what just happened during her time with the group.

A break was given while the staff made their decisions and the group helped to transform the meeting room for when the parents arrived to either console or congratulate their kids. It was always an informal affair and allowed everyone the chance to talk of other things rather than just why they were here.

Elizabeth and her mom had never been closer. Now that her mom had been clean for a month, Elizabeth could see how pretty she had once been and how contagious her laugh was to those around her. In the past, anyone who had met Elizabeth bragged about how much they loved her mom and how special she was to them. She couldn't appreciate it at the time because of the resentment she had felt, but now, she could see how even when her mom was hurting, it didn't stop her from helping others. She hoped that people would think as highly of her one day.

The decisions were always given before the parents arrived so that those who were denied could have time to react and regain their composure before having to face their parents. Elizabeth had never had to deal with that and she began to wonder if this would be the first time she would need to. It felt good to know that at least Paul was on her side and he was doing everything he could to help her succeed. She shook her head as she thought, *this is the same guy who fought me tooth and nail from the day I arrived and now we have this forbidden love thing going.* She wondered if these feelings would be as strong if she knew she could leave tomorrow or would they just fade the moment she was free. She had begun to psychoanalyze everything since coming to the program. It was taught that there was a secret motive behind every thought or action. Elizabeth believed that she had become so used to just siding with whoever could help her get her way that she lost sense of her God-given intuition that led her to people that were good for her for the sake of being good. There was always the feeling of being in a chess match, moving her pawns in an attempt to reach the other side without being destroyed. She could not think of a friendship she had since using drugs that was based on enjoying each other's company and helping each other reach their goals. It was all about who they knew to score weed from or what guy they could flirt with to get a ride somewhere. It had been exhausting never being able to let her guard down because as she was making her moves; the other side was playing the game as well and they wanted something in return. It had left her feeling like a whore at times.

The silly little bell that Mrs. Stein liked to use to signal that a decision had been reached chimed three times. The group reassembled like a swarm of bees buzzing their predictions of each outcome. Elizabeth was tempted to be angry with her fellow prisoners, but realized, this was all they had to look forward to in their mundane lives.

Mrs. Stein was dressed in a long dress that almost touched her ankles. A poor fashion choice in Elizabeth's eyes due to how short Mrs. Stein was. She was barely five feet one inches so Elizabeth thought the dress made her look dwarfish. Nevertheless, she still held her commanding air as she dashed or granted each person's request. Marie had slid into Stage five and the relief of it finally allowed her to smile. Those who were granted their request were given the opportunity to speak if they chose to. Marie who was usually so eloquent could barely muster a thank you before sitting back down. Elizabeth had been kept waiting until the very end for dramatic effect, no doubt. Paul had kept his promise of not being so obvious. He had looked at her just as randomly as he did anyone else while making sure not to walk or stand near her during the proceedings.

As Mrs. Stein cleared her throat, she began by saying, "If Miss Elizabeth Tartaglia could join me, she will be our final student of the day." Elizabeth could feel goose bumps on her arms and was grateful that she had chosen to wear a long-sleeved shirt that day. She held her head high as she approached Mrs. Stein.

"From the moment you entered our facility Elizabeth, you have been a challenge to us but not in the way we are used to. You never got physical or tried to run; you never refused a lesson…you were quite the opposite. The challenge you presented us with was due to your wanting to speed things along, the lack of time you took to relish the stage you were currently on; always looking forward. We had to discuss your behavior with our resident psychologist, Dr. Scott who always had nothing but positive remarks about you. He believes that your drive is essential to your recovery. That if we stifled your progress, you may stop sharing with the group and begin to internalize your feelings. I do not particularly agree with his analysis of you but I also do not have all of the letters behind my name that he does." The group smiled as she admitted herself inadequate in some area. "However, Dr. Scott is only a piece that makes up this puzzle regarding you."

Elizabeth had begun to switch her weight from one foot to the other due to her nerves and the sudden need to pee. *Why doesn't she just spit it out?* thought Elizabeth, *she always has to make things long and drawn out as a reminder that she is in charge.*

As if reading her mind, Mrs. Stein said, "Well let's not draw this out any longer, Elizabeth, the staff and I have reached the decision of allowing you to enter Stage three." Quickly holding up her hand to quiet the murmurs that had already started she continued, "With one stipulation." She allowed a dramatic pause before finishing, "This will be on a 30-day trial basis where we can revoke the stage should we feel it necessary. If after the 30 days you have continued to do well, we will recognize the stage as permanent. We are doing this in part to slow you down a bit. You will not be able to put in for a higher stage during the probationary period.

53

Going back to school is a big deal and we want you to focus solely on that. Do you understand what I have just said Elizabeth?"

Before answering Elizabeth took a look around the room to see the reactions on the faces of her friends and those she thought had been her friends. Trina was obviously seething, although, her face gave nothing away. Elizabeth saw her obsessively picking at her fingernails and cuticles. Something she had witnessed while staying at her house. Dr. Scott should name her the poster child for "internalizing feelings." Marie looked genuinely happy for her. The boys looked like they couldn't care less.

She wished she didn't care what other people thought of her but she did. She should have felt elated from the moment she heard that she had made it, but somehow, it felt like a hollow victory. In part, because it was on a temporary basis and then there was Paul. Although her mom had put her here on the pretense of her drug use, Elizabeth realized the main reason had been to get her away from Marcus. Now here she was beginning to have feelings for Paul. Did that mean that she hadn't loved Marcus after all, if he was so easily replaced? Paul had become her secret rescuer and that was a turn on. The volatility of their feelings towards one another at the beginning should have put her on high alert but she hadn't suspected anything. Paul was 19 so she wouldn't see him at the high school. Maybe it was for the best. Relationships were always the greatest in the beginning stages and it looked like this one would perpetually stay at that stage. They may be able to send subtle messages with their bodies such as their arms brushing against each other in passing causing the sensation of electricity through the body while at the same time not allowing themselves to react.

Snapping herself out of her daydream, she said, "Thank you," and sat back down. What more could she have said? The incredulous look on everyone's faces seemed to demand she say more but, *to hell with them*, she thought. This program had begun to feel like a game; a game she knew she was winning. Why get cocky and ruin things? Let them pull the 30-day trump card on her. The wheels had begun to turn in her mind. She had planned on seeing this whole program through since she seemed to always quit things in the past but now she began to entertain other thoughts. Thoughts of how she might use her newfound freedom to escape completely

.

Chapter 19

The key to this succeeding would be getting her mother on her side. She knew from eavesdropping on her mom's phone conversations that she had become disgruntled with the program. She had begun to question why there were so many stages and why, at the last one, the child had to remain there for six months before being released from the program. Helen thought that it was to try and justify the exorbitant amount of money the parents were paying. Helen could only talk freely to friends she had outside of the program. Even the parents from the program tended to act paranoid around one another. Afraid that one wrong word could be misinterpreted and their child would be set back a level.

Elizabeth would have to think of the best way to approach things with her mom; but in the meantime, she had school to concentrate on. Her tutor had expedited things and Elizabeth was to start first thing Monday morning. Since she had missed half the school year, she was slave to whatever electives they chose for her. She would not get her schedule until the morning she arrived there.

She was not allowed to go to the mall but could be left at home by herself for one hour. This allowed her mom to grab a few items she would need for school. It took Elizabeth a long time to even think of what she would want to wear because she knew her taste in the past would not fly here. To her surprise, she found that she wanted to get away from the all-black clothing and animal prints. She had begun to like pastels and feminine clothing. She knew her mom was on a budget but could not imagine showing up at school with clothes from Kmart. She knew of a few cheapie stores in the mall that she told her mom to check. She played it safe by asking for solid skirts and slacks and thought she could dress things up with the colored tops and accessories.

There were mixed feelings about going to this school. She liked the idea that she would most likely not know a soul who attended but the memories of Fort Myers High still plagued her.

Middle school had been the most positive time of her school years. Although the first day had been hectic due to her mom's car breaking down, they had to take a taxi which caused them to arrive late. The second shock had been when Elizabeth realized that she and Nicholas were the minority. She had grown up going to school with other black kids but seeing so many all at once kind of frightened her. That was her ignorance at the time because within the first few days, she had made some of the best friends she had ever had. There was a funny boy named Malcolm that could light up a room with his smile and a huge guy named Douglas who Elizabeth nicknamed "bodyguard" when he saved her from this bully one day by dropping him in a garbage can head first for calling her names.

She became popular after joining the drama department and newspaper staff. The school had even started an advice column called "Dear Eagle," that Elizabeth was in charge of. Her natural ability to help others really kicked in and within a few weeks, she received more questions than she could ever answer. Only the newspaper teacher knew her identity, which Elizabeth thought was pretty cool.

Imagine her surprise when she began high school all full of hopes and dreams only to be greeted with chants of "go home freshman, go home" by the upper classmen as she walked the halls. The teachers had seemed indifferent to the newcomers and showed open favoritism to the popular kids. Kids whose families were affluent and had attended the high school themselves. Carrying on the tradition of cheerleaders, jocks, and beauty queens.

Elizabeth quickly realized that a pair of Nikes and some Jordache jeans would not be enough to let her squeak by unnoticed with the wealthier kids. There was a new form of segregation that had nothing to do with color but with class. Cliques were formed in the lunchroom; so Elizabeth began to eat outside. Her brother was already at the school but wasn't much help to her. He seemed to be accepted by all the groups and she would often hear people yelling "Yo, Nick!" in the hallways to him. It did not take long to realize that Nicholas was supplying the football players and others with the occasional joint which granted him access to their circle. It was not that easy for a girl.

When her mom returned from the mall, Elizabeth held her breath as she reached into the bag that was handed to her. Expecting the worst, she gave herself away by exclaiming "Oh, these are nice," to her mom.

"Don't act so surprised," her mother responded. "You know, when I played piano in the jazz clubs in New York, I was quite the fashion plate."

"Sorry mom," replied Elizabeth, "I guess this is new for the both of us. While I am getting used to my new style and my limitations to shop, I need to rely and trust in you more. Thanks for going to the mall." She leaned over and kissed her mom on the cheek.

Her mom smiled and gave her a big hug. "I wish you the best at your new high school. I know you are going to do great. Now let's see the new clothes on you, feel like putting on a little fashion show for your old mom?" she asked.

"You bet." Elizabeth raced to her room to try on the new clothes. She was grateful for the few pounds she had gained which caused the clothes to fit the way they were meant to. Elizabeth used to have to use jacket clips and safety pins to alter things in the past due to how tiny she was. Now a size two was a perfect fit.

Chapter 20

Elizabeth's alarm went off at 5:00 a.m. on Monday morning. She wanted to give herself plenty of time to get ready, not to mention the 30-minute drive to the school. She had been allowed to do a facial masque the night before and her skin glowed as a result. Her hair was a little unruly but without permission to use any type of styling product she was forced to make due with bobby pins. Try as she might to put a positive spin on things; the reflection in the mirror could only be described as homely.

Tears welled in her eyes at the memory of how pretty she used to be. She remembered how she and her friends used to walk down Palm Beach Boulevard and count how many cars would honk at them. She knew it had been childish to think that the more honks you got the prettier you were but at the time, it had been a big deal. No matter what they said at Helping Hands; being pretty was important.

She felt as if she were in mourning over the girl she used to be. Before her thinking could get too morbid, she stopped herself and thought, *I can get her back. Just the good parts.* She began convincing herself that the only way to do that was to leave the treatment center. It would take her another eight months if she were lucky to get to Stage six which allowed cosmetics. Certainly, her hair would grow longer by the then but she would still be stuck with the face that was staring at her in the mirror.

It wasn't that she hated her looks completely but makeup helped to enhance what she was born with. Her eyes were definitely her finest feature. They weren't your typical brown but had flecks of hazel in them. Nice on their own but transformed when eyeliner and mascara were added. Her nose was her least favorite. It was quite large, which she had always attributed to her Italian side. Six months before entering the program, she had been drinking with her best friend and as she was getting out of the passenger side of the car she started laughing at something Kristy had said. Her head was thrown back in laughter and as it came back down it cracked the door frame of the car. Her nose was broken and blood began to pour from it. Due to her inebriation, she did not feel the pain right away and didn't even have the sense to be angry when she noticed Kristy laughing again, but this time at her injury.

She had to face the fact that this was as good as it was going to get for now. She heard her mom calling from the hallway and began to quickly gather her things. As Elizabeth got in the car, she knew her mom was just as nervous as she was. After a few minutes of mindless chatter, Helen finally said out loud what she had been thinking; "Now you aren't going to try and run away are you, Elizabeth?"

"Of course not, mom," she quickly replied. "I know this probably sounds messed up but I have left you out of too much in the past so if I were planning on running, I would tell you." Elizabeth glanced sideways at her mom so as not to appear too

57

interested in her response but in reality, she was very interested. Her mom's reaction would let Elizabeth know where her loyalty stood.

Helen said, "That doesn't sound messed up at all Elizabeth. I am actually relieved to hear you say that you would tell me. You and I are in this together and if the time comes that one of us believes we need to end it with Helping Hands, we will come to a decision together."

"Thanks, mom." Inside Elizabeth's head, she was doing the Snoopy happy dance. Her mom was on her side. Knowing this allowed her to feel that she could handle anything that was thrown her way today at school. The car pulled up to the front of the school and without a backward glance she told her mom she loved her and was on her way.

The adrenaline rush she felt as the five-minute warning bell rang was indescribable. She stood in the middle of the courtyard feeling as though a story she had read had come to life. All of this had been described to her by the other students at Helping Hands. The noises that surrounded her were magnified; from car keys rattling, lockers slamming and girls calling to one another.

Elizabeth was armed with the school map so she was pretty confident as to where her homeroom was located. What she dreaded the most was the way teachers were notorious for parading a new kid in front of the class. It was the last thing in the world she wanted to happen, so of course by the final ringing of the bell she found herself being held by the shoulders by her coffee buzzed science teacher, Mr. Bloom.

As her name was told to the class, she heard a shout from the back saying, "Just what we need; another nerd."

Elizabeth could feel her face flush but refused to look down at the floor. Her eyes scanned the room to see if she could figure out who had said it when she saw her counselor, Christy, sitting in the second row. Never in her life had she been referred to as a nerd. A head banger, certainly; a stoner, most definitely but never a nerd.

She found an empty seat and tried to act like her book was the most interesting thing in the world. When the class was at an end, she looked at Christy and raised her hand to her without thinking. It was required at Helping Hands to wait to be acknowledged before speaking but the look of horror on Christy's face as she frantically shook her head "no" let Elizabeth know that it wasn't necessary at school. It wasn't until after class that she knew what Christy had really feared was her cover being blown. She passed as a regular student since she could wear makeup and do her hair. Obviously, nobody knew she was part of Helping Hands and she wanted to keep it that way.

Elizabeth made a mental note to apologize for her faux pas when she saw Christy after school.

Chapter 21

The day flew by and to her surprise, Elizabeth began to care less and less of what the others thought of her. Her fellow students seemed like such kids. The things she had heard them talking about seemed so childish. Her worldliness did not make her feel superior, it made her feel envious. This is what she had missed with the drugs; she missed this whole carefree time in her life. She had been in such a rush to grow up that she completely bypassed a stage in her life that she could never get back. She almost felt like she was pretending to be a student.

Elizabeth had always been known as the countdown queen. It had begun as a child when she had found ways to make uncomfortable situations go by quicker. She thought that the countdown to her freedom was to begin today. Her first order of business would be to get a feel for the school; find out who from the program may be in her classes as well as when she passed them in the halls. She must find out when and where she would go unnoticed from the Helping Hands crowd. Elizabeth was certain they were told to keep an eye on her.

For the next couple of weeks, she would keep her nose clean and concentrate on her studies. She would start dropping subtle hints around her mom about her desire to leave the program and see what type of response she would get. She would turn 18 in four months and by that time, nobody could stop her from leaving but that would only be plan B. To have to stay there for another four months, was unthinkable. Once she set her mind to something, there was no turning back. She had failed enough in the past so it was not an option in this case.

She found everyone waiting for her at the curb of the school where a small van picked them up to take them back to Helping Hands. They were anxious to hear about her day. She was able to make Christy laugh about the mishap in class so that turned out OK. She told them how overwhelmed she had become when she heard about several projects that were due in the next couple of weeks. It wasn't like she had a social schedule so it shouldn't be too hard to complete them on time.

Although she had seen several good looking guys at school, she found that she kept thinking about Paul. It was the first day in months that they hadn't seen one another. She wondered if there might be a way for him to meet her at the school one day. She felt like she was about to betray him with her plans to escape.

In the following weeks, Christy had become her new ally in regards to stealing a moment or two with Paul. She would ask Elizabeth to help with something outside of the room on the days that Mrs. Stein left early. Paul would be waiting for her in the hall where all they were afforded was a brief hug and exchange of words but it was enough to send shivers down her spine. They stood close so they could whisper and Elizabeth's hair would move as his breath came close to her ear. The anticipation of a simple touch of his hand made her catch her breath.

She was pleased at how slow the relationship had to go; it was unlike anything she had ever known. Boys in the past had always wanted to cop a feel right off the bat, so she thought that was how things were in the real world. She had thought that boys that courted girls were ancient history.

Unfortunately, in the midst of the good feelings, Elizabeth questioned whether it was merely the fact that their relationship was forbidden that made it so alluring. She asked herself, "Would it be half as exciting if it were allowed?"

Back in the main room, whenever it was her turn to share her day she would pretend it was just she and Paul in the room; that way she didn't have to waste the precious alone moments on those subjects.

Chapter 22

It was on a Sunday when her plan began to really take shape. It had been a rare weekend where she did not have a newcomer with her. As Elizabeth and her mom were eating breakfast, she nonchalantly mentioned how nice it was not to have to spend her entire day cooped up in the Helping Hands building now that she was back at school. Helen replied with a compliment on how well Elizabeth had transitioned.

Elizabeth said, "It isn't that I'm not grateful but I wonder when the day will come when I won't have to go back at all." She began to get nervous when, after a pregnant pause, her mother had still not responded. Looking up, she was surprised at what she saw.

Helen had a look of relief on her face as she reached across the table to take Elizabeth's hand in her own. "Elizabeth," she said, "I could not bear to be separated from you again. I am not talking about physically but emotionally. This past year you and I were so far apart, I had no clue as to what you were thinking or going through. I could sense the resentment you felt toward me, and everything I did to try and fix things just made them worse. I don't want to be left guessing again; so please promise me that you will include me in whatever plans you make and know that I am on your side."

Her mother had tricked her before in order to get her locked up, *could this also be a trick,* thought Elizabeth. Again, she had the feeling that she was in a human chess match and it was her move. To blurt out what was on her mind, was incredibly risky but it was exactly what her mom was asking of her.

When the hell did I become so cynical and distrusting? she asked herself. *This is my mother for heaven's sake. No matter what her issues are as far as the drinking is concerned, there is no doubt in my mind that she loves me.*

As if a dam had broken, Elizabeth's heart began to tumble out of her mouth, "Mom, I am ready NOW. School is great and I wouldn't have had the nerve to go back if you hadn't put me in Helping Hands, where they helped me regain my self-esteem. I will forever be grateful to them for that but it is killing me to watch these new kids come in and see how the team there just breaks their spirits before building them back up. It is heart wrenching. I don't agree with many of their practices and if I were to leave, I have every intention of involving myself in some sort of support group so that I don't backslide."

Helen had been shaking her head in agreement with everything that Elizabeth had been saying. With a wisdom that Elizabeth had never known, her mom began to work out the details with her. Helen pointed out flaws in Elizabeth's plan that she had not even considered. Elizabeth had thought it would be best if she left school early one day but Helen was certain that Mrs. Stein would have a watchdog on staff at the school to report any schedule changes with students listed with Helping Hands.

"Of course she would, how stupid of me," said Elizabeth.

"You are not stupid," said Helen "I just happened to overhear something one day at the rehab regarding that young boy that recently tried to run from school."

Elizabeth smiled, "Look at us mom, we are just breaking all the rules now. Not only planning my escape but talking about people who have attempted to run themselves."

They both began to laugh but as the reality of the situation began to sink in, they sobered up.

"Can you believe that we can't just walk in there tomorrow and have you sign me out? I know that they would try and pit us against each other with their psychobabble. They would tell you that I am manipulating you like I have in the past and they would tell me that you aren't stable enough to keep me on the straight and narrow. They would assure me that I would be shooting heroin by the end of the week." Elizabeth's voice quivered at the mention of the drug. Heroin was the one drug she never tried. Needles had always scared her. In that moment, Elizabeth knew what she would write about in her Moral Inventory that evening. Although she wouldn't be there much longer, she wanted to complete all of her assignments as not to draw unwanted attention to herself.

The final plan was this: on the following Friday, Elizabeth was to go straight to the office when the final bell rang at school. This would give her a bird's eye view of what was going on at the pickup line. She knew from the rules she had been given that even if someone were to spot her, they were not to try and retrieve her. They were only to report back to Mrs. Stein when they arrived at Helping Hands. Mrs. Stein would then try to be in touch with Elizabeth's mom to confirm whether she was in cahoots with what was going on. The bottom line was that they could not force her back without her mom's cooperation. In Elizabeth's mind, Helen would not pass the test until they had finally passed the Helping Hands building.

She had not wanted to wait until Friday but upon really thinking it through, it made more sense because the school was always crazy busy on a Friday which would help to conceal Elizabeth as she made her way to the office. It would also give her mom time to talk to Fort Myers High about transferring Elizabeth the following week.

It was crucial that Elizabeth did nothing to give herself away. She was to fall back on all of her acting skills. Paul had been on her mind all weekend. She knew he had become a crutch to her and she no longer wanted to rely on a man to make her complete. Men had been the downfall of her mother and she had begun to repeat the same pattern. If Helping Hands had taught her anything, it was to accept yourself for who you are and to hell with anyone else that tried to make you something you weren't.

Pleased with the progress she and her mom had made, Elizabeth decided to start her journal early. On the weekends, you were allowed to pick your own topic to write about. Preparing herself for the emotions that were about to be unleashed; Elizabeth went to her room to find her favorite pen with the pink fluffy troll on it.

Chapter 23

Today, I want to talk about why my taste for certain drugs stopped at heroin. For one thing, there isn't a movie out there that has ever portrayed heroin use as glamorous. I started drinking alcohol and doing drugs to feel prettier, sexier, and happier. The glimpses I had of heroin users were just the opposite. In my neighborhood, there were some girls that were recognizable right away as prostitutes, even though they were only a couple of years older than me. I had even been mistaken for one of these girls as I would walk down Second Street to visit friends. Men in Mercedes would slow down and roll down their windows to try and lure me in. I was so offended at the time that these men could mistake me for girls who sold their bodies. It wasn't until recently that I realized that it wasn't that I had a certain look that resembled a prostitute, it was that those poor girls were just kids so they resembled me. Does that make sense to you? I wasn't them, they were me…only someone got a hold of them and turned them into something from their nightmares.

One of the assholes that would enslave these girls was this Hispanic guy that lived a couple of blocks away. I had witnessed girls coming and going from his house over the years and could guess as to what went on inside. One day, I was cutting through backyards to get to my friend Sean's house when I noticed the drug dealer/pimp opening his back door. I could tell right away he was high and had already begun to plan a change of route so I wouldn't have to get too close. He beckoned me over and as he raised his arm, I could see track marks and a bunch of bruises.

He leered at me and kept saying, "Come here for a minute," and I knew if I did, I was a goner. I did not care if I looked like a scaredy-cat; I ran like the wind. I didn't look back but I could hear him cackling like a maniac. It was a game to him. He was a life destroyer. Have you ever heard that term "my blood felt like ice in my veins?" That is exactly how I felt during those few seconds that I thought I could have been yanked into that house and changed forever.

We humans aren't too far off from the animal kingdom. There were times that I felt like the prey that the predator had in its sights. There were other times that I was the one planning and scheming to get something out of someone.

Anyway, back to the heroin. It was on that day that I recognized what that drug could do and I was smart enough to draw the line there. Too bad I couldn't have done that with the crack, hash, or other crap. If I had, I wouldn't be where I am today.

Elizabeth felt relieved as she put her pen down and closed the journal. For the first time, it felt like a memory had actually been extracted from her brain versus relived like before. The memory had been removed as did the feelings of revulsion that went along with it. *There is something to be said about therapy,* she thought to herself.

Monday came by in a flash and Elizabeth felt like an anxious actor waiting in the wings until show time. She had rehearsed how she would get through the few hours after school that was required of her to be at Helping Hands. She would participate in group without seeming overeager. The hardest part would be when she was around Marie who she had shared everything with since their friendship had formed. She knew Marie would be devastated when Elizabeth wasn't at the pickup line on Friday. It had been a long time since Elizabeth had to apologize to someone for her actions but the need to do so now was overwhelming. Just as she was beginning to think that she would never be given the opportunity to explain things to Marie, a new idea popped into her head. She would never want to jeopardize Marie's position at Helping Hands but maybe rather than addressing a letter to Marie directly, she could mail it to Marie's parents letting them know that she was OK and how badly she felt for not being able to tell Marie beforehand. She could give them the opportunity to say things indirectly to let Marie know what had happened to her. Marie was a smart girl and could figure out what they meant even though she wouldn't know how the information had come to them. Not until she herself had left Helping Hands and could talk freely with her parents again.

Feeling so much better knowing her friend would not be left in the dark for long, Elizabeth's mind strayed to Paul. The last time they had gotten together was in a darkened doorway and things had gotten heated due to the close proximity of their bodies. The warmth of his breath as he whispered caused Elizabeth to purposefully tilt her head to the side so that his lips brushed across her neck. Paul quickly pulled away as if he couldn't trust himself. He had taken her hand and given it a soft kiss before disappearing down the hall. Elizabeth knew he must be struggling with his responsibility as a counselor. She had no idea where he lived so sending a letter to him was out of the question.

Elizabeth knew in her heart that there was no future for them as a couple. She also knew that he had served a need while she was cooped up in the program but the minute she tasted freedom, all the longing for him would disappear. It wasn't that she had purposefully used him, it was just human nature. With that thought in mind, she concluded that there would be no need to get any type of message to Paul when she left. Sure, he would be hurt for a while but with nobody but Christy to share it with, he would soon have to move on as well.

During school that day, she received her midterm report card and was proud to see all A's and B's with only one C. Marcus had worked so hard to convince her that she was stupid that she had begun to believe it. These grades showed her just the opposite and she vowed that nobody would ever be allowed to bring her down like that again. "Allowed" was the right word to use because nobody *made* her feel that way, she "allowed" their negativity to penetrate into her spirit. That was one of the first things she learned at Helping Hands because she was so trained into trying to blame others for her troubles; making it seem like everyone had "made" her do things.

Elizabeth was glad that she would have all of her Moral Inventory books to look back on when she left. The world would try to get her to fall again and it would succeed if she did not keep things fresh in her mind and never forget where she came from. She hated the quote "once an addict, always an addict" but there was a ring of truth in it. If she got cocky and believed that she could go back into the same circles she was involved with before she came to rehab and come out unscathed, she would backslide. One toke of a joint would seem harmless until it needed to be washed down with a beer and then when the warm blanket feeling encased her, a line of coke would not be far behind. Amnesia would set in about how horribly she always felt the next day. Her gasp from this last thought was audible and she realized that her daydream had taken place in her class with Christy. As she turned her head, she saw Christy staring at her. Christy drew an "R" in the air with her finger, then pointed at Elizabeth followed by the "OK" symbol; which Elizabeth deciphered as "Are you OK?" She quickly did her own unspoken language by shaking her head "yes" while holding up her report card and swiping her hand across her forehead. Hoping her gestures translated to "Yes, Whew…good grades on my report card." Elizabeth was reassured by the smile that appeared on Christy's face. For the next four days, she would need to have better control of her thoughts. Another slip like that would have alarms going off at Helping Hands.

Chapter 24

By the end of the day on Tuesday, Elizabeth felt mentally checked out. Her disinterest in the group discussion caught the attention of Mrs. Stein as she came into the room to give some papers to Paul. She leaned over to whisper in his ear.

Elizabeth glanced up in time to see him shake his head in understanding and he locked eyes with her. She knew that she had been avoiding him for the last couple of days but she was in self-preservation mode and could not risk any action on her part to give herself away. It had become apparent that her inaction was gaining attention anyway.

Paul had slipped out of the room twice the day before probably hoping that she would excuse herself on the pretext of using the bathroom. He had returned a few minutes later when he realized she wasn't planning on meeting him.

When Mrs. Stein finally left the room, Paul's eyes showed signs of being hurt. He abruptly cut off a boy who had been in the middle of speaking and said, "You're awfully quiet today, Elizabeth."

Could you be any more obvious? Elizabeth thought to herself. She shrugged her shoulders and said, "I have a little bit of a headache." In an instant, his look turned to concern.

"Can I get you an aspirin?" he asked.

You mean a chewable children's aspirin, thought Elizabeth. It was the only type of medication they were allowed. She shook her head and replied, "No, thank you." She felt mad at Paul. He was acting like a puppy dog and she didn't like it. Her ex was very abrasive and demanding and Paul was beginning to show signs of being the complete opposite. Would it ever be possible to find someone right in the middle, she wondered. A guy that would never raise his hand to her and would help her through life's obstacles like a teammate rather than someone who thought she was some poor, defenseless damsel in distress.

Tears were beginning to well up in her eyes and she brushed them away with the back of her hand. She felt like she was on an emotional rollercoaster. One minute she was thinking of how much she would miss Paul and the next she couldn't stand the sight of him. One minute she was ready to take on the world and the next ready to fold like a deck of cards. "It's just the stress of the situation you are in," she told herself. Fear had begun to creep in regarding her leaving the shelter of Helping Hands. It had not dawned on her until just then that she had been spending all of her time and energy in planning this great escape and had not even considered what her game plan would be once she was free. She had never been good on her own. She had always relied on the companionship of friends or boyfriends. When she was very young, she had no problem playing solitaire for hours on end or reading the day away but as she got older, the silence of a room made her extremely uncomfortable to the point of fright. At first, she had tried to stifle it with loud music but that would only agitate her more. She learned at the program that she had suffered from abandonment issues. Without ever being aware of it, even her father's murder had left an emotional scar as if he had willingly walked out on her. Her mother's bouts of drinking and leaving at all hours of the night would cause Elizabeth's imagination to go into overdrive; always preparing her for the day she would be told that her mother had died in a car accident, of alcohol poisoning, or at the hand of another. Not being able to count on Nicholas who always ran out the door at the first sign of trouble.

She was becoming suspicious of her mother's willingness to help too. Was this a way for Helen to start drinking again? The moment the spotlight of Helping Hands was off of her, would she begin her downward spiral again? It was something she would have to openly discuss with her mom that night, if she didn't have a newcomer to bring home with her. She had one the night before and hoped that they might do one night on, one night off. She didn't like the distrust and doubt that was beginning to take residence in her head. There had always been an unseen enemy, but it had remained dormant for the past few months. *What has woken you from your slumber?* thought Elizabeth. Maybe leaving was not in her best interest. Helping Hands had pounded into their heads that if they continued the lifestyle they had been leading before they came there, they would either end up in the hospital, dead, or in jail. Just when she thought she was about to snap and break down completely, a staff member announced that it was parent pick up time.

Chapter 25

Trying not to break into a run, Elizabeth finally approached her mother's car. As she climbed in and felt secure that the darkness outside was obscuring her, she began to cry hysterically. She was unable to control her breathing as the wracking sobs overtook her. Helen knew enough to drive out of the parking lot before launching into a bunch of questions.

Elizabeth had begun shaking her head "no" without stopping. Her voice came out in a whisper which caused Helen to have to strain to hear her words. "I can't do it," began Elizabeth, "I can't do it, mom."

"You can't do what?" asked Helen

"What if I go back to the way I was? What if I were to die? I would go to hell. I just know it. What if Helping Hands is the only place that can help me?"

"Elizabeth, calm down!" Helen said sternly. She grabbed Elizabeth's hand and squeezed really hard. It startled her just enough to get her wits back.

"Mom, I really screwed up. I think they know. Mrs. Stein was whispering to Paul and then he seemed to be watching me closer than usual."

"Sweetie, it is only reasonable that you would start to get cold feet. This place is all you have known for over six months. I have no regrets for sending you there but I do think the time has come for you to branch out. They have stifled you to the point of oppression and *that* I don't agree with."

Elizabeth had calmed down but had begun to hiccup. "I feel like there is a double standard at Helping Hands where they tell you to stop playing the victim but at the same time, want to keep you a victim at their hands so they can control you. We were asked the other day to list some things we liked to do and I couldn't tell if the things I named were things I really liked or what they would like me to like." Elizabeth began to cry again and wailed, "I don't even make sense when I talk anymore. I can't get my point across. What I mean is that I don't know if I am the real Elizabeth or the one they have molded."

"Don't you worry," said Helen, "I have been catching glimpses of the real Elizabeth more and more as each day passes. It sounds to me like the two Elizabeths are having a showdown but I know the carbon copy does not stand a chance and the real you will be triumphant."

They had just pulled into the driveway when Elizabeth leaned over and hugged her mom and said, "I don't know about you but I am exhausted. Mind if I hit the sack early tonight?"

"Not at all darling. A good night's sleep is exactly what you need. When you wake up, you will see everything fall into place. You will regain the confidence that had begun to waiver and will know just what to do tomorrow."

As she entered the house, she went straight to the bathroom and brushed her teeth. Stifling a yawn, Elizabeth said, "Goodnight mom, see ya in the morning." She flopped onto her bed and without changing into pajamas, fell into a deep sleep.

A dream began to form almost immediately in a kaleidoscope of images and colors. It finally stabilized into a scene that Elizabeth recognized. The dream was a memory. After her father's death, they had moved several times ending briefly in a trailer park in Fort Lauderdale, Florida. It did not take long for Elizabeth and Nicholas to find other kids who were in the same boat of having parents that were M.I.A most of the time. There was another brother and sister; Michelle and Larry that lived a street over and it was there that Nicholas tried a cigarette for the first time. Elizabeth's dream was capturing that very moment so vividly that she would have no trouble recalling it the following day. It was late at night and Nicholas was sprawled across one of Larry's couches. The soundtrack to the movie "Grease" was playing on the stereo. Elizabeth was sitting on the arm of the couch as Larry walked in. "Want to try a smoke?" he asked Nicholas "I know where my mom hides them."

"Sure," said Nicholas as he began to play air drums to "Grease Lightening."

As Larry left the room, Elizabeth sidled over to him and said, "I don't think you should do that Nicholas; you might burn a hole in the couch or something."

"Quit trying to tell me what to do," was his response.

Shrugging her shoulders, she went to join Michelle who had walked out of the room. She found Michelle in her mother's room. Throwing the closet door open, she said, "Let's play dress up."

Hearing the beginning lyrics of "You're the one that I want" from the next room, Elizabeth's eyes lit up as she added, "Why don't we dress up like Sandy from the movie and lip synch to this song?"

Michelle shook her hips and snapped her fingers to the beat and the girls fell to the floor in a fit of laughter.

The dream shifted to them strutting into the living room, now smoky from the lit cigarettes held by both boys. Coughing, Elizabeth fanned the smoke away from her face and announced that the boys were to judge her and Michelle, who were performing the same song.

In Elizabeth's mind, she *was* Olivia Newton John. She closed her fist making it her microphone. She danced in the high heels only stumbling once and froze as if on cue when the song ended. To her surprise, when all was said and done, Nicholas voted that she was the best one. After his declaration, she noticed his face had taken on a greenish hue although he was trying very hard not to act as if anything were wrong.

Quickly making up an excuse as to why they should be leaving, Elizabeth ran to the bedroom to return Michelle's mom's belongings. When she returned to the living room, her brother was clutching his stomach and groaning softly.

Once they were out the door and into the dark night, Nicholas allowed himself to be supported by Elizabeth. There were only a couple of street lamps which illuminated them every so often but it appeared that the fresh air was helping Nicholas and his skin looked a shade more normal. "You better get that makeup off your face before mom gets home," he said and then with a crooked grin added, "You actually were really good tonight."

"Thanks," said Elizabeth. Walking past the last lamp, they were plunged back in to darkness but not before Nicholas caught sight of the smile that spread across Elizabeth's face.

The smile did not end in the dream; it was on Elizabeth's face as she lay in bed, followed by a small giggle that was enough to wake her. She sat up in bed and replayed the scenario in her head. What a great feeling it was to have a dream that left her happy. Helping Hands would have wanted her to focus on the darkness of the situation: poor helpless kids whose parents left them alone, God forbid, trying a cigarette at such a tender age, singing to unwholesome music. For shame! She laughed again and decided at that moment that whatever her next Moral Inventory topic would be, she would shed the light of happiness on it. "Two days and counting," she said aloud. She curled back up in bed anticipating another great dream.

Chapter 26

Rising to the smell of bacon, Elizabeth shed the blankets that had been covering her to her chin. Looking at the bedspread with Strawberry Shortcake images on it, she made a mental note to ask her mom for something a little more age appropriate. Dragging her feet into the kitchen, she saw her mom busy with the preparations for breakfast. "Can you believe it is already Wednesday?" Helen said over her shoulder.

"I know," she said as she grabbed a piece of bacon that was draining on a paper towel. "You know, I will most likely be bringing a newcomer home tonight, so we need to be careful what we say in front of her. When you are new, you are desperate to make brownie points, and if she were to hear something she thought she could report on, she would do it in a heartbeat."

"I don't think there is much more to say anyway. We know the drill for Friday by heart. You are to go straight to the office when the final bell rings. You are to keep your head low and make eye contact with no one. You are to wait in the office for me. I will already be in the parking lot but will wait until I see the white van pull away before going in to retrieve you. By the time we get home, the phone will be ringing off the hook with them trying to reach us in regards to your disappearance. I will then inform them that it was I who took you out of the school and the program." She flipped fried eggs onto the empty plates at the table and with a nod of her head added, "End of story."

"Geez mom, ever think of being a criminal?"

"No, I left that up to your older brother Mark." They both began to laugh because Mark was quite a character.

Mark was the eldest of Helen's children from her first marriage and was at least 20 years older than Elizabeth. From what she had heard, he had been in trouble since he was a young kid. Always drawn to the tough guys who rode motorcycles, it was no surprise that as he got older, he became a member of the Hell's Angels. He had been arrested and put in jail a couple of times, and although that part wasn't funny, one story as to how he got there was. Elizabeth was recalling the morning that Helen received a call from him informing her that he had been arrested for bank robbery. Apparently, the getaway driver made a wrong turn and wound up on a dead end street where they were sitting ducks for the police who had been chasing them. Mark's final words were spoken solemnly as he said, "Ma, I knew it was going to be a bad day when I put my ski mask on, and the eye and nose holes didn't match up." Replaying that day in her head, Elizabeth snorted and thought, *really, Mark, that was your only clue to the way the day would end?*

Mark was no longer with them, having died from a gunshot wound the previous year. His girlfriend was serving a sentence for his death, but it was still unclear as to what really happened. Her mistake had been that she lied to the police the first time, so therefore looked guilty when she finally came clean. Her first story was that

71

during one of their fights, Mark had come into the room waving a gun and threatening to kill himself. She said that as she was trying to wrestle the gun away from him, it went off, shooting him in the head. When the autopsy was done, it proved that the trajectory of the bullet did not match her story, so she then said that Mark had been threatening to shoot her, and it was self-defense. Either way, it was really sad because Elizabeth had witnessed in the past how abusive Mark was to his girlfriends, and adding heroin into the mix was a deadly combination.

Just another example of how you gravitate to those who are the worst for you, and then, the drugs just muddy the water even more, causing normal people to do crazy things, thought Elizabeth. She shook her head as she thought of how tragic her family was. She had heard of generational curses and wondered if that was the reasoning behind her family history.

Maybe I can break this curse, she thought, *maybe if I have kids one day, they won't have to repeat our history. They would have one thing going for them, and that was that due to everything Elizabeth had done and tried, the little suckers wouldn't get away with a thing*, smilingly, she thought, *try sneaking out on my watch...not going to happen.* She thanked her mom for breakfast and began to get dressed for the day.

Was it really Wednesday? Two days to go, Elizabeth repeated once more. Today was one of the last days that she would have the chance to reassure Paul. She knew that she couldn't promise anything regarding a relationship with him, but she hoped to tell him what he had meant to her during this time as well as what a great guy she thought he was. She hoped that it would soften the blow when he realized that she was gone. If he was anything like her, she knew that he would replay their last conversation over and over in his mind. He would dissect each phrase trying to find meaning as if there had been a hidden code. As Elizabeth thought of those last two words, it gave her the idea that maybe that is exactly what she could give him. Who knew what the future would hold, maybe Paul would leave the program one day soon, and if he still had feelings for her, he could find her. *Hopeless romantic*, Elizabeth thought and smiled as she gathered her books for school. She glanced at the bare walls in her room, noting that a decorating project was definitely in order.

The drive that morning allowed Elizabeth to reflect on her time at Helping Hands. It was like a mini movie playing in her head, which began with her crazy look – as she first came to the facility: blue boots, denim jacket with the paisley lining – and then to her getting her hair chopped off and the climb to Level Three. It did bother her to think that she would be quitting Helping Hands just like she had quit so many other things, but she justified it as being different because it would be a positive change.

There was a church in their neighborhood that Elizabeth thought she would like to join. If there were a teen group, that would be even better. The idea of a clean slate with complete strangers had a strange appeal. Normally walking into a room full of strangers freaked her out, but now thinking of people who had no idea about her past was refreshing.

As she got out of the car, she smiled at her mom and said, "See ya later, alligator," and waited to hear: "after a while, crocodile" from her mom before shutting the door. She seemed to be looking at everything with new eyes as she walked to the side door. The thought of attending school without the attachment to

Helping Hands would be so freeing. She was actually excited about the prospect of decorating her locker. She hadn't bothered to use the one assigned to her at Mariner High because she feared it being searched, and God forbid she had put a picture of the Beatles or something in there; she would have been bumped right back down to Level One. Just not worth the risk.

Knowing that freedom was close at hand, Elizabeth was getting excited about the little things that she had taken for granted before. She would soon be able to listen to the radio while doing homework or walk to the little bakery store down the street to buy tiny cherry pies. She laughed as she thought, *I hope I remember how to use the telephone.*

Just then, Christy had walked beside her and asked, "What's so funny?"

Frozen for a split second, Elizabeth regained her composure and lied, "I was just thinking about how funny my cats are."

"I'm allergic," said Christy, "hey, I have a meeting with Paul today right after school to plan for some future assignments. Did you want me to pass any messages to him? I don't know what is going on, but he seemed a little down this week."

Elizabeth could feel her cheeks heating up and sat down on a bench that they had just walked up to. "Please tell him I am sorry about how weird I have been acting lately. I have been a little paranoid lately (true enough) about someone finding out about us (not so true). I will excuse myself today to use the bathroom and hopefully will have a chance to tell him as well."

Christy smiled, "You know, I only have three more months of being on sixth phase, and then I am pretty much done. I think I would still like to be a counselor at Helping Hands but not if it means Mrs. Stein will keep treating me like a patient."

"I get it," replied Elizabeth. "Thanks for always being so fair to me. It is funny how I hated Paul in the beginning and actually thought your brother was cute, only to fall for Paul in the end."

Realizing how chummy they looked on the bench, Christy glanced around nervously and began to rise, "Well, I better get going. I will be sure to give Paul the message."

"Thanks, see ya." Elizabeth continued to class and decided that she would do a mental practice run that day to prepare for Friday.

Chapter 27

Elizabeth picked a table outside to eat her lunch later that day. It gave her a view of the office as well as the pickup location of the van. As she ate her loaded baked potato, she took inventory of the school staff that she could see inside and which chairs in the lobby would give her the best cover as she waited for her mom. There were two entry doors; one on either side of the office but the one facing the north had a small window which was tinted compared to the other side which was clear.

She got up to throw away her trash and purposely walked to the north side to see just how dark the tint was. It was beautifully dark and all she could see of someone seated inside was more of a silhouette than actual features. Perfect, she thought.

Before she knew it, the final bell rang and it was time to head to Helping Hands. She allowed everyone else to get in the van first so she could pay attention to how absorbed they were as to who was there to be picked up and to her surprise, found that no one even flinched when a kid named Joshua kept them waiting an extra minute. They were all too engrossed in sharing their day with each other, fully aware that these few short minutes from the school to Helping Hands was the only time they would have to talk about non-drug related topics.

Elizabeth gave herself an imaginary pat on the back for a reconnaissance mission that had been a success. She was confident that Friday would go without a hitch.

As Elizabeth was exiting the van to enter the facility, she saw Paul getting out of his car, a yellow Mustang. She noticed he had a deeper tan and was beginning to envy the free time he had when she remembered that she would too in just another few days. As he turned around, he noticed her looking at him and gave her a curt nod. She flashed a quick smile to let him know she was happy to see him and crossed her fingers that an opportunity would present itself that day where she could talk to him for just a minute.

The moment she walked into the building, she could tell something was different. There was usually a quiet buzz around this time as Mrs. Stein, the queen bee, was always giving out orders to the staff and they were normally buzzing around from room to room. Today there was a calmness that was rarely there and the voices she heard through doorways were a little louder in volume, not to mention, less strained. Before she could guess as to the meaning of it all, it was made clear as Christy announced that Mrs. Stein had been called away and a little more trust would be given to the students that day since they were also short staffed. Relief seemed to sweep through the room and kids' faces that were always prepared for a poker game relaxed and Elizabeth saw real features for the first time in many of them. One girl who had always seemed so homely looked positively radiant as she smiled toward Christy. Another boy who had been brooding in the last row for weeks, walked up to the front and took a seat.

Elizabeth smiled and thought to herself, *this is going to be quite an interesting day.*

Christy turned toward Elizabeth and added, "Because of us having a skeleton crew today, I have chosen Elizabeth to be my helper."

"Wow, thanks," said Elizabeth. "What can I do for you?"

"I need some copies made on colored paper, but I would also like you to cut these cards I have made for another project. You can use the conference room near the bathrooms but I will need you to have it all done in a half hour, does that seem doable?"

"Sure," she responded.

It was apparent that Paul had heard the conversation because he immediately began to assign team leaders to his group of boys and told them that he had to catch up on some work in the front office.

Everything seemed to be falling into place perfectly...too perfectly. The old Elizabeth would have become suspicious but the new Elizabeth believed it to be fate on her side. Her palms had begun to sweat and she caught herself holding her breath a couple of times and had to remind herself to breathe. As she gathered the papers together, she glanced at Marie. After today, she would be the only person that Elizabeth had to focus on. Marie had been a little preoccupied lately but Elizabeth had been too busy with her own plans to even inquire as to what was up with her.

Elizabeth was anxious to see how she looked but there were no mirrors in the group hall. She asked to use the bathroom and upon closing the door she looked at her reflection. She noticed that her skin had cleared up considerably and although she was not tanned, the natural blend of olive tones from her Italian side and the fairness from her Scottish side looked just as nice. The program had forced her to embrace her more natural qualities and it surprised her how she had grown to like herself without all the extras.

Before she turned to go, she rubbed her lips together a few times to give them a little color, shook out her hair and smiled. She gathered the things that Christy had given her and proceeded to the conference room.

Elizabeth saw that the door to the conference room was slightly ajar. She wondered if Paul was already inside. A surge of emotion ran through her as a scene from Casablanca flashed through her mind; with Humphrey Bogart and Ingrid Bergman locked in a romantic embrace. Just like in the movie, only one character knew what was going on; in her case Paul was the one completely in the dark.

Opening the door further with her foot, Elizabeth peered in and saw Paul leaning over the desk intently reading something. Wearing his usual striped polo shirt, she noticed how it stretched across his back as he leaned over. She could see his brow furrowed in concentration and as she cleared her throat, he jumped slightly.

Upon recognizing her, Paul let his guard down and gave her a big smile. She quickly closed the door and before she could reason her way out of it, she crossed the room and hugged him. They had never fully embraced with both arms around each other; it was always a hurried side type of hug. His hands began to rub her back up and down and they began kissing. It was rather hard to continue due to the conflicting voices Elizabeth kept hearing in her head. Between the 'that's what I'm talking about!' and 'what the heck do you think you are doing?' her body kept starting and stopping. Sensing the change, Paul held her away from him while holding both of her shoulders in each hand. He took a moment to just look at her and it was then that Elizabeth knew she had to finish what she came to do. She smiled and gave him a quick peck on the cheek and began to spread the cards she was to cut on the table in the center of the room.

Coming up behind her, he whispered, "I miss you now that you are in school all day."

Turning around to face him, she said, "If we are going to make this time alone work, you need to be doing something in case someone should walk in."

Recognizing his momentary lapse in judgment, he went back towards the desk.

"I have something I want to say to you Paul," said Elizabeth as she busied herself with the paper and scissors. "This time with you has been great and I don't regret a second of it…especially what just happened." She glanced up to make sure he was listening and when she was assured that she had his rapt attention, she continued. "I think you already know that I have never been into preppy guys like you before as I am sure you were never into head banger girls like me." They both gave a small laugh confirming that what she had said was true. "I don't want you to be hurt by what I have to say next…so please always remember how I started this conversation, OK?" Looking at him again Paul shook his head "yes."

"Your position here is very important to you and as much as I would have hated to admit it earlier on; you're great at what you do. I will not allow what we have been doing to jeopardize it. I will cherish every moment we shared but think this is where it needs to end," seeing his crestfallen face she hastily added, "…for now."

"What does that mean…for now?" Paul asked.

"Just that, this is not the environment to see if what we have can really work; it is doomed to fail in these circumstances. However, what the future holds is a mystery. Where you and I will be in the next year is unknown."

They both turned abruptly at the sound of the doorknob turning. Taking a step or two away from each other, they busily attended to the papers on the table. At that moment, Christy stuck her head in the door and said, "You have maybe two minutes and then I need Paul to help start the last group session."

"I'll be right there," said Paul as he exhaled loudly. Had it been anyone else who had walked in, it still would have been considered highly inappropriate for him to have been in the room alone with Elizabeth, staff member or not. When the door had closed again, he walked right up to Elizabeth and clasped both of her hands in his. "Listen, Elizabeth, I think I love you," his voice faltered on the last two words but his eyes never left hers. "That is the only reason I am willing to follow your lead on this. I don't agree with us not having a moment to steal away and see each other, but you have always taken more of a street approach to things and could see things at a different angle than I could so I am going to respect your wishes on this and see where it leads us." At these final words, he turned to leave the room when Elizabeth whispered "I need a favor."

Having rarely heard Elizabeth ever ask for help, Paul did not hesitate before saying "Ask anything."

"Could you please assign an open topic for our Moral Inventory assignments today? I want to share some things with you." She lifted her arm and brushed the back of her hand against his face. He closed his eyes for a moment before answering,

"Of course." Leaving the room, he turned to say "Goodbye," not realizing how true those words were.

Elizabeth's mind was in a jumble for she didn't hear much after he had stated that he thought he loved her. The conversation had not really gone as she had planned but considering she didn't really have a plan, she figured it could have gone a lot worse. Completing the bogus project she had been assigned by Christy, she returned to the main room to join the others for their group session.

Now that Elizabeth had finished with Paul, she figured she could now focus on Marie. Although her communication to her wouldn't happen until after she left; she hoped to be able to express how much her friendship meant to her without being too obvious. *I wonder if this is how a spy or double agent feels,* thought Elizabeth, *I have been wandering down school hallways, peeking around corners, eavesdropping on conversations, and all the while trying not to get caught.*

Something inside of her wanted her to remember every detail of Helping Hands. As she walked back into the main room, she smiled at their attempt to paint the boards that blocked the windows in soothing colors. One was a sea foam green and another a pale pink. Elizabeth remembered how those boards seemed to glare at her when she had first arrived. It had seemed that they were talking to her and saying "don't even think about it." As her body was detoxing, she believed the boards were mocking her, chanting, "What are you going to do now, little girl?" She had not regarded those boards in months. It was amazing to her how quickly the mind adapts to its surroundings, making whatever adjustments it needs to in order to stay sane.

The topic of the group discussion was "coping mechanisms" and each person was asked to describe theirs. Marie was the first to raise her hand; "Mine was music," she stated, "the louder the better." The group laughed, shaking their heads in assent. Smiling, Marie added, "I know it is not the most original form of a coping mechanism but it was all that I had. My family never talked about the problems that were staring us right in the face. I would get so pissed about the emotions they were forcing me to keep inside so that we could blend with the rest of the country club clan. I was drawn to lyrics that spewed hatred and anarchy."

The group was encouraged to speak up at any time during someone's dialogue and a new boy who had only been there a few days said with a sneer "You don't look like someone who listens to death metal; I would have pegged you as a John Denver fan or something."

Marie, who had no trouble matching anyone's intellect, was unmoved by his aggression and without missing a beat said, "Your ignorance of others is clear or you would have been onto your parents when they told you that they were taking you for a ride to get Metallica tickets when in reality your bags were in the trunk and you were headed here."

The mention of two musical artists (not allowed) within 20 seconds of each other caused Paul to stand up abruptly, waving his hands while repeating, "Whoa, whoa, whoa; that's enough you two. These sessions are not set up for people to bait each other." Turning to the new boy, he said, "Kevin, you're apparently still angry about being brought here but I will not allow you to bring others down with you."

Kevin, looking like he wanted to take a swing at Paul, had second thoughts as Paul took a step toward him. He unclenched his fists and sat back down.

77

Addressing the group again, Paul said, "We have time for one more person. Does anyone else want to share?"

Elizabeth, who had not planned on participating in this group topic was surprised to see her own hand rise. Paul nodded to her and said, "Go ahead, Elizabeth." He returned to his director's chair and leaned forward showing his eagerness to hear her speak. Elizabeth was struck again with how different girls were from guys. She knew that Paul's guard was down due to Mrs. Stein not being around but was sure that any other female in the room with any sense at all would see that his interest in her crossed the line of staff member and into the area of attraction. Elizabeth was grateful that she only had a couple of more days to go or Paul was likely to send her spiraling back to Level One with no chance of escape.

Clearing her throat, she began with a smile, "I totally get what Marie was talking about with the music; but for me, that came much later. Before I had music, I had…," she raised her voice for dramatic effect, "…FORTS!" A few people giggled, others looked confused, then she added, "Let me explain. As many of you know, I was left alone a lot due to my mom's work and drinking schedule." She saw some kids nodding their heads because they could relate to having one or both parents with addictions of their own. "Sometimes, I would be alone on a beautiful clear blue day and others were more ominous because storms would be raging outside or it would be the middle of the night with noises I couldn't distinguish, let alone know where they were coming from. Needless to say, those times scared the SHI…CRAP out of me." Everyone laughed then and they settled in to hear the rest of her tale.

"My forts started out as basic tents and grew to be epic. My brother had this captain's bed that was built up to where you had to climb a ladder to get up to it. There were drawers on the bottom part, but one day, I wondered what was behind the drawers because they certainly weren't the depth of the bed. Being so small, I was able to squeeze between the bed and the wall and discovered a cave like fort. I began to move in right away. I brought flash lights and comic books; snacks and a few toys. You would think a space like that would have creeped me out even more, but for some reason, I felt secure because the way I saw it was that nobody would ever know I was there which meant they couldn't get to me." I also made outdoor forts for the times I was locked out of the house. There was this field near a school in my neighborhood that had these folded-up bleachers. My brother, Nicholas, and I retracted a few of them where it wasn't too obvious to anyone who may have walked by, but when you crawled inside, it created a large covered fort. At that time, we were living in a rough part of town in Hartford, Connecticut, so this fort wasn't for fun, it was for safety."

Shrugging her shoulders, Elizabeth scanned the group and said, "I know it sounds weird but that became my coping mechanism." She was proud of herself for sharing and it felt like she had given something back to the group that she knew she would no longer be a part of in a couple of days. She felt a real kinship to these kids, well most of them anyway. Trina had remained a thorn in her side and would be the one person Elizabeth would have no regrets never having to see again.

Chapter 28

Paul was as good as his word and made that evening's Moral Inventory topic to be whatever the writer chose it to be. Elizabeth had been assigned a newcomer that night but she didn't mind because it happened to be her favorite girl named Marcy. She recalled the first night that Marcy had stayed with her and how she had cried most of the time until Elizabeth had let her hold her cat Cali. There had been an instant bond between Marcy and the cat and Elizabeth's house had become Marcy's favorite as well. It seemed as though the speech that Elizabeth had first given her about the chance of her rapidly moving to second stage had fallen on deaf ears. Marcy was a great houseguest but terrible student at Helping Hands. She would not participate in group sessions as often as Mrs. Stein would have liked and had stubbornly refused to talk to her mom for the past three weeks after she had found out that the rest of her family had just taken a vacation without her. Elizabeth never believed that Marcy was a hardcore drug user but her promiscuity with older boys had been enough to freak her parents out and they responded in the extreme.

Once they arrived home, Elizabeth decided to take a bubble bath before she started her Moral Inventory that evening. She knew it would be such a tease to Marcy who was still forced to take quickie showers but reassured herself that it would be a great motivator for Marcy to get off her butt and get with the program, no pun intended. Getting undressed in front of newcomers was still uncomfortable for Elizabeth because, although she was older than most of them, they were more developed than she was.

She was too embarrassed to ask Marcy to turn around while she climbed in the tub so she distracted her by pointing to the linen closet and saying, "Marcy could you hand me a towel from that cabinet?" As Marcy turned away, Elizabeth tried to climb into the tub but in her haste sent bubbles over the edge and onto the floor. "Whoops!" she said and couldn't help but laugh at herself.

Marcy bent down to mop up the floor with the towel she had just taken out of the closet. Glancing up at Elizabeth she asked, "Why am I still on Stage one? I thought you said it would be easy for me to get to Stage two?" A tear had formed and began to slide down Marcy's face. Elizabeth knew exactly how she was feeling, not because her climb had been as long as Marcy's but the feeling in limbo part.

"Do you promise not to get mad at me if I tell you?" asked Elizabeth.

Marcy shook her head up and down and said, "Of course, you're like the only person I feel like I can trust at Helping Hands."

To give any of her secrets away this close to leaving, was a huge risk, but Elizabeth was a giver to a fault so she proceeded to tell Marcy her thoughts on the matter. Taking a deep breath in, Elizabeth said, "Well, to begin with, you are stubborn like me. Unfortunately, or fortunately, depending on the way you look at it, you do not have a conniving side to you like I did. I was able to give the counselors what they thought was the whole truth when in reality I only told them the parts I wanted to; that way I could not be resentful about them **making** me do something because I knew things that they didn't. Does that make any sense to you?"

Marcy shrugged, uncertainly.

"I mean, I still felt like I was in control and had the power. I learned to cry when that is what they were expecting and after a while it was actually fun. Now don't get me wrong, there came a time when I knew that the life I had been living was destructive and I had paid a huge price to continue living that way. I found myself waking up one morning actually wanting to change and to better myself. I enjoy group sessions and no longer worry about being judged about who I had sex with or whatever."

At the word 'sex', Marcy visibly flinched. "I just don't know if I can go there." she said. "I know our parents hear about most of what we share in group and if my mom heard about some of the stuff I did; I think she would disown me."

Elizabeth leaned over to give Marcy a hug and said, "I think she may surprise you. Promise me you will try." She looked into Marcy's eyes and felt like she had reached her.

"I will," she said, "maybe just with the girls to start with and then I can work up to discussing more personal things in the group sessions."

Smiling, Elizabeth said, "That, my friend, will guarantee you Stage two within the next couple of weeks."

The thought of that brought fresh tears to Marcy's eyes and, as if on cue, Cali walked into the room. Marcy scooped her up and said, "I sure will miss Cali though." Both girls laughed as Elizabeth splashed the two of them with water.

"Could you grab me another towel?" she said.

Having dried her hair and slipped into comfortable pajamas, Elizabeth prepared to write in her journal. *How shall I title it?* she thought. *Times Gone By? Bygone Times? The Life and Times of Elizabeth?* The perfect title popped into her head and she began to write:

Menagerie of Memories

Within these walls of Helping Hands, I have become a martyr, blaming others for my shortfalls. I know through my sharing I have helped others but that is only because we have been forced to listen to each other day in and day out. When the time comes that I am outside of these walls, my stories would not draw others closer to me but would cause them to push me away. Who would want sobriety by seeing what I have become? I have learned to tread lightly in sharing certain memories with the group, not allowing too much comedy to enter into them. I will therefore be pushing the envelope in this Moral Inventory entry because I feel that it is important for you to see all of me. None of these memories are earth shattering nor will they be life changing for anyone, but they are memories I do not want to leave behind or untold.

You will undoubtedly raise your eyebrows because one or two of them occurred during the times of my drug use, but underneath it all, the real Elizabeth was there. I am a clown, a romantic, and a dreamer. Before I continue, I want to thank all of the staff at Helping Hands who, through all the hours of discussions, unknowingly helped these memories to resurface. I hope they willingly or unwillingly bring a smile to your face.

Compared to most of my friends; I was a late bloomer in the boy/girl department. Having an older brother, I had always hung around guys and even though I had no experience with them, I knew from an early age what attraction felt like. It was kind of weird to be physically innocent but to mentally feel mature and wanting in these areas. I had a crush on a neighborhood boy for over a year and had to endure the agony of watching him date a mutual friend in seventh grade. His name was Tom and he was tall with feathered hair and an accent from New Hampshire. He had moved into the neighborhood the year before and what started out as friendship ended in us being boyfriend and girlfriend. Luckily, I lived one block away from him compared to his girlfriend who lived across town so it was inevitable that we would spend more time together as he and her grew apart over the summer.

We would always meet each other at the end of an alley between both of our homes and whenever he would walk me home, we would say our goodbyes there. Up until this point, the two of us would give each other a quick peck on the lips when parting but both of us knew we wanted a little more than that; it was just up to one of us to make the first move. I had been practicing French kissing with my pillow at home, but come on, when has that ever really prepared anyone for the real thing? I wish I could tell you it was pure perfection when it finally happened but that would be an utter lie. Our nerves got the better of us one day when we mutually seemed ready to give it a try. Standing at the edge of the alley already having said our goodbyes we were facing one another and holding hands. Tom began to lean in for a kiss and I saw his head tilting to one side; I quickly tilted my head to the other side. His mouth was beginning to open and I knew this was it. Like two planes coming in for a crash landing, our teeth clanked together due to our nerves and inexperience. There was no recovering from such an epic fail and we both mumbled good bye, turned in opposite directions and headed home.

I can't remember how the heck we overcame that but assume it was the usual kid routine of pretending it never happened. I am happy to say it did not discourage us from trying in the future and although he does not rank as the best kisser I have ever known (that title goes to the last boy I kissed), he was detrimental in my learning how to do it. The reason I decided to share this with you tonight is to give you a glimpse of who I was before I became the girl you knew walking in here almost a year ago.

Now this next one is one of my favorite memories because we were wild kids who thought we were invincible. I imagine I was about 13 here and not sure if I was still dating Tom, but we were still inseparable at this time. It was Tom, his brother Sebastian, me, and my best friend, Mary. We were bored and were brainstorming on what we should do next. One of us came up with a plot to steal, I mean borrow, a neighborhood kid's canoe. We knew he leaned it up against his shed so we could grab it with no problem. He was a brainiac kid from school who looked up to us and would never narc us out even if he found out what we had done.

I came up with the brilliant idea of grabbing some homemade wine I knew my brother had been fermenting in the attic at home. Now that my head is clear, I can see what idiots we were in planning on stealing a "friend's" canoe, rowing in open

81

water in the Caloosahatchee River with a bottle of wine to boot; but remember how I used the word invincible earlier? That was us. So here we are, lugging this canoe two blocks to the river while one of us is carrying the wine. The plan was to row to this island that was about a quarter of a mile out in the water.

We took turns rowing and quickly got on each other's nerves yelling which way someone should paddle or who was holding the oar the wrong way. I had been a contributing factor in all this with my adding my two cents in but knew a way to keep the peace. Naturally, I uncorked the bottle of wine and began to pass it around. It was disgusting. Nicholas had used oranges is his concoction and it tasted rancid but we could still make out a taste of alcohol so continued to drink it. Before long, we had a good rhythm going with the oars and as our buzz kicked in; I started humming aloud the theme to Hawaii Five O. I sure hope you guys remember that theme because it is what makes this story so funny. We were cruising across the water when everyone began to hum it loudly. It helped make the labor of rowing so much easier; the faster we sang it, the faster we rowed until we couldn't take it any longer and all busted out laughing. We made it to the island and did what we did best; hang out.

On the way home, we were all a bit drunk from the wine and my dramatic side kicked in. Although I had liked Tom first, his brother was easy on the eyes too and at that moment I didn't care which one of them gave me attention. I had started rocking the boat, literally, when Mary dropped her paddle into the water. The boat kept going and Sebastian was having a hard time slowing it down and trying to turn the boat around to get the oar back. Tom started yelling at me to stop but I was having too much fun. Giggling my head off, I rocked the boat again only to toss myself overboard. I was a strong swimmer but didn't want to miss the opportunity of being rescued. (All of this revelation is in hindsight of course; at the time, I was totally caught up in the moment). I began to flounder in the water dipping my head under and sputtering as I came back up to the surface. Sebastian jumped overboard and grabbed me around the waist. (Now that is what I am talking about). To me, at the time, it proved he cared but once we were back in the canoe he was furious. Nobody talked to me for the rest of the way back. I remember sitting there smugly, not affected at all that I had pissed everybody off. What a brat, right?

Last but not least, was the time I and a group of friends, ages between 11 and 15, were all hanging out at the house of a girl named Donna. Like Nicholas and me, she lived in a one parent household, although with her dad. He was a truck driver and would be gone a week at a time. She had two older brothers; Jimmy and Shawn who were always arguing as to who was in charge when their dad was gone. Their dad would stock the fridge with food before he went on the road and would yell about the rules of the house that he knew good and well would not be followed during his absence. Once word got out in the neighborhood that their dad was leaving, a small army of us would head over to hang out.

One night, Donna's brothers headed out to the local Kiwanis club. The building was locked up, but somehow Jimmy and Shawn found a way in. As the rest of us were hanging out in the front yard, we could hear some hooting and hollering going on, but due to the darkness, couldn't make out who it was. The sound of something rolling down the street was what our ears picked up next followed by an image of both Jimmy and Shawn pushing something together. We all clambered to the fence as they got closer, but the cylindrical object had no label on it. Jimmy called for *some help to carry the canister in. I assumed it was pretty heavy, from the grunting noises coming from the people who were lugging it. With a flourish, Jimmy ripped off the top of the canister to expose vanilla ice cream...more than we could possibly eat. Grabbing spoons and vying for position, we all began to feast. Yes, it was illegal, but what a happy gang of kids we were that night. We could always count on Jimmy and Shawn to liven up a boring day or to try and help when the cupboards were bare. Their solution to no food in the house was to jump in the river, swim to a crab trap that was marked with a colorful bobber and drag it back to the house for us to boil up lunch or dinner. Due to us not having authority figures around all the time, we really felt that certain rules did not apply to us. We never sat around talking about what laws we wanted to break but followed whatever whim we had at the time and as long as nobody got hurt or caught, we had lived to hang out for another day.*

I wish that I could transport you into these memories so that you could join in the laughter and camaraderie that I shared with different groups of misfits at certain times of my life. We may have looked rough around the edges with our bare feet and uncombed hair, but let me tell you, I felt protected by the boys, Donna played the part of the den mother, and I was astounded at how smart a few were; both book and street smart.

I just wanted to set the record straight that I am not someone to pity. Due to my parent's choices, I have been put in terrible positions and have suffered psychologically from them, BUT it helped to shape me into the person I am today. I am not a quitter, I am a fighter. I have turned crying into laughter and I look forward to a happy and healthy future.

Chapter 29

As Elizabeth put her pen down, she began to rub her aching hand. She glanced down and saw an indent in her middle finger from all of the writing she had just done. A little voice was whispering a warning in her head. "Are you sure this was the smartest thing to do right before you plan to jump ship? You have blatantly rubbed everything they are against under their noses. You realize you are going to get called out for this journal entry, right?" She justified her writing as unfinished business.

Glancing at the clock that stood on her nightstand, she couldn't believe it was almost 11 o'clock. Marcy had fallen asleep on top of the covers; the book she had been reading was lying across her chest. It rose and fell with her breathing. Cali had curled up near her feet and Elizabeth could hear her purring softly. She took this moment to say a little prayer for Marcy; asking that she be looked after once Elizabeth had gone. It was a nice feeling to pray for someone else for a change. Elizabeth smiled thinking that God probably appreciated that prayer a whole lot better than the ones she had prayed in the past. They usually took place as she was hugging a toilet bowl swearing that if God would help her to stop throwing up, she would never touch another drink again.

Exhaustion hit her the minute she had crawled under her blanket. Tomorrow marked the last day that she would return to Helping Hands after school. Once this was all behind her, she could concentrate on the letter to Marie. Clicking off her lamp, Elizabeth lay in bed, thinking of what her last day at Helping Hands would be like. Turning on her side, she hoped for a dreamless sleep.

Hearing the creak of her bedroom door, Elizabeth opened her eyes and quickly shielded her face from the sun that was streaming in through her bedroom blinds. She must have forgotten to close them last night. She smiled as she saw her mom stick her head through the door bearing a steaming cup of coffee in her hands.

"Good morning," Helen whispered with a mischievous grin on her face.

Elizabeth could tell her mom was feeling the excitement of the countdown as well. She was sure her mom would not miss the long drives to and from the center anymore. Grateful that her mom was in the room to watch over Marcy, Elizabeth dashed out to use the bathroom. Her mom was waiting at the foot of her bed when she returned. She was glancing at Elizabeth's Moral Inventory book. Elizabeth had not allowed her to read any entries; although she was aware that there had been one or two that Mrs. Stein had copied and shown her throughout her treatment. It had been explained that "it was for her own good."

"I promise I will let you read it once I leave the program," she told her.

Helen nodded and passed the coffee to Elizabeth.

"Thanks mom"

"You're welcome."

"I mean for everything," said Elizabeth.

"I know." Smiling, Helen left the room.

Marcy had begun to stir so Elizabeth didn't feel guilty as she flung a pillow at her to help her along. From the giggle she heard come from under the covers, she knew that Marcy didn't mind either.

My last full day, thought Elizabeth as she headed to the closet to pick out her school clothes.

It had begun to rain as her mother pulled up to Helping Hands but having no fear of mascara running down her face; Elizabeth didn't mind. She quickly got Marcy situated in the main room before returning to the front entrance where the infamous white van would take her to school. She had deposited her Moral Inventory in the basket for the staff to peruse while she was at school. She was a little nervous as to the reception she might receive when she got back that day.

She saw Paul as he walked into the front door shaking out his umbrella. There was a squeal from those who the cold water had splattered followed by laughter, which helped cover their own smiles as they looked across the room at each other. Elizabeth had unconsciously taken a step toward Paul when she saw him but he had been alert enough to avert his gaze and head in the other direction.

Climbing into the van that had just pulled up, Elizabeth took the first available seat and began to go over some notes for a quiz she had in first period. Christy slid beside her and said, "Good morning." Elizabeth nodded and continued to study for the short drive to Mariner High while simultaneously praying that this day would fly by. Swallowing the breakfast that kept threatening to come back up her throat, she willed her nerves to calm down.

The day went by like a dream. Elizabeth was thrilled with the 90 she received on her quiz, the cafeteria had served her favorite lunch, Mexican pizza, and she was given zero homework from all of her teachers. The only thing that had momentarily threatened this seemingly perfect day was an announcement made by one of the boys in the van on the way back to Helping Hands. Carl was a pimply faced boy that nobody seemed to pay much attention to, but Elizabeth was all ears when she heard him say to the boy sitting next to him, "I just got the after-school office assistant job."

"That's cool," said the kid sitting next to him.

It was obvious he was proud of himself by the way he had puffed out his chest and how loudly he had spoken so no one in the van could help but hear his announcement. This had actually helped Elizabeth not to seem intrusive when she said, "Excellent, when do you start?"

"On Monday," he said.

Elizabeth let a rush of air come out of her nose as she exhaled. *What a freaking close call,* she thought to herself. She did not know how much more of these emotional ups and downs her heart could take. Steeling herself for the remainder of the day, Elizabeth chose not to speak for the rest of the ride.

When she walked into Helping Hands, it was just as obvious that Mrs. Stein was back as it was yesterday when she was away. Instead of the calm, low volume voices and relaxed atmosphere of the day before, this one held clipped tones and murmurings with everyone acting "busy" in hopes that they wouldn't be called out by her.

85

Elizabeth went back to the basket to retrieve her Moral Inventory for that evening's entry. Having shifted each book out of the way and double checking that she hadn't overlooked it; it was clear the book was missing. Scanning the room for Paul, she found him jotting something down on a small piece of paper on his lap. Looking up, he saw her and quickly glanced at the paper he had just folded. As if he was trying to send her some sort of message, he coughed into his hand that held the note, walked over to the bookshelf against the wall, and in Elizabeth's opinion, did a very poor imitation of someone looking for a certain book by pulling one book out and barely glancing the title, and return it only to pull another out. She saw him slip the paper inside the third book he had pulled down as if it were some sort of bookmark. He then walked straight out of the room without another glance in her direction.

What in the world was that all about? thought Elizabeth, although she knew in her heart it had to do with her missing Moral Inventory journal. Christy had just announced that group would start in one minute when Elizabeth crossed the room, waved to Marie, and snatched the book from the shelf. Unfolding the paper, she looked over her shoulder to make sure everyone was absorbed in their own affairs. Figuring this was her only chance to read it, she kept the book open with the unfolded paper inside. Grateful for Paul's clean handwriting, she was able to read at top speed, "Mrs. Stein joining group today. Topic…your journal…thanks for the compliment…P."

Elizabeth smiled, happy that Paul had read between the lines when she had explained in her journal that her last kiss had been the best yet. That had been her personal message to him; kind of like a going away present. She hoped it would take some of the sting out of her disappearance tomorrow.

She knew that she had run the risk of being called out today by what she had written the night before. Mrs. Stein was probably fearful that Elizabeth's journal topic might open the door to others trying to be free thinkers. Taking her normal seat at the front row, Elizabeth wiped her sweaty palms on her pants and prepared to finish her last after-school day at Helping Hands.

86

Chapter 30

Mrs. Stein loved to make an entrance and today was no exception. Sweeping into the room with her long skirt bellowing behind her, she greeted the room with her patented "Good afternoon, my dear students," followed by a full turn worthy of a runway model on the catwalk. Flashing her overly white teeth into what was as genuine of a smile as she could muster, she ran her eyes over each and every girl and boy in the room, stopping at Elizabeth. It was then that her smile faltered a bit and a cough from the group broke her gaze.

"I was called away on business yesterday but have been assured by the staff that you all were on your best behavior. Thank you for honoring the trust that I have given you. I know that you have all been guilty at one time or another of rebelling against our rules here at Helping Hands. I believe whether you are willing to admit it or not, you know that these rules are in place for a reason. The same goes for our curriculum and the program's guidelines and stages. I will have to admit that I was a little taken aback to hear that Paul had given an open topic for last night's journal entries, but I have always encouraged the staff to follow their instincts when I am away. I was very impressed with what many of you chose to share and confused by only one or two, who I feel wasted a great opportunity." Mrs. Stein had begun to pace back and forth as she spoke. "I found one journal entry in particular that seemed to glamorize the past."

Kids began to shift uneasily in their seats as their eyes darted around in an attempt to figure out who Mrs. Stein was talking about.

Mrs. Stein turned her back to the group and made her way to the area where the other staff members were seated. She reached toward the tall table that was beside an empty seat and raised the lone journal that had been placed there. Rotating to face the group again, she continued to hold the journal up and said, "This is the journal in question and it comes from a student who I have been defending for months now. The normal procedure would be to pull the student aside and talk to them, but I feel in this case, I need to make an example of...Elizabeth." There were audible gasps from the girls' side of the room. Continuing with her dialogue, Mrs. Stein said, "Although I am very curious to hear your motivation for last night's entry, Elizabeth, I think it only fair that the group hear what was written before we proceed." With that, Mrs. Stein read the entire journal entry to the group.

Elizabeth was tempted to look around to see the reaction the journal would have on the others but knew it would be no use due to her knowing that everyone would do whatever they had to do not to show any emotion, whether for or against the entry. People had been tricked in the past thinking if they took Mrs. Stein's side they would be in the clear only to find her turning the tables and asking them to go into detail about their opinion. That is when they would usually get tongue tied and Mrs. Stein would reprimand them for their rush to judgment.

87

To make matters worse, Mrs. Stein was reading the entry using her own inflections. Adding a conceited tone in areas that Elizabeth never intended and slowing down the areas that held the action parts which caused the entry to read flat. Elizabeth realized then how smart Mrs. Stein really was. She knew enough not to have Elizabeth read the entry because she would have made the stories come to life.

"So, Elizabeth, why don't you share with us all what in the world you were thinking when you chose your topic for last night?"

The question allowed Elizabeth to look at the staff and she could tell both Christy and Paul were worried for her. Elizabeth wasn't too concerned because even if Mrs. Stein decided to move her down a stage, it would allow her to still go home that night and even though school wasn't allowed on Stage two she figured Mrs. Stein would allow her one more day of school to notify her teachers and line up another tutor to come to Helping Hands but by then it would be too late and she would be home free.

Clearing her throat, Elizabeth began her defense. "Well, like any piece of writing, I knew my entry would be interpreted differently depending on who was doing the reading. I do think I explained myself pretty clearly that it was not meant to be life changing but more of a 'hey, this is a part of me you never knew about.' My intent was never to offend anyone." Looking at her fellow peers she asked, "Did I offend any of you?" There was a lot of head nodding back and forth with Trina being the only one to kind of shrug her shoulders. She felt a surge of relief until she saw the look on Mrs. Steins face. It was obvious that this lecture was not going in the direction that Mrs. Stein had hoped and Elizabeth figured that she had made her point and if she wanted to end this unscathed, it was time to eat some humble pie.

Elizabeth dropped her head to her chest and stood in one place as if inspecting her shoes. As she looked up, she made sure to make direct eye contact with each staff member albeit skimming quickly by Paul. "I feel that an apology is in order…actually more than one apology. First I would like to apologize to Paul," she squared her shoulders and looked right at him, "You were kind enough to give us a little freedom last night in regards to our journal entries. I am sure you thought that we would keep in mind the strict standards that the program has taught all of us."

Paul sat with his hands clasped on his legs, but she could see how his fingers would tighten and loosen as she talked. Elizabeth did not want Paul to wind up in trouble for what she had done and had finally recognized how reckless her journal entry had been.

"Maybe the lines got blurred a little with the freedom I am given to write at school compared to here. I lost sight that this is my recovery program not my English Lit class." Looking at Mrs. Stein again, it appeared that this last comment had appeased her a little. Continuing she said, "I would also like to apologize to the group and to you Mrs. Stein." First, addressing the group, she began, "I have come to regard you all as my brothers and sisters." Her eyes had begun to tear and she was surprised to see the same reflected in many of the faces that were looking up at her. "Sometimes I feel so down on myself after sharing my past with all of you and I got to thinking that if I feel this bad at times, then you must too." Using her fingers to demonstrate quotation marks Elizabeth continued, "The "fixer" in me wanted to help show a lighter side to our dysfunction…but I shouldn't have gone down the road I did."

Turning to face Mrs. Stein, Elizabeth concluded, "I am sorry Mrs. Stein that I didn't run my idea by one of the staff first. My gut knew that it might not have been the wisest choice but I wrote it anyway. I did notice that even though I thought I was going on my own path, the things that I have learned at Helping Hands managed to creep into my writing." She smiled and was happy to see Mrs. Stein returning it.

"I will not deny that I saw how hindsight had kicked in for you. You did share your experience while at the same time sharing what you did not know then, but know now in regards to your behavior. Unfortunately, if these became the memories you kept the closest to you; it is certain you would return to that lifestyle." Mrs. Stein said, "You mentioned stealing multiple times, faking accidents, and drinking alcohol; yet in the same breath made it seem as though this was before things got real bad for you. I found the piece you wrote very sad in the fact that even at this point you couldn't recognize where your actions were leading you. Granted you had very little supervision and guidance then, but with the time you have spent here, I would have thought that your mind would have cleared enough to know the danger of flirting with these types of memories."

Mrs. Stein began her pacing again and only stopped to glare in the direction of Paul before saying, "With that being said, there will never again be an open topic for Moral Inventories. Coming in today, I had every intention of punishing you Elizabeth and possibly putting you on suspension, Paul." With her usual pause for dramatic effect, she finally added, "but having seen how we were able to turn this into a real learning lesson, I have decided no punishments will be issued."

There was an audible sigh of relief from the majority of the group, which caused Elizabeth to be swept with gratitude. She wished she could give everyone a hug but knew it was impossible especially with the opposite sex. As the group disbanded for the night, she looked one last time at Paul who gave her another smile. All was well again…another disaster averted. She had learned a very important lesson about thinking things through before jumping in head first. The rebel in her had reared its ugly head and could have sent her plans for tomorrow down the drain.

Elizabeth knew she would not be telling her mom about this group session unless she wanted another tongue lashing. Which she did not. The newcomer that had been assigned to her was a girl named Frances who was still in her "I hate this place" phase. Luckily, she reserved that attitude for the staff members but could still be a little mouthy when the rules were discussed. As they climbed in the car, Frances started in right away with "Wow, I thought you were going to get shot down to my level tonight for sure." A quick glare from Elizabeth was signal enough for her to shut her mouth.

"What was that dear?" asked Helen.

"Nothing mom…what's for dinner, I am starving."

"Well," she began, and Elizabeth knew that to be the sign for "all clear" and happily nodded and gave one syllable responses throughout the conversation. It was enough to keep Helen going for the remainder of the ride home.

Once inside, Frances was given the tour of the house and was introduced to all of the animals. The phone rang and Elizabeth thought about how cool it would be to actually answer the phone tomorrow if it were to ring. Her mind instantly amended that thought, seeing as tomorrow would NOT be the day to answer the phone as her mom was anticipating an onslaught of calls from Mrs. Stein once it was determined that Elizabeth had not joined the others after school.

"Tomorrow," she said in her head, "Tomorrow, I am free." Goosebumps had broken out on her arm as those words were repeated over and over in her head. She had begun to get giddy like a child on Christmas Eve. It made her a great companion that evening for she listened as Helen and Frances spoke; inserting her own dialogue only after hearing them out completely. She had always had a habit of interrupting others mid-sentence but that habit had seemed to die on its own tonight. Although the conversation flowed effortlessly, sleep would not come as easily. Elizabeth lay in bed replaying every move that she would have to make the next day, trying to foresee any problems that may occur. Unlike her days of acting on stage, she knew there would be no dress rehearsal tomorrow. She would need to drop off Frances before going to school, she would have to act carefree in her classes that she shared with Christy, and she would have to slip unseen into the office. The key would be to just blend with the crowd…merge with them to get to her final destination. That was the last thought that Elizabeth remembered before opening her eyes to a bright and beautiful morning.

Chapter 31

Looking across the room, Elizabeth saw Frances still sleeping with a dribble of drool running down her face. *How can she not feel the electricity in the room that I do?* thought Elizabeth, who was so full of energy she didn't quite know what to do with herself. Elizabeth began to peel Frances from the bed and with the promise of bacon, finally got her to move. Frances appeared confused for a moment as she yawned and began to pick the sleep from her eyes.

Elizabeth knew what she was going through. When she herself had been a newcomer, she would find waking up each morning a surreal experience. It would take a minute for her mind to catch up with what her eyes were seeing. Her surroundings were constantly changing. The Program did not want a newcomer getting too familiar with a certain area, so they would frequently change the locations that they would be staying in. It was crazy the range of emotions that would assault her each morning. Confusion followed by realization, and then sadness over the loss of friends and family. Hopefully, Frances could get to the part where determination kicked in for that is when she would find herself moving up in the program.

A feast awaited them as they entered the kitchen and Elizabeth knew that this was her mother's way of celebrating. Food revolved around all of Helen's moods, whether good or bad. Making eye contact with her mom, they smiled simultaneously. Frances was oblivious to the silent communication and was content with digging in to the platefuls of food that filled the entire kitchen table. Between bites, there was light talk about the day ahead of them with frequent compliments on the food. Pushing back their chairs and contentedly patting their stomachs, both Frances and Elizabeth gave Helen a hug.

Climbing into her mom's beat up car, Elizabeth was so glad that the van from Helping Hands took her to school each day. She remembered the time when she attended Fort Myers High and her mom had dropped her off right in front of the school in her 69' Rambler. When Elizabeth was walking to her class, a boy had yelled "Tell your grandma she needs a new car!" Elizabeth was horrified not only by the comment about the car but his reference to her mom as her grandma. She had run to the bathroom to catch the tears before they had a chance to ruin her mascara. When she came out, she saw the boy standing at his locker and to her relief she saw her brother, Nicholas. Before she could even consider the consequences of her actions, she ran up to Nicholas and while pointing at the boy, regaled him with the scene that had just taken place. She had just wanted to vent and was completely taken aback when Nicholas charged toward the boy, slamming him against a locker. While gripping the boy's shirt in his fist, Nicholas said, "If you ever make fun of my mother or sister again, I will kick your ass." Resembling a frightened sixth grader rather than the tough bully, the kid began to nod his head rapidly to show that he understood Nicholas completely. The scene gave Elizabeth a fleeting moment of vindication, but the voice in her head reminded her that what the boy had said was true. Her mom always bought beater cars and she was…old. It was times like those that Elizabeth felt hatred toward her mom for having her at the age of 40. She had wished her mom had thought about the taunting that Elizabeth would have to endure in future years. Those were always her thoughts when her mother's age was addressed and it wasn't until just now that Elizabeth thought, that perhaps, her mother had NOT chosen to have another child but was forced into sex and then became pregnant. With Elizabeth and Nicholas being only 11 months apart it would mean that Nicholas was only about three months old when Helen became pregnant with her. What woman in her right mind would want that?

Elizabeth had witnessed first-hand, as a child, how aggressive her father had been towards her mother. The only thing visible to Elizabeth from where she sat in the car was the back of her mother's head. Elizabeth felt a surge of love toward her mother because whether her mother chose to get pregnant or not, she most definitely chose to have the baby. Elizabeth felt grateful to be alive and was happy at the revelation that this thought would forever replace the previous one when her mother's age was brought up. Elizabeth, in her selfishness had never considered anyone else and what they may or may not have been forced into.

Of course, her mother would be picking her up today but Elizabeth figured most of the kids would already have gone by then, not to mention this was to be her last day at Mariner High and she wouldn't have to face any of her fellow students again. *I can handle getting into my mom's junker today,* she thought to herself.

Chapter 32

By the time Elizabeth had gotten Frances situated at Helping Hands, she had to immediately load into the white van. It struck her that she would no longer see Paul on a daily basis. Trying for a quick glimpse at the parking lot as she climbed into the van, she saw no sign of Paul's Mustang. She felt a pang of sadness and a part of her knew that she would miss the familiarity of the place and even some of the routine. There was something to be said about knowing what is expected of you from day to day.

As she stepped down from the van, she was swept downstream by the sea of students that were there to greet her. It seemed like her senses were heightened as she listened to weekend plans being made. Her upcoming freedom would allow her to be the one making plans next. Looking down at her boring clothes, everyone else's seemed so vibrant. The different fashion statements walking past her no longer filled her with envy because she knew, as of tomorrow, she could strut around in anything she chose. She began to make mental notes as to what she would like to go shopping for with her mom. She hadn't dared to write anything down because she still had classes with some of the Helping Hands crowd.

Elizabeth found herself with no appetite come lunch time. Doubt had begun to creep in and the trust she had in her mother that very morning seemed to falter. It wouldn't be enough to see her mom at the school that afternoon to convince Elizabeth that she was in the clear. It would be passing Helping Hands that would prove her mother was totally on her side.

Her attention span was nonexistent in class because she couldn't help but wonder what going back to Fort Myers High would be like. She was close to a year behind so anyone she knew from the old neighborhood would have graduated and those who had been younger might very well be in the same classes with her. *It will just be another hurdle you will have to jump,* she thought. Fatigue swept through her as she reached her last class. Her old enemy, fear, was rearing its ugly head again but having come this far, Elizabeth knew there would be no turning back. Either her mother would be there to get her after school or the jig would be up. Christy was waiting for her at the door to the classroom. Her face had a look of concern on it as she said, "Elizabeth, can we talk for just a second?" Following her back outside, Elizabeth was determined to let Christy speak first since it was she who had suggested they talk.

"It's about Paul," she began, "I have noticed you two distancing yourselves from each other and I just wanted to make sure it wasn't because of something I said or did."

This was so far from what Elizabeth thought Christy had wanted to talk about that it took her a second to regain her composure. With her smile back in place, she shrugged her shoulders and said, "What the heck would give you that idea?" Without giving Christy a chance to answer she said, "You have been nothing but the most trusted friend I could ask for at Helping Hands." She had lowered her voice to a whisper at the mention of Helping Hands because she knew Christy's desire not to be linked with the place.

The bell shrieked the fact that they were now tardy, but having never even been given a warning, both girls were unfazed. Elizabeth finished with, "I'm glad you stopped me today because I feel like I have never properly thanked you for being my ally where Paul is concerned. The truth of the matter is that I do still care for him a lot, but I did not want him to jeopardize his position for me. I am carrying enough guilt around from stupid mistakes I made in the past and don't want to add anymore to the list." Tilting her head toward the door, she finished by saying, "What do you say we get back to class before we get a detention or something?"

Laughing, they turned toward the classroom and out of the corner of her eye, Elizabeth caught Christy smiling. *I guess I am destined to always be the fixer*, she thought; and for once she was okay with that.

Christy whispered, "Maybe we can study for Monday's quiz today after school."

"Sure," said Elizabeth, rushing to her desk before Christy could see the color rising in her cheeks. Her heart was pounding as she took her seat. Watching the clock, the final countdown was upon her.

The clock that hung on the wall in Elizabeth's last class had always been rather loud but today it was like something out of an Edgar Allen Poe story. Tick, tock, tick, tock the second hand boomed in Elizabeth's ears, causing her to glance up at it every few minutes. Elizabeth felt like a crazy cartoon character as her hands began to sweat, her throat began to itch, and her shirt gave away the pounding of her heart.

Thoughts like, *what if Christy tries to walk with me towards the van once the bell rings?* ran through Elizabeth's head. Christy had never done that before; always choosing instead to meet her brother in the main courtyard. Still, this was one part of the plan that Elizabeth hadn't considered. Having riled herself to the point of hysteria it wasn't until the bell had rung and students were filing out of the classroom that Elizabeth finally noticed that Christy had already exited the room.

Rising from her desk, she quickly snatched at her books only to watch them fall to the floor. Scrambling to pick them up, she told herself to settle down. Concentrating on her breathing, she began inhaling through her nose and exhaling out of her mouth. She could feel the tension easing up a bit. If the plan was to succeed, she knew she had to have her wits about her.

As she was leaving the room, she was thankful for her acting skills which enabled her to memorize a ton of information. The plan was in motion and she was mentally checking off each step as she physically reached certain areas. Fridays were always a bit crazier in the halls due to the excitement of the weekend for the students. For once, Elizabeth was grateful for being short. Joining the students at the end of the hall, she was packed like a sardine with the taller students providing a human barrier around her.

She pulled the rubber band that had been holding her tiny pony tail and shook her head to allow her hair to fall a little more toward her face.

94

Chapter 33

Elizabeth saw the school office straight ahead and aimed for the tinted door on the side. Her peripheral vision could see the white of the van and what appeared to be two or three students. Not wanting to risk turning her head for a better look and getting caught she focused instead on her target.

The rush of cold air that hit her as she opened the door was a welcome relief. She loved how quiet it was compared to the noisy hallways. An office assistant looked up from her work and asked if she needed help with anything. Elizabeth smiled and replied that she was just waiting on her mom.

Taking a seat in one of the cloth covered chairs, she continued her breathing exercise. It was all up to her mom now. Would she betray Elizabeth or follow through with the plan?

Within a few minutes, Helen breezed into the office with the energy of a woman half her age. With a vibrant smile, she announced to the office lady that she was there to pick Elizabeth up. Holding her arm out, Elizabeth grasped her mother's outstretched hand. Teenager or not, this was definitely a day that the reassurance of a mother's touch was needed.

They found themselves whispering through the parking lot only to be bent in half a minute later laughing uncontrollably. Their nerves were shot and Elizabeth became aware of the fact that she and her mother were much more alike than she had ever thought.

"Thank you, mom," she began as they sat in the car. Since her mother had not been drinking for a while, she had become reliable again. There had been so many times in the past that Elizabeth had found herself stranded at work, school, or social events due to her mother forgetting to pick her up during a stint of drinking. "I have to admit, I wasn't sure if you were going to see this through."

Smiling, Helen turned to face Elizabeth and said, "There wasn't a second that I thought of reconsidering Elizabeth, but before I start this car and head home, I want to hear from you that you are sure this is what you want."

"Absolutely, mom. I have been at a standstill for some time at the program and I want to stand on my own two feet now. I won't let you down mom."

Cranking up the old car, they headed home. There was no way to avoid passing Helping Hands because there was only the one main road to head back into town. Glancing at the building, Elizabeth was struck by how unassuming it appeared. No sign announcing what type of place it was, only two cars in the parking lot; just your average home or business. It was amazing to think that another kid in town could just disappear today without any word to friends or even certain family members and wind up there. Elizabeth said a silent prayer for all of her friends she was leaving behind. She knew they would be briefly questioned to make sure that they had not seen this coming and then a quick announcement would be made or possibly not and the program would continue without a hiccup.

"I don't mean to corrupt you right out of the gate," said Helen "but there is this great show I watch called "Murder She Wrote" with Angela Lansbury that I think you will love. Wanna watch it with me tonight?"

"Sounds good to me," said Elizabeth as she rolled down the window and held her arm out to catch the wind. She stuck her head out next and just breathed the fresh air, feeling freer than she had in months. Watching TV would be the highlight of her night and then the task of writing a quick letter to Marie would be next.

Murder She Wrote turned out to be a great show and Elizabeth was pleased with herself for not showing signs of excess by wanting to watch back to back TV shows. Mysteries had always intrigued her. She used to chalk it up to her father being murdered, but had actually enjoyed cartoons like Scooby Doo before that had even happened. Her father's death had become like a crutch to her; she used it in the past as an excuse for everything from bad decisions to equally bad relationships and drug use. The program had helped her to see that although that was a catalyst, she would not heal or conquer her drug use if she didn't start to take responsibility for her actions.

Soaking in a tub and mentally preparing herself for the letter she wanted to get to Marie, Elizabeth absentmindedly grabbed a disposable razor that had been left on the edge of the tub. She prepped underneath her arm pit with soap and gave a gasp as she made the first downward stroke and rinsed the blade. She had not been allowed to shave while in the program and had been momentarily frozen with fear with the thought of whether she would report herself or not in the morning. Snapping out of it, she was angry with herself for the way her brain kept switching gears; one moment knowing she was free and the next feeling like she was breaking rules. *This must be how prisoners or captives feel once they have been released,* she thought. Out loud she said, "I am allowed to shave, it is not a crime," and continued with her new routine.

96

Chapter 34

The time to write to Marie was at hand and Elizabeth felt important to be sitting at her mother's roll top desk which sat in the front room. Elizabeth had spent a few minutes just walking in and out of rooms for the sheer enjoyment of it. No newcomers to look after and no alarms going off. That had reminded her to rip the alarms from her bedroom doorway and windows. What pleasure it gave her to feel in control. After several attempts to start the letter, she finally began with a shaky hand:

Dear Mrs. Fleming,

I am writing to you so that you may somehow convey to Marie that I am all right without risking her position at Helping Hands. I will not even be signing my name so that you can truthfully say you can't be certain who this letter was from.

Marie is the truest friend I have had in a long time. Your family treated me as one of your own during my visits and I can never thank you enough for that acceptance.

I am now focusing on rebuilding my relationship with my own family and to stop blaming them for my past hurts. Life is much harder than I thought it would be, but I am now ready to face it sober and not in a drug induced stupor.

The sadness I feel at the realization that I will no longer see Marie is overwhelming, but I had to make the sacrifice. It just was not the place for me to be in anymore.

I wish I could share more detailed memories with you so that you can really grasp how influential you have been in my growth but know that would cross the line into the danger zone.

Sorry to be so cryptic but if anyone could understand why I am doing it this way, it would be you.

Wishing you the brightest future.

Elizabeth frowned at how abruptly the letter ended, but there was no way to include a signature and even an initial would be too risky. She would not drag that family down. A good cry was in order, but somehow, it wouldn't come. Grief was not something that was new to Elizabeth, but she could not move from the emotional fatigue that struck her so suddenly. Peace would come in time and that was something she had plenty of right now.

The phone sat on the edge of the desk and it occurred to Elizabeth that it hadn't rung all night. Flipping the phone over, she saw that the ringer had not been turned off. She and her mom had been so sure that Mrs. Klein would have been driving them crazy with calls. On a hunch, she followed the phone cord to the wall and saw that sure enough, her mother had disconnected it. It was times like these that

Elizabeth admired her mother's foresight. It was sporadic, but when it kicked in, it was right on the money.

Although Elizabeth was thrilled that she did not have to return to Helping Hands, there was an underlying nagging feeling that she wasn't out of the woods yet. It was then that she missed her Moral Inventory. There was something about writing your feelings down that helped you to pinpoint where an issue lay. *I guess I will start my own diary again,* thought Elizabeth.

Once Marie's letter was addressed and stamped, Elizabeth gathered a couple of her cats in her arms and carried them to her bedroom. Luring them with her blanket they were all settled within minutes. With pen and paper in hand, Elizabeth began her diary that she titled: "Post Helping Hands."

This journal entry marks my first day away from Helping Hands. I attended school today and mom brought me home. Yes, there is a hell of a lot more detail that goes into today's events but I am writing in this journal to try and gather my thoughts as to why the elation that I was so looking forward to hasn't set in. There is a sense of dread rolling around inside of me and I think I know why.

Mom was truly my hero today by not turning me back into the program, but I realize that I was not the only one set free...mom was too. Helping Hands has been monitoring her just as much as me, making sure she doesn't "fall off the wagon," so to speak. I love the new relationship she and I have shared over the past couple of months and I don't want to wind back up to where we were at the start of all of this.

The burden I am now carrying is how to manage my own sobriety, let alone my mother's. I am scared for the both of us. Marcus had such control over me whenever drugs or alcohol were involved. From the first moment, I lay my drunken eyes on him, I was hooked. I was at a Halloween party that my then boyfriend's band was throwing. I was dressed as Pebbles from the Flintstones. My boyfriend Chris had already cheated on me with an ex-girlfriend which hurt, but my environment made me believe that this is what people do to one another. That night, I did the same to him. Marcus and I were openly holding hands in front of Chris within the hour. I felt little shame due to the alcohol induced state I was in. I was overwhelmed with the sheer masculinity of Marcus. He was a grown man with large muscles, long hair, and full lips. Chris's scrawny teenage body became glaringly apparent in the presence of Marcus.

The following day, Marcus gave me a card that showed a bunny sitting on a cloud and inside it said, "I am on cloud 9 since meeting you." As the saying goes, "that's all she wrote." We became inseparable; kind of us against the world. When my mom met him, she was in hysterics due to his age and size. From then on, she was the enemy. I had tried to explain to her that I was in love and she told me that it was lust not love that I was feeling.

I never want someone or something to have that kind of hold on me again. I wish I could say that the love I felt for him lasted until the day I was sent to Helping Hands, but in reality, the love turned to hate rather quickly. Our drinking caused him to be suspicious of me when I hung around any other guys, while he, on the other hand, openly flirted with other girls. In one instant, we were cursing each other and in the next seeking each other out for comfort.

With my new eyes, I can see how sick and twisted the whole thing was, but man I was so lonely at the time. Journal...I feel lonely right now. All that has been my world these past six months is now gone and I don't want to run back to my past. I pray that my mom will stay with her AA meetings and we can work all of this out together.

Chapter 35

After a good night's sleep, Elizabeth felt like she could take on the world; last night's anxiety having been swept away by Mr. Sandman. Church seemed like the most logical place to start in her effort to clear a new path for her life. She still loved downtown Fort Myers and remembered a beautiful red bricked church just off of First Street that she thought she would like to try. Finding the church's name and phone number in the phone book, she dialed the office. She learned that there was a youth group for teenagers that the office assistant thought would be a good fit for her. They would be meeting again the next day at noon.

She found her mom in good spirits when she entered the kitchen. Hearing the familiar meows at the back door, Elizabeth opened it to see Cali who was not alone but had another cat that looked to be a boy standing next to her. "Mom, look what the cat dragged in."

Helen came to the door and with a sigh said, "That will make nine of the little scamps running around here. Where do they all come from?"

"News travels fast," said Elizabeth, "Hey, do you remember that time I was looking out the front window and saw that dog that looked like Benji from TV walking down the sidewalk?" They both began to laugh before Elizabeth even had time to complete her thought. "Without a pause, he turned right onto our front walkway and straight up to the door. I tell ya ma, these animals talk and the topic of their conversations is about the little lady who lives on Michigan Avenue who would feed anything that came calling." Laughing again, she kissed her mom on the cheek and told her of her plans to attend church the following day.

Helen was supportive of her decision, but she herself had not attended any type of services in a long time. Just like her AA meetings, Helen was sporadic; attending when she hit bottom or when, just the opposite, she felt a renewing. It seemed that right now Helen was going to try things her own way.

Hearing a car door close outside, she knew it had to be Nicholas who said he would stop by on his way to work. Elizabeth wondered if he may want to move back in now that there was nothing stopping him from doing so. As he walked in the door, a mischievous smile appeared and he waved what looked like a VHS tape in his hand. "Hey sis, I brought a movie I thought you would like to watch."

"What is it?" asked Elizabeth.

"Escape from Alcatraz." Nicholas burst out laughing at his wit.

"You are soooo original," she said as she reached to snatch the tape from his hands.

"Would you like something to eat?" asked Helen, and the kitchen bustled with the activity of her preparing a meal for the family. These were the times that Helen was truly happy, when surrounded by her children and cooking.

Preparing for church the next morning, Elizabeth was seized with apprehension. Kids her own age left her very unsure of herself. Her appearance was no longer an issue because she could now do her hair and makeup properly and was content with what she saw in the mirror. Her clothes were still very conservative but that is exactly what this occasion called for. It was mainly the topic of conversation she struggled with. She felt so out of touch with society not having been able to watch TV or read a newspaper for months, not to mention that before the program, she hung around people in their twenties versus teenagers. *Well, these kids are supposed to be Christians,* she thought, *let's see if they act like one.*

Staring up at the beautiful house that was part of the church that held the teen groups, Elizabeth could picture herself living there. The red brick reminded her of books she had read that talked of simpler times and there had always been something deep inside of her that felt she was born in the wrong era. She loved the idea of how people would have calling cards when they wanted to visit someone or even a letter of introduction when coming to a new city. Sighing at the romanticism of all of that, she pulled the front door open.

She was greeted by a grand staircase that stood on both sides of the room and wound itself to meet at the top where a balcony stood. There were three teens looking down on her from above. Two girls and a boy. The tallest girl looked like a life-sized Barbie doll. She wore a pretty white dress and black ballet flats. Were it not for the smirk on her face, she would have appeared quite innocent and approachable. By their whispers and soft laughter, she felt that they weren't just literally looking down on her but also metaphorically. This was not quite the start she had in mind. Should she wave and risk rejection or just pretend she hadn't noticed them? She was spared from making a decision when the chime from the church bells began and a woman with pretty features approached her.

"You must be Elizabeth," she said. "The front office told me to look out for you. Follow me and I will show you to the class that has kids your age in it." A shrewd glance up at the balcony caused the three kids to disperse. "You look a bit frightened...don't be. Most of the kids here have known each other since childhood, but it won't take you long to feel included."

Elizabeth was shocked at how frank the woman was being with her. In the politest of ways, she let Elizabeth know exactly what to expect and that her first impression of the three kids above had been spot on.

All eyes were on her as she stepped into the room and found a seat. The topic that was discussed that day was on forgiveness. Other than the fact that Bible scriptures were used to reference things; the class was outlined a lot like the program.

Elizabeth couldn't help feeling a bit critical toward the other kids in the room as they discussed what they needed to forgive others for. "My sister took my favorite lipstick," or "my parents wouldn't give me my allowance," were the topics being batted around. As Elizabeth was thinking that these kids didn't have a clue, a thought struck her that it was she that didn't have a clue. What seemed so trivial to her at the time was, indeed, what normal kids were dealing with; that it was these small concerns that would help mold them for future conflicts. Elizabeth had dealt with such adult concerns at such a young age that this was yet another area that had completely bypassed her. As much as she wanted to relate to this class, she just couldn't. There was no way to undo what was already done. She thought that if she

101

were to try and share with this innocent group of teenagers, they would be repelled by her.

The three kids that she saw earlier spent much of the time whispering and giggling to each other to which the teacher seemed oblivious.

She became angry at the teacher for not telling them to shut up and be more respectful. Her emotions were spinning out of control and she jumped to the conclusion that the church was run by a bunch of hypocrites. She vowed to never return to this class or the church again. She knew she was being childish for letting one scenario form her opinion of the church as a whole, but the dark mood that had taken hold was hard to shake.

A bathroom break was issued and that was Elizabeth's cue to leave. Slipping down the hall unnoticed, she left by a side door and walked the two miles home. When her mother asked her how it went, she simply shrugged and they both let it go at that.

Unfortunately, the experience left her feeling like a quitter again. Yet another thing she couldn't see through. She just wanted a sense of belonging and the only place she knew to turn was her journal.

Chapter 36

Well, journal, what the hell do I do now? I haven't had to think for myself for over half a year and now I am completely free to do what I want, yet I have no clue as to what that is.

Mom seems to be doing good with her AA meetings so maybe that should be the next step for me as well. I can't imagine us both attending the same one so I will seek somewhere else to go.

Don't even ask me how church went today. Some stupid kids were sizing me up the minute I walked through the door. One was this blonde girl who was obviously the ringleader with her perfect hair and clothes. I could tell just by looking at her that she has gotten anything she has ever wanted from mommy and daddy. I wanted to slap the smug smile off her face. Yeah, I know, in church.

What a bitch I have become. I have only been out a couple of days but still feel like a prisoner, but this time it is of my own making. I am chicken shit to go anywhere or do anything for fear of running into someone from my past.

I have heard doctors say that wherever you were in your maturity level when you started doing drugs is where you stay while using. Like it stunts your ability to grow up. I kind of understand that when thinking of my foolish reaction at church today, but then the other part of me gets confused because I have had to do adult things since a young age, like cook and look after my own safety. If it is true, then maybe, there is hope for me now that I don't do drugs anymore. Maybe my brain can start to catch up with my age. I am too exhausted to think about it anymore. I will just chalk it up to one of life's little mysteries.

Mom signed me up to return to school but that has its own nightmares to be defeated. Life is so hard. I hear Nicholas outside so I am going to cut this short.

Love Elizabeth

Peering out of her room to see who Nicholas was talking to, Elizabeth caught her breath at the sight of Robby. Robby had not only been Nicholas' best friend but one of the cutest boys at Fort Myers High School when she was a freshman. Every type of girl from cheerleader to goth had a crush on him. The most amazing thing was that he was also one of the nicest guys around and not conceited in the least. To top it all off, while his peers chose to drink and do drugs, Robby politely declined and nobody ever gave him a problem.

When he saw Elizabeth, a big grin spread across his face. Without hesitation, he walked quickly towards her, picked her up, and spun her around. As he set her back on her feet, he said, "I am so proud of you Elizabeth." He gave her a long hug and then held her at arm's length while his eyes seemed to take her all in.

Nicholas had begun to shift uneasily at this sign of affection; then punched his friend in the arm and said, "Enough already Robby, she is the same Elizabeth you have always known, just a bit squarer."

The trance was broken and Elizabeth responded with a curt, "Gee, thanks."

They all laughed and wound up hanging out together in the living room to discuss what each other had been up to.

It was a disappointment to Elizabeth to realize that Robby still looked at her as a little sister and nothing more. She knew a relationship was something the program had always warned against and it brought back memories of her and Paul. He probably hated her right now, she thought.

Glancing at the clock on the wall, Robby stood up and said that it was time for him to leave. Within minutes, he was gone, Nicholas was holed up in his old room, and Elizabeth was surrounded by silence. She had found that silence continued to make her antsy and uneasy. Discontent surrounded her and she retreated to her room for a good cry.

Tomorrow, she was to return to school. The good thing was that all of her old cronies would be gone because she was now a year behind since she had quit. There was someone in the neighborhood who had been Elizabeth's best friend for several years before she had gotten involved with Marcus. Her name was Mary and she was one year younger than Elizabeth. They would now be in the same grade and Elizabeth wasn't sure if she could bridge the gap between them. The way they had parted was mutual; Mary had a boyfriend before Elizabeth had even met Marcus. When Elizabeth had started going out with Marcus, she thought it would be a great idea to introduce the two people who were most important to her. It was obvious that Mary hated him on sight. The last time that Elizabeth saw Mary was when she and her boyfriend were supposed to buy some weed for her and Marcus. They came back with a cock and bull story that they had been ripped off and that is when Elizabeth knew things would never be the same. Mary had banded together with someone else and her loyalty did not lie with Elizabeth any longer. Marcus had been furious about the transaction and called Mary and her boyfriend some pretty rotten names and for once, Elizabeth did not come to Mary's defense. Mary's mom and dad had been like a second family to her. Their home had been so secure for Elizabeth over the years. The fridge was always stocked and with them having central air and heat, the temperature inside their home was always perfect. Elizabeth had to always defend her food against the roaches at her house and with no air conditioner and only a fireplace and furnace with one vent in the floor, summers and winters were treacherous.

As if in a trance, Elizabeth reached for the phone, still having Mary's number memorized. After several attempts at dialing before hanging the phone up each time, Elizabeth finally got up the nerve to complete the call. *I guess the worst thing that could happen is that she could hang up on me*, thought Elizabeth.

After three rings someone answered, "Hello."

"Hi, is this Mary?'

"Yes, who's this?"

Taking a deep breath Elizabeth said, "This is a blast from your past, it's me Elizabeth."

104

There was a sharp intake of breath followed by silence that lasted several seconds. "Elizabeth!" she screamed, "I can't believe it is you. I have heard so many weird rumors but didn't know what to believe."

"Other than the one about me dying in New York, I think it is safe to say that the rumors were true. Are you and your boyfriend still together?

Mary laughed and said, "Hell no! Girl, I am single and happy about it. So, what's up? Are you back at Fort Myers High? I go there now."

Elizabeth couldn't believe how easily the conversation had turned right into the topic she most wanted to talk about. "As a matter of fact, that is why I am calling you. I plan on starting back tomorrow and was just checking on whether I would see a friendly and familiar face." It was as if time stood still the way both girls seemed to have picked their friendship back up from where they had left it before they had boyfriends.

"You bet. I drive my Camaro to school and can pick you up if you want."

Elizabeth remembered the blue Camaro that had sat in Mary's driveway months before she was even of age to take the driving test. Mary was the youngest in the family with her two siblings already grown and moved out. Mary had always been spoiled which had caused Elizabeth quite a bit of jealousy over the years. The Camaro as a gift to someone too young to even drive had been too much for Elizabeth to handle at the time. She remembered being less than enthusiastic in congratulating her and became too busy to hang out for several days following.

After a few minutes of catching up, Mary interrupted Elizabeth saying, "What are we still doing talking on the phone? Get your butt over here."

For the first time since she left the program, Elizabeth felt she had found her place. Tying her sneakers, she yelled to her mom, "Guess who I just got off the phone with?"

Helen, who had been drying the dishes, crossed to Elizabeth's room and with a smile on her face said, "I don't know, but from the sound of your voice, it was someone I will approve of."

Laughing, Elizabeth said, "It was Mary mom. Mary." Tears spilled from Elizabeth's eyes as she hugged her mother. Her emotions were so raw. She hadn't realized the relationships that she had been mourning. Mary had been the one person that Elizabeth did not have to pretend around. She was fully aware of Helen's drinking problem, having witnessed some embarrassing moments firsthand. She had always been there for Elizabeth without feeling sorry for her. The one thing that Elizabeth had not taken into consideration was that Mary was also the first person that she had experimented with drugs with.

"Well, nobody said this was going to be easy, but I have to face a test in order to pass one, right?" she murmured to herself.

Walking over to Mary's house; Elizabeth spent the rest of her Sunday reminiscing with her until the conversation finally turned to the present. Mary reassured Elizabeth that Fort Myers High would be a great experience the second time around. Elizabeth left feeling less unsure about returning to school now that she would have Mary by her side.

Chapter 37

It was only 6:45 a.m. and the sound of Motley Crue singing 'Live Wire' outside of Elizabeth's house could only mean that Mary was there to pick her up.

"What is all that racket?" yelled Helen from her bedroom. She had worked the graveyard shift at the hospital the night before and was just getting settled into bed to get some rest.

"Sorry mom," she said as she waved frantically from the door for Mary to lower the volume. A dog began to bark and the next door neighbor's light had just turned on. This was not the way Elizabeth had planned on starting her day.

As Elizabeth approached the car, she could see another girl inside that she did not recognize. Cigarette smoke was billowing out of the windows but Elizabeth didn't care as long as it wasn't pot smoke. Naturally expecting Mary to tell the other girl to move to the back seat, Elizabeth was taken aback when she opened the door and folded the front seat down in order to let Elizabeth climb into the back.

The school was less than five minutes away so there wasn't much time for Elizabeth to get a feel for whether she liked the other girl or not. She had been surprised to see her because Mary had made no mention of her driving anyone else to school. She had been naïve to think that Mary had no other friends and that Elizabeth could just step right back in as being her best friend again.

Mary yelled over the music," Show Kim your schedule and we will see if we have any classes together." Having perused her schedule, it was confirmed that the two of them did not share one class with Elizabeth.

Silly thoughts started to fill Elizabeth's head like…what if I forgot how to work a combination lock and can't get into my locker? What if, at lunch, all the tables are taken and nobody invites me to sit with them? What if I am not the only one a grade behind and I see someone I knew from my past? This was one of those times that Elizabeth wished she could just go with the flow and handle things as they came. She always felt like she had to prepare for life's 'what ifs' and have three possible solutions to events that rarely ever happened.

Fear was a bitch and at that moment, Elizabeth was convicted to never let it grip her this way again. If she did, it would be the beginning of the domino effect to start using drugs again. Reciting the serenity prayer in her head, Elizabeth controlled her breathing in time for their arrival at school.

All of this went completely unnoticed by both Kim and Mary. The age of self-absorption was still alive and kicking.

Walking into school, Mary looped her arm through Elizabeth's. It seemed to be what most of the girls were doing as they strutted down the hall. It felt awkward to Elizabeth but she didn't want to risk upsetting Mary by pulling her arm back.

"Want to hit the bathroom real quick?" asked Elizabeth

"Sure," said Mary.

Entering the second floor bathroom, Elizabeth saw that nothing had changed. The mirrors still gave off a strange reflection like something from the hall of mirrors at the circus.

Glancing at herself, Elizabeth liked what she saw. Her makeup application was very different from the past, but it seemed appropriate since she was making a fresh start. Gone was the thick black liquid eyeliner and heavily made up face. What she saw now was a touch of bronzer, brown eyeliner and long thick eyelashes. Rather than a garish red on her lips, she had a light peachy pink.

Having completed the girl ritual of touching up makeup and chatting about boys, they parted ways at the end of the hall. She couldn't believe she had to do all of this by herself, wishing that her mother was there with her.

The day was pretty uneventful with none of Elizabeth's fears coming to fruition. Her new appearance seemed to attract others rather than keep them at arm's length. A girl from her English class invited Elizabeth to sit with her at lunch, she opened her locker on the first try and she didn't recognize anyone that she used to hang out with. All in all, it had been a pretty good day. She couldn't wait to get home and tell her mom all about it.

Elizabeth was surprised not to see her mother's car in the driveway when she returned home. She thought she would have been excited to hear the day's news. Putting her books away she walked into the kitchen to see if Helen had left a note, but there was nothing.

Paranoia about her mother going back to drinking had Elizabeth listening at key holes for the past couple of days. Last night she had been sure she had heard the telltale signs of her mother filling a glass with ice but nothing being poured in the glass could be heard. In the past, her mom would fill her glass with ice and nonchalantly walk right past Elizabeth as though it made complete sense to have a glass with nothing but ice in it. The sound of a beer can being cracked open in her room would be unmistaken as would her continued migration from the room to the kitchen and back to the room. There was a sick comedy in the way her mom would walk normal for the first trip but then gradually get more and more zig zagged with her hanging on to door frames for balance with each trip that followed. That had been part of the reason Elizabeth would get so angry with her mom; because she felt that she was insulting her intelligence.

She heard car tires crunching on the gravel driveway and peered out the window to see who it was. Helen appeared to be having difficulty in centering her car as she tried to park. After several attempts at putting the car in reverse and then drive, she, eventually, just left it askew by the back alley.

A lump had formed in Elizabeth's throat as her mind scrambled around for the right reaction. She stuffed down the rage that had begun to bubble up only to feel fear take its place. Fear became a living thing inside of Elizabeth's head. She could hear the sound of tapping fingernails as the seconds ticked by and then the voice of fear saying, "Whatcha gonna do? Whatcha gonna do?"

After pacing back and forth, her instinct to help kicked in and she responded to fear with "This is what I am gonna do bitch." She opened the back door and planted a smile on her face as she said, "Hi mom!" This had startled Helen who had been struggling with her balance as she was reaching into the car to retrieve her purse.

107

She bumped her head on the door frame and Elizabeth quickly ran down the back steps to assist.

The first thing she did was hug her mom because in her heart, she had known all along that her mom didn't stand a chance with the alcohol. It had been her comforter for too long. Over the years, Elizabeth had found out about how much sadness her mom had endured. She understood her need to forget.

It was very hard to decipher what Helen was saying due to her slurred speech, but Elizabeth answered with noncommittal um hmmm noises and helped her up the stairs. Propping her on her bed, Elizabeth began to remove her mom's shoes. Helen's head was lolling forward as she kept repeating, "I'm sorry." Tilting her mom's face up with her hands, Elizabeth made her mother look at her as she said, "Mom, it is okay. It is you and me against the world okay?" As tears welled in Helen's eyes, she shook her head in comprehension.

Elizabeth leaned her back into her pillows and Helen was out like a light. Sinking to the floor Elizabeth wrapped her arms around her knees and began to sob. She felt a breeze hit the back of her neck and looked up to see the curtains just billowing in the wind. It was such a beautiful day. She couldn't understand how bad things could happen on such a beautiful day.

Her poor mother. Elizabeth had recently found out that at an early age her mother's parents had made it very clear that they had wished she was a boy. They already had a son, but back then a boy could earn more etc. Her mom had to leave school in the eighth grade in order to work and help the family. From what other family members had told Elizabeth, Helen's dad was a drinker…no surprise there, it had to come from somewhere. If her mother had hoped to be set free from this tyranny by getting married at the age of 17, she was wrong. Her first husband was verbally abusive and to this day, Elizabeth did not know how but he was given custody of their three children when they divorced. This caused Helen to have a nervous breakdown and back then psychiatry was quite primitive and her mother was subjected to shock therapy. All of this history, Elizabeth had learned when she reconnected with other family members through letter writing while in the program.

She knew she was not qualified to help her mom, but felt that she wanted to return the loyalty that her mother had recently shown her. This moment felt very surreal as Elizabeth knew that there was no one that she could confide in or turn to for help.

The isolation she felt was magnified by the quietness of the house. *Well,* she thought to herself, *the best thing for me right now is to just sleep it off, I guess.*

Getting back up, she wound her way back to her room. Starting on homework seemed like the sensible thing to do, so she opened her history book and began to read. She had finished two chapters without retaining a bit of information. Closing the book in exasperation, her eyes fell on her journal. *My trusted friend,* she thought. Her hands were shaking as she reached for the book. After five minutes had passed where her pen was held in midair above the blank page, Elizabeth experienced, for the first time, a complete loss of what to write. She had always written with the belief that a solution would come or at the very least she would feel better after a journal entry. She felt abandoned by the last thing that she trusted.

Throwing the journal across the room she began to cry again. Collapsing on her bed, she cried until her pillowcase was soaking wet. She awoke two hours later.

Elizabeth sat up in bed and picking the crust from her eyes, stood up and walked to the bathroom. The bathroom was adjoined to both her and her mother's bedroom. Peeking her head through the second door, she saw that Helen was still fast asleep. Rubbing her temples to try and ease the throb that had started, Elizabeth thought to herself, *I have heard the term 'crying yourself to sleep' but have never actually done it.* Hoping never to do it again because she felt like she had a hangover; Elizabeth was startled by the ringing of the telephone. Thinking that it could be Mrs. Stein, Elizabeth refrained from answering it.

Chapter 38

For the next few weeks, Elizabeth found her mother succumbing to the alcohol more frequently. On one of these nights, she had just gotten Helen to bed when the phone began its incessant ringing. Rushing to grab the phone before it woke her mother, Elizabeth snatched up the receiver with a whispered, "Hello?"

A deep male voice responded, "Can I talk to Elizabeth, please?"

As her automatic reply of, "This is she," tumbled out of her mouth, she recognized the voice on the other end.

"Where the hell have you been, I have been looking everywhere for you?"

It was Marcus…several seconds of silence ensued and he must have thought he had scared her off. Lowering his voice, he hastily added, "Are you OK?"

Despite everything she had been through with him, despite everything she had learned from Helping Hands; to hear Marcus ask if she was OK breathed new life into her. His gravitational pull was unmistakable. The emotions he could evoke in a single sentence had Elizabeth's head reeling.

Taking a deep breath to allow her voice to remain calm she finally answered, "Yes, I'm OK." Gripping the receiver, she waited to hear what he had to say next.

She heard a choking sob as Marcus began to speak again. "It was just like you were there one minute and gone the next Elizabeth. First I thought you were dead because some asshole told me you had been hit by a car, but then your brother told me you were OK…but that is all he would tell me." The choking sobs returned.

Hearing him sound so vulnerable caused Elizabeth to want to comfort and reassure him. She began to murmur as she would to a child, "Shh, shh, shh, it's all right Marcus, everything is all right." Continuing in a whisper she said, "I am back and now that you know that I am OK, you can go back to your life."

Was it her imagination or had she just seamlessly transitioned right back to her dramatic side? A warning voice she began to hear in her head was the influence that Helping Hands had on her. It was blunt and to the point. As her heart hammered in her chest, she scrambled to figure out a way to undo this whole conversation.

"Go back to my life? What life!" screamed Marcus who had now begun to hyperventilate on the phone. "Don't you get it, Elizabeth," he heaved between words, "I love you and I need you!"

Elizabeth was praying desperately in her head, "Please God, help me, please God, help me," but said nothing to Marcus.

The Helping Hands voice kept repeating, "Remember what he did to you, remember what he did to you. He cracked your rib…he cheated on you. He did things you never even dared share with your group."

Her plea to God stopped as she switched gears to deal with the voice, "Shut up! Shut up!" she yelled, although only in her head.

Having gotten himself together, Marcus continued in a calmer voice, "Elizabeth, I know you are scared about something, can't you just tell me where you have been?"

"Drug rehab."

His voice rising again, he said, "What? Who the hell put you there? Oh, never mind, let me guess, your mother?" There was no hiding the snide tone he used when saying the word "mother."

He had been expecting the Elizabeth she had been when he had last seen her. The Elizabeth who acted like she hated her mother and was quick witted when it came to mocking her mother's drunkenness.

As with most cases of dysfunction, it was OK for Elizabeth to say ugly things about her mother but not OK for others to. She snapped back with, "She was trying to save my life, Marcus. Are you actually going to sit there and deny that I had a problem?"

Sensing a shift in her mood, Marcus quickly brought down the volume of his voice saying, "I am sorry Elizabeth, of course she was only trying to help and yes, I guess we were all getting out of control with the drugs and alcohol, but all I do now is smoke a little weed and have a few beers. When can I see you?"

Sighing, Elizabeth felt so weary as if she had been talking to him for hours. The paranoia of being caught by her mom as she peered around the corner every few minutes to make sure she was still asleep was exhausting. She leaned her back against the wall and slid to the floor.

"It is not that easy, Marcus. I won't lie by saying it has not been good to hear your voice. I have been so lonely these last few weeks. You wouldn't like the new me; they cut all my hair off." She was crying again but trying hard for Marcus not to know.

"I don't give a shit about your hair. Elizabeth, we can get back to the place we were at when we first met…I promise. We belong together."

Unable to contain her emotions any longer, Elizabeth cried openly. She tried to muffle the sound with her hand but not before Marcus heard her and the ripple effect started with the sound of his cries too.

She had no idea how much time had passed before their cries subsided but was aware that they had been replaced with the two of them saying "I love you" to each other. First in a jumble with one "I love you" running over the other, and then taking turns so that they both heard each other's confession. Laughter rang out after about a minute of this; a giddy, dizzying laughter.

Marcus pressed on with his request to see her and she finally consented to meet him at a record store that they both were familiar with. She refused to allow him to pick her up in his car for fear of being seen by a neighbor who would undoubtedly inform Helen right away. The record store was located a few blocks from the high school so Elizabeth opted to walk instead.

It took all of her remaining energy to convince Marcus that he couldn't just come by that minute. She shared with him all that had occurred to get away from Helping Hands and in the end, he conceded to wait until the next day.

Finally replacing the phone in the cradle, Elizabeth remained sitting on the floor, trying to make sense of what had just happened. There were two conflicting voices raging in her brain. She felt like the cartoon character that had the devil on one shoulder and the angel on the other.

111

What was done was done and rising from her sitting position, Elizabeth walked over to one of her sleeping cats and began to stroke his soft fur. She gently picked him up from his perch and carried him back to her room. *Time to find the right outfit for school tomorrow,* she thought to herself. Setting the cat down, the angel voice responded with "Who do you think you are kidding? More like time to find the right outfit to see Marcus in tomorrow."

"Nothing wrong with that," responded the little devil. With a mischievous grin. Elizabeth walked into her closet and began throwing pieces of clothing on her bed. Although that morning she had been completely content with her look, she now felt that Marcus may mock her for appearing too docile. Her mind was racing with ideas of how to redesign her clothing. Before long she had split the sides of a couple of skirts with a pair of scissors, layered a few blouses and mismatched different materials together. She crossed her arms and took a step back to observe her handiwork. Elizabeth liked what she saw and more importantly, liked how she felt.

Elizabeth pretended to be asleep when her mother woke up several hours later. She just couldn't cope with the seriousness of the situation just yet. She had enough on her mind with having to meet Marcus the next day. She heard the familiar sounds of her mother preparing for work. Elizabeth had no idea how her mother would get through her shift after the binge she just had but had witnessed many occasions where Helen seemed to pull it off. Elizabeth cringed when she heard her mother retching in the bathroom.

Wishing for sleep to really come, she squeezed her eyes shut to try and block out all the images that were racing before her. Images of being right back where she started with not only Marcus but her mom too. What Helen had done that day was a betrayal but Elizabeth had been a betrayer as well by not hanging up the phone the moment she had recognized Marcus' voice.

Elizabeth began to list all of the pros and cons of meeting Marcus the following day. He had admitted to still smoking pot and drinking. He had been an ugly drunk who had taken all of his frustrations out on Elizabeth. He was still much too old for her. She knew there was no way he had been celibate the whole time that Elizabeth had been gone. The cons seemed to come so easily and she found herself struggling to come up with any pros. Elizabeth remembered the intimate conversations they used to have when they first met, how they shared their dreams with each other. Maybe if they really could get back to where they used to be, those types of conversations could resume.

Thinking of the lies she knew she would start telling as of the next day made her stomach feel queasy. It hadn't occurred to her how hard it would be to go back to her old ways. It had felt good to be trusted by people again, to have a clean slate.

As drowsiness began to overtake her, she thought of Paul. If she could have him that moment over Marcus, she knew that she would choose him. There was no long history with him in which to repair and they both shared the same goal of not going back to drugs and alcohol. The only advantage that Marcus had over him was that he was physically available. Sleep finally came and was considerate enough to provide no dreams to torment Elizabeth further.

The alarm clock rang at its usual 5:30 the next morning. The memory of the day before swam in Elizabeth's head before her feet even hit the floor. The smell of fresh coffee greeted Elizabeth as she shuffled into the kitchen. Helen was winding down from the night shift by cooking. Elizabeth always considered cooking as work and failed to see how it produced such a calming effect on her mom. She wouldn't dare argue the point since she was about to reap the rewards of Helen's handiwork: poached eggs, fresh toast, and hash browns.

Watching her mother out of the corner of her eye, Elizabeth could tell she was hurting from the night before. Helen had yet to produce any excuses or apologies which led Elizabeth to believe that they were back to the denial phase in which she would be expected to pretend nothing had happened. Her chest ached from the desire to talk things through; the way she had been taught at the program. Instead, she ranted and raved about the food which brought a smile to Helen's face. Excusing herself from the table, Elizabeth gave her mother a big hug and told her to get some rest.

As she looked at the clothing choices for the day, Elizabeth began to doubt whether it was such a good idea to draw attention to herself this way. She had only been back to school for a couple of weeks and liked the fact that, although she wasn't popular, she wasn't an outcast either. These clothes, even with their subtle changes, would send a certain message that she belonged to the rebels. *Maybe I can sew the seam back where I ripped the skirt,* she thought to herself. As Elizabeth grabbed a needle and thread, she saw that Mary had pulled into the driveway. Curious as to why she was a half hour early, Elizabeth headed to the front of the house and opened the door for her.

"Sorry to get here so early," began Mary, "but when I got to Kim's house her mom said she was sick as a dog so I thought rather than head back home, I would just come here."

Elizabeth put her finger to her lips and pointed at her mom's door to let Mary know to keep her voice down.

Continuing in a whisper, Mary said, "Wow, I haven't been here in forever." Glancing at the steep staircase she laughed, "Remember when Nicholas' friend fell through the ceiling when they were goofing off in the attic? It was genius for your mother to have had stairs put where he crashed through rather than patch the hole."

"I know," Elizabeth whispered back and signaled for Mary to follow her to her room.

"You have had every bedroom in this house over the years. How do you get your mom to go along with it?"

Shrugging her shoulders, Elizabeth said, "I guess my mom understands the need for change. We have moved enough over the years, so going from one room to another isn't such a big deal."

"I was thinking that after school, we can hit the mall," said Mary.

"I can't," Elizabeth quickly responded.

Mary's head shot up at the abruptness of Elizabeth's answer. "Why not?" she asked.

Lie number one was tumbling out of her mouth before she could stop herself, "I plan on talking to the guidance counselor after school today to go over classes and maybe even talk about career choices." Where that utter nonsense came from, Elizabeth did not know but was grateful for her ability to ad lib on the spot. Her acting skills seemed to be as sharp as ever.

The excuse seemed to mollify Mary who moved right on to the latest music and gossip from school.

Having fixed her skirt, Elizabeth announced that she was ready to go.

Chapter 39

On the drive to school, it struck Elizabeth that there was a chance that Marcus may not even look the same as she remembered him. She was sure that his hair would still touch his shoulders and that his general physique would be the same, but the concern was more about how her perception of his looks may have changed after being in the program. She did, for instance, fall for Paul who was as preppy as you could get. Her brain began to go in reverse which caused her to question where the two of them even stood with each other. Yes, officially they had still been a couple when she entered treatment but the relationship itself was in tatters, filled with distrust and resentment. Though she hadn't even been enjoying her time with Marcus, it was just part of her routine to go over and see him each day.

Elizabeth retained nothing from each of her classes that day but spent the time going over her upcoming meeting with Marcus. The logical side of her was quick to point out that it was a bad idea and that she should just be a "no show." The other side of her wanted to see for herself if he had really missed her as much as he said he had during their last phone conversation.

Part of her wished she could just start over somewhere else where she knew no one. Having witnessed Helen's attempt at geographical changes only to fall into old habits was her wakeup call that the same would happen to her. Since Elizabeth's father had died, they had moved from Florida to Connecticut back to Fort Lauderdale, Florida then to the boonies of Pioneer Plantation, on to Clewiston, and finally to settle in Fort Myers. Through all of those moves, Helen continued to drink, get in minor fender benders, and even lost a job or two.

At the age of 17, Elizabeth was on her own again with zero guidance from a reliable adult. She was smart enough to know that this decision of hers to meet Marcus would only end in misery but it was all she knew. If not comforting, it was at least familiar.

As the day progressed, Elizabeth felt a sense of déjà vu. It was so like the last day at Mariner High when she was leaving the program, except this time she was dodging Mary. Every corner she rounded seemed to bring her face to face with Mary and paranoia was kicking in as though Mary knew exactly what she was planning.

Luckily, they did not share the same lunch shift so Elizabeth would be free to go over her plan then. After circling the salad bar three times she finally decided on a loaded baked potato. Exiting the cafeteria, she found an unoccupied picnic table where she placed her tray and spread out a sheet of paper in order to organize her thoughts a little more.

On the first line, she wrote "Mary" and put a check mark beside the name. Having already given Mary her excuse for the day she felt that she had that base covered. The next line read "Mom." Helen was off that day but had told Elizabeth she would be home around four after seeing some friends at the flea market.

Elizabeth figured she had about an hour to spend with Marcus before she would have to start her three-mile walk home, unless he really did have a car and then maybe she could have him drop her off a few blocks from the house which would allow her more time with him. After careful consideration, Elizabeth placed a check mark beside her too.

Having so few friends put Elizabeth at an advantage where this day was concerned. As she began to slip the paper back into her folder, she thought, *how could I be so stupid?* Pulling the paper right back out, she jotted, "Nicholas." Elizabeth knew that Nicholas still worked downtown but did not know his schedule. She would have to make sure that if she was stuck walking home, that she would have to skirt around the few blocks that surrounded the restaurant that Nicholas worked at. "Whew," she said aloud as she placed her third check mark on the paper.

Her appetite had left her but she made herself eat her baked potato anyway. She had to admit she was scared. Marcus seemed like a stranger even though she had shared her most intimate moments with him. Flashes of the girl she was when she entered Helping Hands appeared in her mind and she was repulsed by herself. She remembered how twisted her face had looked in the bathroom mirror as she was forced to remove her clothes and be searched for drugs. The bitterness she had felt within the first few hours kept see sawing from the loss of Marcus to her grudgingly missing her mother.

The past few weeks she had at least felt semi-content; that is, until last night when the anguish hit her from her mother coming home drunk. Elizabeth kept asking herself if she wanted to risk losing the self-respect she had gained by returning to Marcus. Her heart ached and as usual the loneliness won out. She had to admit that she would rather be miserable than lonely. *How twisted am I!* she thought and started to cry. She put her legs up on the bench and placed her face between her knees so that nobody would see her if they walked by.

Grabbing her napkin, she blotted her cheeks and then blew her nose. Elizabeth threw the napkin on the half eaten baked potato and carried the tray to the nearest garbage can where she got rid of the evidence of her weakness. The warning bell rang and as she walked to class, she wished that she were anyone other than Elizabeth Tartaglia.

To her surprise, the rest of the day flew by and before she knew it, she was walking towards the record store where she was to meet Marcus. It was a gorgeous day with a slight breeze that helped Elizabeth feel like all of her misgivings were being blown away by it. Passing the hospital, she could see the rooftop of the record store ahead. Reaching the final corner, she just stopped and stared at the storefront window wondering if Marcus was already there. It was impossible to make out the features of the people she could see walking around inside the store.

The light turned red, allowing her to cross the street. Barely taking the time to look both ways, Elizabeth picked up her pace. Trying to appear calm, she opened the front door slowly and said, "Hello" to the guy at the register. The store was small enough for Elizabeth to assess that she was the first to arrive. She was just looking at the record jacket for Pink Floyd's "Dark Side of the Moon" album when she heard the door open. Looking up, she saw Marcus half walking, half running toward her. His hair was a bit longer than when she saw him last and it blew behind him from the speed that he was traveling at.

Before she knew what was happening he had lifted her off of her feet and had her in a bear hug. Snatching the album from her hand he placed it back in its spot and led her straight out the door.

Outside, he led her to a fairly new yellow Toyota, not something she thought he would have ever chosen. He quickly explained that a friend had lent him the car and they would head to that person's apartment because it was right around the corner.

When they were inside the car, Elizabeth saw Marcus' hands visibly shaking. Placing his head on the steering wheel he said, "I just need a minute to take this all in, Elizabeth." In the quietness that followed, Elizabeth had time to look at him unobserved. Marcus had a deep tan which Elizabeth guessed was from his time at the beach not from an outdoor job. Marcus had always loved his free time, never having held down a real job in his entire life. Although Elizabeth could not hear Marcus crying, she heard the drips from his tears hit the top of his jeans.

Without warning, he quickly reached across her to open the glove box where he grabbed a tissue and blew his nose. His arm had grazed her chest and she felt goose bumps form on her arms.

Just as quickly, Marcus leaned into her for a kiss. Embarrassed, Elizabeth pulled her head back to avoid contact. Ready to explain herself, she was cut off in mid-sentence with Marcus apologizing profusely. "I am sorry, Elizabeth, I know...I know, I am moving too fast. Let me just look at you for a minute."

Cupping her chin in his hand, he whispered, "I forgot how beautiful you are."

Blushing, Elizabeth grabbed his hand and suggested they get going.

With a steadier hand, Marcus started the car. It barely took two minutes to reach their destination and Elizabeth found herself extremely anxious about who she was about to meet. She wished they had some time to themselves before she was put on display. In the back of her mind, she knew this was probably better because it meant that Marcus would have to keep his hands to himself.

Running around to her side of the car, Marcus opened her door; something he had never done before. *Wow, this must be what people refer to as the honeymoon phase,* she thought to herself.

Upon entering the apartment Elizabeth was greeted by Marcus' best friend, Wayne. He looked about the same as he did the last time she saw him, although his blond hair did appear to be receding a bit. He approached her like a stranger; not sure if he should hug her or shake her hand. She relieved him of his discomfort by standing on tip toe and wrapping her arms around his neck and giving him a big squeeze. Whispering in his ear, she said, "It is so nice to see a familiar face. Thanks for being here."

"No problem," he replied. "It was the only way to get Marcus to shut up about you."

Punching him in the side, Marcus told him to knock it off. Luckily there were only two other guys in the apartment and they were busy getting ready for work so they said a quick "Hi" and were gone.

Marcus offered Elizabeth a beer which she declined. It did not bother her that he and Wayne were slugging down beer. She did not want to become that person who quit drugs and expected everyone else to quit too.

Out of nowhere, Wayne starting cracking up laughing. Unable to speak, he could only point at Elizabeth.

117

"Glad to see you're enjoying your private little joke over there," she said to him but couldn't stop smirking herself.

"I was just thinking about the first time I met you. I had been discouraging Marcus from seeing you when he told me how young you were. He finally dragged me to meet you and you were wearing that shiny black skirt, looking all innocent."

By this time, Elizabeth knew exactly what memory he was reliving and she began to snort with laughter as well.

"We had just finished a joint and you grabbed some kid's bicycle and started peddling in circles screaming, "I'll get you and your little dog, Toto, too." You looked absolutely hilarious with that skirt past your knees and your legs peddling so fast, you could barely steer."

Marcus joined in the laughter and pulled her to his chest. She did not resist him but allowed her body to just rest against him. She could feel his body heat through his shirt and could hear his heart beating.

Any tension that had been in the room was finally released. More memories began to flow with each of them taking turns telling their own versions. Only the good memories were shared and Elizabeth's cheeks had begun to hurt from all the smiling she was doing. With their laughter subsiding, Marcus excused himself to go to the bathroom.

Wiping the tears from his eyes, Wayne suddenly turned serious. Glancing behind him to make sure Marcus was out of the room he continued, "On a heavier note though, Elizabeth, Marcus has been worried sick about you. I couldn't get him to eat for days after he realized you were missing. I know things were rocky between you two at the time you disappeared but he never stopped loving you, in his own way that is."

Not knowing where all of this was leading, Elizabeth wasn't sure how to respond.

"Just don't go breaking his heart again, OK?"

Bristling a little from this last comment, Elizabeth sat up straighter; all laughter forgotten. "I'm sorry did you say that **I** shouldn't break **his** heart? I am not the one who blatantly cheated. I am the one who tried to cope with his cheating by consuming way too much alcohol and swallowing whatever pill was passed my way. I disappeared because my mom didn't know how to handle my coming home and threatening to slit my wrists in the bathroom."

Standing up, Elizabeth was preparing to leave. Wayne grabbed her wrist but one look at her face caused him to release her as if he had been burned.

Waving his palms in the air in surrender, he urged her to sit back down. "If you storm out now, he will never forgive me…please sit down."

The memories that had flooded her mind hurt as if they had just happened. Marcus reentered the room with a fresh beer. He was oblivious to the change in the atmosphere due to his semi-inebriated state.

"So, what do you guys wanna do?" he asked.

Standing up for the second time, Elizabeth said, "I really have to get going, Marcus. I wanted to reassure you today that I am doing well, but my mom will be very suspicious if I break my normal pattern by too much. Right now, I am an hour later than usual."

Marcus was looking at her as if she were speaking another language. He responded by shaking his head in disbelief and saying, "No way, I just got you back, Elizabeth."

Staring into his eyes, Elizabeth recognized the hurt only because she had felt it so many times herself in the past. It had been his careless actions that caused that pain and as a flash of anger showed in her eyes, she turned to leave, saying, "Are you able to take me home or should I start walking?"

Startled by her abruptness, Marcus turned towards Wayne for help and then quickly back to Elizabeth to make sure she wasn't bolting for the door. Frantically, looking to Wayne, comprehension began to dawn on him and in a tone of anger, he said, "What the hell just happened? What did I miss when I left the room?" In his agitation, he swayed a little on his feet. Crushing his beer can with his hand he threw it across the room, spraying beer as it hit the wall.

Elizabeth felt like rolling her eyes at this silly man/boy drama. Marcus was as gifted an actor as she was when it came to getting his way. Unfortunately, he had a tendency to cross the line into violence. Looking like a caged lion, Marcus faced Wayne and in fear of what he was capable of, Elizabeth was forced to intervene. She placed herself between both men, pressing her palms against Marcus' chest to move him back a step. She felt a thrill of power knowing that she and she alone could diffuse the situation.

Locking eyes with Marcus, she used her soothing voice to say, "It was nothing, Marcus. Really, it has just been such an emotional day for all of us. Please…if I don't go home now we may never get another chance to see each other again. Is that what you want?" When he didn't respond, she repeated "Is that what you want?"

Slowly he shook his head and his body sagged like a deflated balloon. "I can take you home," he said. "I'll go get the keys."

When he left the room, Elizabeth looked back at Wayne and with a shaky smile, she wiped pretend sweat from her brow.

Wayne knew how close he had come to getting his face punched in. He gave Elizabeth a quick hug, releasing her just as quickly. It would not have been a good moment for Marcus to have walked in on them in any form of embrace.

Elizabeth was not very comfortable with the idea of Marcus driving after he had consumed so much alcohol, but she only lived a few miles away and if he took the back streets, they would be at her house in five minutes.

The ride home was spent in silence which suited her just fine. Adrenaline was still coursing through her body and although she knew the stress was not healthy, she loved how alive she felt. Being in the middle of the drama was exciting and even though it was all dysfunctional, she enjoyed the role she played in it. She had become "the fixer" again. It was what she knew best.

Finally finding his voice, Marcus asked, "When can I see you again?"

It amazed Elizabeth how docile and tame he appeared just then when only moments ago he was crazed and wild.

"Let's just take it one day at a time, OK?" Had she just used one of her mother's lines? "Who are you?" she asked herself in her mind. It was like she had morphed into several different Elizabeths. There was the shiny new drug free Elizabeth, the drama queen Elizabeth who had remained dormant for a while, and now this Elizabeth who was a reflection of her mother.

119

Nearing her home, she directed Marcus to let her out in the back alley behind her house. Grabbing her school books, she debated as to whether she should kiss him goodbye. *A peck on the cheek won't hurt anything,* she thought.

As she turned to say goodbye, the sun suddenly broke from a cloud and a stream of light shone through the windshield of the car. Elizabeth was struck by his beauty. The same beauty that had ensnared her the first night they met. The same beauty that had her cheat on her first real boyfriend.

Marcus was all Greek and his mane of hair glowed in the sunlight and his perfectly full lips waited for her. His muscular arms were involuntarily flexing through his shirt as he gripped the steering wheel. His long eyelashes blinked as he stared at her and she sensed it was taking all of his will power not to grab her and hold her. It was as if he realized the importance of her being the one to make the first move.

Having every intention of just giving him the peck on the cheek that she and her mind had agreed on; Elizabeth was just as shocked as Marcus when she found herself nuzzling her face in his neck. "Thank you for seeing me," she whispered as her fingers entwined themselves through his hair. Although Elizabeth was no virgin, she had never enjoyed the act of sex. It was always about the guy and servicing him. There had never been any intimacy in her sexual encounters but the closeness of their bodies in the car now and feeling the heat of her own breath gave her more of a sexual pleasure than the act itself. She suddenly felt a possessiveness towards him. Reeling herself in, she finished with the peck on the cheek, nothing more.

In that moment, she knew that she would be seeing Marcus again. Meeting his eyes for the last time, she recognized the desire he had for her. *He is mine,* she thought to herself. *He is mine and I now know how to keep him mine. No other girl will ever draw him away from me again.*

Feeling completely in control, she said to him, "You understand you are mine?" "Yes."

"I will not share you, do you understand?"

"I don't want anyone else, Elizabeth."

She knew that he meant what he said at the time, but wasn't going to let him off so easy. "I mean a month from now, a year from now."

"I know, I know!" he nearly shouted.

Smiling, she opened the car door and told him the best times to call her. She walked to the house self-consciously aware that Marcus wouldn't leave until she was out of sight. She hoped that he felt a pang of regret for his past mistreatment of her.

Chapter 40

As she cut across the backyard, Elizabeth was relieved to see that her mom's car was not in the driveway. She wasn't too surprised that she had beat her mom home because she knew her past drinking patterns and now that her mom had gotten bombed again, it was only natural that a bender was at hand. Mentally going through the calendar, Elizabeth searched for the cause of her mom's downfall. It was typical for Helen to struggle during the holidays since her father had died so close to them. Shrugging her shoulders, she figured it was the same type of voice plaguing her mother that had caused her to rationalize seeing Marcus again. If that was the case, the voice her mom was hearing was bent on her destruction so what could that mean about her and Marcus getting back together? It had felt so right in the car.

Letting herself in with her key, she headed to her room. All of this overanalyzing was giving her a headache. Throwing her books on her bed, she began pacing the room while massaging her temples. "Was I not happy five minutes ago?" she yelled to the room. "Why do I feel like I am in a dungeon now?"

Elizabeth wanted someone or something to blame. *It's this stupid house,* she thought to herself. Walking from room to room, the loneliness enveloped her again. The living room reminded her of the Christmas that her mom was so drunk that she had given her and Nicholas each other's presents by mistake. The bathroom where she locked herself in screaming for the razors. The dining room where one Thanksgiving her mom had slammed the dinner on the table while muttering that nobody had helped her prepare it, which caused everyone to eat in guilty silence.

She began to cry at the silliness of blaming a house for her unhappiness and confusion. She was ashamed at the fact that she couldn't seem to be content with her own company. Marcus' apparent need of her was what caused her to be so possessive of him that day. She felt no self-worth unless she was in the midst of someone else's crisis.

Across the room lay her journal looking as dejected as she felt. She had thrown it in a fit of anger because she felt that it had abandoned her. Wiping a tear from her face, she bent down and picked it up. Elizabeth skimmed through the pages, reading passages describing the journey she had been on for almost a year.

Hugging the journal to her chest she said, "How could I have discarded you so easily? You are the only one I can share my secrets with now."

Propping her pillows against the headboard, Elizabeth made herself comfortable. Taking a few deep breaths, she opened the book to the next clean page and began to write.

Dear Journal
Sometimes I think that I should give you a name other than journal because you feel so real to me. You stir in me all the same emotions that a loved one does. I have

always written in you as if just recording events in my life, but going forward, will write to you as a friend.

I want to apologize to you for throwing you so rudely to the ground the other day. I was mad at you. After leaving the program, I expected you to be able to help me sort out all of my emotions and keep me on track.

It was foolish of me to expect that of you and I know that I have been ignoring all of the other resources that are available to help me. The thought of AA meetings make me cringe. Another group of strangers. I imagine that appeals to a lot of people; a place that they unload all of their emotional baggage to a bunch of people they don't know. What they don't consider is the possibility of running into those same people somewhere else and having to pretend you don't know each other as well as the realization that that person knows stuff about you.

At least with the program, you knew everyone was trapped there so there was no risk of them running and telling people your secrets. I guess now that I think about it, an AA meeting would be similar; those folks wouldn't want that either. Wow, see how you help me? For some reason, I think clearer when I am writing in you and I contemplate things a little more before jumping the gun. Maybe if I had you with me the other day at the church, I wouldn't have been so quick to judge everyone. Then again, I would be replacing one crutch for another wouldn't I?

I had hoped to share you one day with my mom, but now I can't, because of something I have done. I have seen Marcus. Not just in passing or by mistake, he called and I came running. Something has changed though, something in me. I know who he is at heart but am not so naïve as to not know what he becomes under the influence. Who am I kidding; he has had a wandering eye whether drunk or sober. But like I said, something has changed. I never had the strength to stay away from him but with my involuntary imprisonment at the program he got to feel what it was like to really miss me. I wish you could have seen the way he looked at me today and he couldn't get close enough on the couch we were sitting on. I know this will fade in time so rather than me wish to change him, I have to figure out a way to change myself.

In a moment of reckless abandon, I basically claimed him as my property today. He wasn't offended or anything; in fact, I think it turned him on a little. I have to make sure that in the future, I react differently when faced with a potential female threat. In the past, whenever any girl appeared to be a bit more sophisticated than me, I just folded. I pretty much handed Marcus to them on a plate. I would run to another room so as not to witness their flirting which gave the other chick free reign to sink her claws into him. They never lasted long and he always came back to me but the damage was already done by then. I have to figure out a way to make him laugh in their faces.

I know what you must be thinking, "What kind of relationship is this if you have to change who you are in order to try and make your boyfriend stay loyal to you? Shouldn't that be a given?" You're absolutely right, journal. My brain knows this is sheer insanity while my heart feels trapped by the fact that I have now chosen Marcus over my mother and my friendship with Mary. If I had the strength to stay away from him, which I willingly admit I don't; he would wind up causing a big scene at the house and my mom would know I met up with him. I made my decision today and now have to suffer the eventual consequences. I will try and juggle all three relationships but know it is just a matter of time before everything comes crashing down.

I am also tired of feeling sorry for myself. Do you know I just walked through this house and drudged up a negative memory associated with each room? How pathetic is that? Why not instead walk through them and remember the fun? My old room that mom uses now had the coolest spray paint job on it at one time. I had such a blast working on it with the gang. The bathroom where me and three of my middle school friends filled the tub to the rim with bubbles and plugged mom's portable spa in it which caused all the bubbles to run all over the floor. I still have a picture of that somewhere because Nicholas had crashed through the door with a camera, hoping, I am sure, to catch a glimpse of one of my friends in the nude. Little did he know we had our tops and underwear on. And I can't forget the kitchen where another friend and I got into a cottage cheese fight one night…I have no idea how that got started but we had it up our noses and in our hair. Another picture of that is somewhere as well. Maybe I will go through some of our boxes in the attic tomorrow and try and find them.

I love you journal and I can't begin to tell you how much better I feel after spending this time with you. I promise to visit more often and won't hold anything back as things unfold with Marcus and I.

Love,
Elizabeth

Standing up to stretch, Elizabeth heard the front door close and her mom call out in a clear voice, "Hi honey, are you home?"

Never feeling the need before to hide her journal, Elizabeth now slipped it under her mattress. She did not want to risk anything so early in the game.

She peered around the door in order to inspect her mother's state. A big smile greeted her, "Sorry I got home so late, but I had a little birthday shopping to do for someone I know." Elizabeth would finally be turning 18 in another two weeks. The impish, playful look on her mother's face caused Elizabeth to feel the first pangs of guilt and regret. Two feelings she had hoped not to feel ever again.

Hugging her mom, she squeezed her eyes closed willing to turn back time. *Why is everyone in my life so inconsistent?* she thought to herself. It had such a yoyo effect on her. In Marcus' time of need, she made herself available until a time came that he would discard her. Then the charm of her mother when things were going well. Elizabeth was never given fair warning of when the tides would turn for the people in her life, but when they did, she was swept out to sea with nobody throwing her a life preserver. Even though she knew it was not in her character, Elizabeth wished she could stop caring. That is where the drugs helped in the past; they made her into a hard ass. Of course, it was very short lived and when the drugs or alcohol wore off, she would be curled up in a ball crying like a baby thinking of what she had said and done to those she loved.

Licking her lips, the thought of a drink was very appealing. Her daydream was so strong that she swore that the smell of gin had just wafted past her nose. That had been the drink of choice for her back in the day. Her first drink would feel like a warm blanket had enveloped her; keeping her safe. The second drink turned her into a real extrovert with a slight comedic side. That third drink, however, was the game changer. Elizabeth would be filled with such a melancholy that it could not be contained in her spirit. It had to be released; sometimes in tears but just as much in anger. She would muster up the harshest criticism to whoever was in her path. Dredging up secrets and spitting them out to the room for all to hear. Seeing the shock on people's faces gave her a real sense of power. She became the evil queen whose hatchet was quick to fall.

She must have tensed up during this reverie because her mother suddenly asked in a serious voice, "Is everything okay, Elizabeth?"

Quickly recovering she said, "Yeah, yeah. I was just thinking that I can't believe I will finally be 18. I have been wanting it for so long. Guess it is time for me to consider finally getting a driver's license, huh?"

Laughing, Helen said, "That would be the proper order Elizabeth; unlike the time you showed up at the house with a car you just bought from the neighbor. You saw no reason why you couldn't drive without a license."

"Well that lasted for about a month, didn't it? I got busted with Andrea at the mall when I accidentally bumped that other car in the Sears parking lot. Serves me right."

Giggling at the memory the two of them went in to the kitchen to discuss dinner.

Chapter 41

They had both opted for a simple can of clam chowder and Elizabeth found it extremely easy to push the thought of Marcus from her mind. When he was with her, she couldn't seem to relax. The energy between the two of them was almost palpable at times. It felt good to relax.

Between mouthfuls of chowder, Helen had turned the conversation to school. "Does it feel weird to only be back at school a few weeks only to have summer break in another week?"

"A little. I mean, I knew what I was getting into when we planned on my transfer. I have my senior year left and then I can put all of this behind me." Picking up the bowl to take a last slurp, Elizabeth placed the bowl on the floor for Cali to lick at the cream on the bottom.

Reaching down to stroke her head she added, "Thanks for putting up with me mom. I am glad to know that no matter how bad I screw up that you will always be here for me."

With a knowing look Helen said, "Thanks for putting up with me too kiddo. I hope the days of screwing up are over for us both."

This last sentence was said very sheepishly as Helen knew that just the day before she had come home drunk.

Since the conversation had turned serious, Elizabeth threw caution to the wind and asked, "Why do you think we are both attracted to the wrong men?"

Staring at her hands, Helen couldn't seem to meet Elizabeth's eyes. "Because the wrong guys seem to possess some energy and life that the rest of us don't have. It is only natural to be attracted to it…like a moth to a flame."

"That's it, exactly! Like a moth to a flame, but then, rather than getting burned when we get too close, it turns into a fly caught in a spider web. You struggle to free yourself but it is impossible."

Reminiscing in a memory of her own, Helen looked up at Elizabeth saying, "Oh, but when the times are good they are oh, so good." Shaking her head, she added, "Almost good enough to erase the bad." With a whisper that Elizabeth had to lean in to make out, she heard the final word, "Almost."

Not trusting herself to say any more without arousing suspicion and with a need to get back to their happy place, Elizabeth raised her glass and in a mock English accent said, "A toast, to moths and flies!"

Helen boisterously added, "Hear, hear!"

Mary had not called once that night and Elizabeth knew that she was being given the silent treatment. Mary wasn't fooled by the excuse Elizabeth had given her for why she couldn't hang out after school that day. Elizabeth wasn't as concerned about it as she thought she would be. Having secured Marcus for the time being had bumped Mary to second or maybe even third place. Elizabeth justified that she was not a "user" but more of a person readjusting her priorities. These thoughts would never fly on paper so she had zero intentions of sharing them with her journal.

With only a week left of school, Elizabeth didn't want things to end on a sour note between her and Mary, so she went to the phone, prepared to face the music. After four rings, Elizabeth was just about to hang up when she heard Mary's voice say, "Hello."

"Hey Mary, it's me, Elizabeth. I didn't interrupt you doing homework or anything, did I?"

In a flat tone Mary answered, "No, my teachers seem as excited about the summer as we are and have really been slacking at school. I actually watched a movie in Biology today."

After an awkward pause, Elizabeth cleared her throat and started with her second lie of the day to Mary. "So, my meeting went pretty good after school today…I…"

"Yeah, about that," Mary interrupted "I didn't want you to have to walk all the way home today so I decided to wait for you outside of the office…only, you never came out. Can you imagine what a jerk I felt like when I finally walked in to ask how much longer you might be only to find out you weren't there?"

Having been caught off guard Elizabeth had no reply.

"What the hell?" Mary added.

Her natural instinct at being cornered like this was to be on the defensive even when she was in the wrong. She caught herself before she could say something she knew she would regret. If she were to confide in Mary, she knew she would not be an ally, having hated Marcus from the start. *Maybe a half truth?* she thought to herself.

"I met a guy," she began, before quickly adding, "Nobody you know. I am not supposed to be in any type of relationship while in recovery."

"Wow, you do work fast," said Mary, but her tone had softened and Elizabeth knew she had followed the right track.

"Nothing serious of course. It's just that I have been pretty lonely since I have been back. I feel like a stranger in a strange land. When I was away, everyone else's lives moved forward while I was locked in a holding pattern. I am trying to find my place again."

Although most of what she had said was the truth, Elizabeth's main goal was to pull at Mary's heart strings.

"I guess I never thought of it like that," said Mary "Well, whoever he is, I hope he makes you happy. It is a relief to me to hear that you have someone to spend the summer with since I plan on heading to Georgia with the family."

"No matter what happens, I just want you to know that you have been the greatest best friend anyone could ever ask for."

Chuckling, Mary said, "Geez, don't sound so cryptic Elizabeth. I am only going to be gone a few weeks and unless you plan on falling off the face of the earth again, we will see each other next month."

"Of course, of course." Wanting to end the conversation on a happier note, Elizabeth said, "I can't wait to see you in the morning. Let's grab slurpees on the way home tomorrow…my treat."

"Now you're talking," said Mary.

After a final goodbye, Elizabeth hung up the phone. A noise just over her shoulder caused her to spin around. Helen was just coming out of the laundry room and seemed very intent on the basket of clothes she was carrying. Without a word in passing she carried it to her room and shut the door. Was Elizabeth just being paranoid or had her mom heard part or all of her conversation with Mary?

In her desperation to clear the air with Mary, Elizabeth hadn't taken proper precautions not to be overheard. *Crap,* she thought to herself, *just when I thought I was tying up one loose end, another comes apart.*

Later that evening, Elizabeth joined her mother in the living room to watch a little TV. Helen was mending some socks and let a few audible sighs escape her between stitches. Those alone confirmed Elizabeth's suspicions that she had heard at least a bit of what Elizabeth had talked about on the phone. During a commercial break, Elizabeth decided to just come out and ask her mom what she had heard.

"Mary and I had a bit of a falling out today," she began.

Feigning innocence her mother asked, "What about?"

"I kind of lied to her about what I was doing after school."

"And what may I ask, were you doing after school?"

"Don't you know?"

"Know what"

Tired of the back and forth Elizabeth lost her patience, "Just spit it out mom. I know you heard something between me and Mary!"

Losing her patience as well, Helen dropped the sock she had been working on in her lap and yelled back, "For crying out loud Elizabeth, why are you putting this on me?" I wasn't eavesdropping, I was just bringing the laundry in!" Releasing one last sigh she finished, "I assume it has something to do with a boy; at least I hope a boy and not a man."

Steeling herself for her mom's reaction when she admitted a boy was involved, Elizabeth said, "Mom, I was flattered that someone took notice of me and when he offered to meet up for an hour after school, I found myself saying, "yes" before I had thought it through." When Helen did not answer right away, Elizabeth finished, "We just walked to Rainbow Records and looked at a couple of albums and then I walked home."

When Elizabeth was done, she looked at her mom and noticed how much older she appeared that night. Weary was more like it. Her posture was stooped and her face just kind of sagged. She had turned 58 that year, but to Elizabeth, looked closer to 60. She knew she had contributed to that with her nights of not coming home in the past or coming home and falling all over things. Her mother had shared with her once that she had a dream where she saw Elizabeth lying in a coffin. With tears in her eyes, her mom had begged her to stop carrying on with the people she had been hanging out with. Having not reached what the program referred to as "rock bottom," Elizabeth was only moved momentarily by her mother's concern, but was right back to what she was doing the same day.

Having found her voice again, Helen said, "I knew you would eventually get involved with a boy sometime or another but had hoped it would be further down the road. With the summer coming up, I am not going to allow you to run the streets at all hours of the night. Even though you will have turned 18 by then, you are still living under my roof and will need to abide by my rules."

Shaking her head in agreement Elizabeth smiled and said, "Of course mom…and anyway after yesterday, I have decided to stay away from any boys from my school." Shocking herself at the audacity in which she just spewed that deception she rose from the couch and picked up the socks that had been folded in the basket at her mom's feet. "I'll just go put these away, OK?"

"Thanks," said Helen, who's face still showed signs of distrust, "I'll see you in the morning then."

In the safety of her room, Elizabeth punched her pillow. Her evening had been spent jumping one hurdle to the next. It appeared that she had cleared them all but at a price. Even though her current stories seemed to appease both her mother and Mary; she had a feeling they no longer completely trusted her. In a single swoop, everything had changed. She had always heard that for every action there is a reaction, she just hadn't counted on the ripple effect of it all. She felt like her one action caused ten reactions. She hoped her mother wouldn't say anything to Nicholas because he would lay into her without mercy. He would want a name and that is something she would not give up.

Not wanting to write in her journal twice in one day, she opted to hit the sack early. Changing into her nightgown, she gave her pillow one last punch and drifted off to sleep. It was not a restful sleep, but one filled with many images. Like someone fast forwarding a video tape. Elizabeth was jolted awake by the last scene of her mother slapping her across the face. Breathing heavily, it took a minute for Elizabeth to make sense of where she was. Clicking on the lamp and reassuring herself that she was in her own room, Elizabeth began to calm down.

She remembered that last image vividly. She was at the apartment where she had met Marcus for the first time. There were about 15 people hanging out with loud music blaring in the living room. Her mother had come looking for her and she had tried to hide out in a back bedroom. Elizabeth was blitzed having smoked pot and been drinking all night. She was sitting on the bed when Marcus entered with her mother hot on his heels. At first, Elizabeth was embarrassed to think that her mother had crashed the party she was at, but she was also scared because at the time, her mother did not know that Marcus was who she was seeing. She had thought that Elizabeth was still seeing this skinny kid who she had been introduced to a month or so before.

Helen tried to stay calm for the first few minutes and used what she thought was an authoritative voice; telling Elizabeth it was time to come home with her. Elizabeth's words were slurred as she refused to leave with her mother. When her mother tried to stand Elizabeth up by pulling on her arm, Elizabeth had screamed, "Leave me the fuck alone" and WHAM! Her head swung back as her mother's slap made contact. Stunned at first because she couldn't think of a time that her mother had actually struck her, Elizabeth swayed on the bed while holding her cheek.

Tears were spilling down her face and she went berserk. It was Helen's turn to be stunned as the vulgar curse words flowed from Elizabeth. She was ranting like a lunatic and finally Marcus was the one begging Helen to just go and reassuring her that he would make sure she got home safely. Helen allowed him to lead her from the room completely unsuspecting of his role in this drama.

That is all that Elizabeth remembered of that night. She woke up the next morning in her own room and her mother didn't speak to her for the entire day, but left notes on the table instead, telling her where she was going and when she would be back. Even angry, she had showed more consideration toward Elizabeth that she herself had shown her mother.

When Elizabeth could trust that she was completely awake, she replayed that night in her head again. *"If I don't get my act together, history could repeat itself here,* she thought, *if I can remain sober, I won't be the crazy girl I was then and maybe my mom won't have such hatred for Marcus. She blamed him for my downfall but I had been doing drugs at least six months before I met him.* Rolling over onto her side Elizabeth gripped her pillow tighter. The shame of the past had bullied her once again; trying to convince her that she was doomed from the start. She knew that she was not the only person in the world who had had a sucky childhood and there were many who had far worse. Although there had been times that she was placed in dangerous situations, she had never been molested or beaten and any confrontations with girls consisted of verbal matches, never escalating into the physical.

Startled by the ringing of her alarm clock, Elizabeth hastily reached across the bed to turn it off. As she rummaged through her closet for something to wear to school, she was overcome with a desire to have a little order in her life. She had gone from totally boring to totally out of control in one fail swoop; all of her own doing, of course, but nonetheless, she wanted to reign the craziness in a bit.

Her main priority was completing her school year and seeing Mary off with her family. Marcus would just have to understand that he would need to wait a little longer until he could see her again. In her mind, she thought that keeping him hanging a little longer while giving him teasers over the phone would ensure that his longing for her would mount. She planned on calling him straight after school while she had the house to herself and there would be zero risk of being overheard…again.

Her final decision of the morning was that she would ask to join her mom at her next AA meeting. Maybe showing each other support would solidify their relationship even more, preparing them both for what was to come. With that settled, Elizabeth took her time applying her makeup and was sitting on the front porch with all of her things when Mary pulled up 30minutes later.

Feeling a bit more in control, Elizabeth was able to relax and she had a great time on the way to school talking of nothing more serious than the football team and laughing as they passed a house that had been TP'd the night before. She had never personally snuck out at night with the sole purpose of covering someone's yard with toilet paper, but had to admit, while admiring the person's handiwork, that it sounded like great fun. Catching Mary's eye in the rearview mirror she could tell she was thinking the same thing. They both nodded their heads as if in agreement and began to laugh again. The ride came to an end as they pulled into the school parking lot while shouting the lyrics to Def Leopard's "Rock of Ages."

Chapter 42

Elizabeth had not been home from school a half hour when the phone rang. Answering it, she was only half surprised to hear Marcus on the other end. He had lasted all of one day before breaking their agreement and calling her house.

"What if I had been my mom?" she questioned him.

"You're the one who told me she usually doesn't get home until five."

"I also told you that I would call you on Friday since it will be my last day at school. You know…part of me thinks you want me to get busted."

Marcus protested, "That is the most ridiculous thing I have ever heard Elizabeth. Forget it, if you don't want to talk to me I will just hang up now."

Determined not to take the bait he was so obviously dangling, Elizabeth decided to bait her own hook, "That is fine with me. I know what day we can meet again, but I can just tell you on Friday. Bye."

She was lowering the receiver towards the cradle of the phone when she heard a frenzied, "When? What day, Elizabeth?"

"Do you promise to never call the house again Marcus?" she cooed into the phone.

"Don't play with me Elizabeth. When?"

She counted to the number three in her head before answering, "How does Sunday sound?

"Why not Saturday?"

"Because I have some friends I need to say goodbye to for the summer."

"Girls or guys?"

Ah, she had him right where she wanted him. It was like an old familiar dance between the two of them. They would sway back and forth, sometimes in a nice slow rhythm but most of the time it was more of a dizzying spin.

She decided to stroke his ego a bit, while at the same time keeping him off balance. "I have already made it clear to my guy friends that I am unavailable. I told them that I am into men, not little boys." Smiling she waited for his response.

"I hope you know that even though you are quite a few years younger than me Elizabeth, that I have never thought of you as a kid. From the first time that I looked into your brown eyes, I saw intelligence and maturity. Hell, you were teaching at that modeling school at 16."

His last words caused a pang in Elizabeth's chest because she really had enjoyed that job. The last time she had shown up late, she had arrived in a taxi with Marcus in the back seat. One of the parents had taken one look at Elizabeth's disheveled state and the grown man she had kissed goodbye and promptly called the owner of the school. Elizabeth was let go the same day.

"Thanks," was all she could mutter in return. "Listen, I have to go, so how about noon on Sunday? I can meet you at the Village Inn for a coffee."

Marcus agreed and after hanging up, Elizabeth tried to gauge her feelings. She knew she was being very clinical about their exchange, but the program had taught them how to self-analyze to help distinguish what was healthy and not healthy.

She knew they both had a tendency to become childish no matter what Marcus has said about her level of maturity. They also seemed to tear each other down only to help build each other back up again. The bond that they did share was that they both had fathers who had died while they were young. Marcus idolized a father that he had no memory of, only parroting stories he had heard his mother tell. She had both good and bad memories of her father, but in the end, felt angrier at him for leaving. Even though he had been murdered, she still felt that he had abandoned her.

It was obvious that Marcus did not have any type of job and Elizabeth wasn't so sure she wanted to spend her summer just hanging out anymore. She herself wanted to get back to work but didn't want to pay her boyfriend's way anymore. At that thought, she reached into her nightstand and grabbed a five-dollar bill in case Marcus didn't have the money to pay for her coffee on Sunday. Placing it in her wallet she realized that she had no specific feelings in anticipation of meeting him. She was glad she had somewhere to be but kind of dreaded where their conversation may lead them.

If they were to ever live together, she didn't want a bunch of roommates hanging around. She wanted to feel like she was in a real grown up relationship.

Wanting to snap out of this line of thinking, Elizabeth decided to do something nice for her mom. After opening the fridge for a quick snack, it was obvious that this was an area of the house that could use some help. By the time Helen walked in the door, the fridge was sparkling clean and the freezer had been completely defrosted.

After peering into both the fridge and freezer, Helen said, "I can't tell you how much I appreciate this Elizabeth. I have been meaning to get to it but am just dead on my feet after my shift at the hospital." Pulling her close, Helen gave Elizabeth a big hug. It lasted a little longer than Elizabeth expected and when they pulled apart, she saw tears in her mother's eyes.

Panicking at the sight of the tears, Elizabeth asked, "What is it mom, what's wrong?"

Grabbing a napkin from the table, Helen wiped her eyes and reassured Elizabeth that it was only her emotions getting the better of her.

"I am just so grateful to have you home with me again, I don't know what I would do without you."

This was not the reaction that Elizabeth had expected and the initial pride she felt from her hard work was swiftly replaced by the guilt of knowing that she was seeing Marcus behind her mother's back again.

A meow at that back door saved Elizabeth from having to come up with something else to say. She opened the door and two of the cats rushed in and headed straight for their bowls. Helen spoiled them by giving them milk. Even though people insisted it was not good for them, Helen was convinced that cats and milk went hand in hand.

Elizabeth pushed any negative thoughts to the back of her mind and was determined to enjoy the moment. There would be plenty of time on Saturday to think of where she wanted things to stand after her talk with Marcus.

Stroking one of the cats, she asked her mom, "When do you think you will be going to your next A.A. meeting?"

Taken aback, Helen replied, "Why do you ask?"

It was obvious that her mom thought that she was suggesting that an A.A. meeting was in order after her recent behavior.

In an attempt to get things back on track, she quickly said, "No, I was only asking because I would like to join you. I think it's time, don't you?"

Happy that the spotlight was on someone else, Helen told her that she would be attending on Saturday and that she would be happy to have Elizabeth join her.

"You don't even have to mention that we are related if that would make you feel more comfortable, Elizabeth." she said.

"I am sure we are not the first generational addicts, mom. I have no problem letting them know who I am. The only other thing I have to do on Saturday is see Mary off, she will be in Georgia all summer."

"That is very sweet of you. I am glad that you to rekindled your friendship. Good friends are hard to find."

Another tug at her chest at her mother's last words had Elizabeth giving a quick excuse to escape the kitchen.

Finding herself in the refuge of the bathroom, she stared at her image in the mirror. Searching her eyes, they withheld their intent even from her.

She was smart enough to know that the feelings of guilt, anguish, and shame were happening for a reason. She knew better and it was her body's way of reminding her that she was out of balance somewhere. This self-inflected nonsense had to stop.

There was no way that she could continue with the emotional rollercoaster that her life had become. It was time to get serious and ask herself what it was that she wanted and then decide who may or may not be in her best interest in fulfilling it.

The games she had been playing with Marcus had to stop. She was not helping matters by always trying to get the upper hand with him. Nobody won when they played that game. Any victory that was felt was short lived. She would confide in her journal after school on Friday and seek the reassurance she needed.

Running a tub and filling it with bubbles was a quick fix and as Elizabeth sunk in to the depths of the water, she could feel the tension of the day sliding off of her skin. She concentrated on her breathing and repeated the word, 'peace' in her head over and over.

It had been a while since she had read a good book so after her tub, she headed to her mother's bookcase and pulled out a V.C. Andrews novel titled, "Flowers in the Attic." Staring at the cover, Elizabeth remembered it being a dark tale about a family even more dysfunctional than her own so she decided to pick something else. There was a nice stack on the floor before she found one with a pretty jacket cover showing beautiful cottages. It was a nonfiction book about Scotland, the country her mother had been born in. Never having an interest in this side of her heritage before, Elizabeth became curious to know more. She brought the book back to her room and proceeded to flip through the pages. She was transported to a place that seemed so simplistic, where people's routines rarely varied but at the same time did not seem boring. There appeared to be a sincere sense of community where everyone looked out for one another.

Elizabeth gave the book a good dusting off when she was done reading it. Rather than put it back where she found it, she placed it in her nightstand drawer. She told herself that if she felt like she was getting down in the dumps she would reach for this book rather than always running to her journal to whine about how unfair life was.

There was a knock on her door and as it opened, she heard her mother say, "The Carol Burnett Show is about to come on. Do you want to watch it with me?"

"Heck yeah," she said as she headed back to the living room with her mom. "Where did you get that cool book about Scotland? It seems like an amazing place."

"Most likely the flea market. I would have to look at it to remember."

Sitting on the couch together, Elizabeth told her she would show it to her later.

They laughed until they cried as they watched Carol Burnett portray Scarlet O'Hara from Gone with the Wind. It was a well-known fact in their house that Gone with the Wind was Helen's favorite movie. Elizabeth was surprised that her mother had not named her Scarlet or Tara in memory of it.

It was only eight o'clock when the show ended, but Elizabeth's eyes were tired and her brain needed a rest to take on the days ahead. Kissing her mom good night, Elizabeth headed to bed.

Saying her prayers, she did not feel worthy of having them answered. She felt like the betrayer, Judas. The crazy part was that she had no idea what she was supposed to gain at the end of it all. She wondered if the outcome would be worth the pain that she would cause and endure to get there.

The sound of crickets finally lulled her to sleep. She awoke surprisingly refreshed and ready to take on the last few days of school.

Chapter 43

The last bell rang on Friday afternoon signaling the start of summer; it was followed by the cheers of the students. Someone brought a boom box and Alice Cooper's, 'Schools out for the Summer' was blasting down the hall. Everyone knew the lyrics and it was comical to see that the cliques had at least this one thing in common. Elizabeth had heard it said that music was a universal language and it looked as if it were true. It seemed to momentarily join people together too because cheerleaders were wishing head bangers a good summer and jocks were high fiving the nerds. Shaking her head, Elizabeth couldn't understand why this camaraderie wasn't shown all year long. Not needing another problem to solve she headed toward the side door for her final ride home with Mary.

Mary was a chatterbox the entire way home. Her plans for the summer were all she could think about. Mary was a country girl at heart and she loved everything about Georgia. She had just launched into the category of food and was regaling Elizabeth with her favorite diners.

"Then there is this little pancake restaurant where they serve warm maple syrup on the side. Real maple syrup, not that fake stuff you get from the store."

Looking toward Elizabeth with her big bright eyes and licking her lips as if she were tasting the syrup as she spoke, Elizabeth laughed. "OK there, chatty Cathy, so what you're saying is that you really love Georgia."

Joining in her laughter, Mary yelled, "Yee Haw."

Elizabeth had really enjoyed this last week of school. Kim's parents had insisted on driving her the last week so Elizabeth was in the front seat where she felt that she had belonged from the start. It wasn't that she did not like Kim, it was just different when she was around. Elizabeth was grateful that Mary had Kim as a friend, especially since she did not know what the future held for her.

Getting out of the car, she turned to wave and said, "I'll be at your house tomorrow morning at eight to see you off."

"Sounds good." And with a roar, Mary shot down the street.

Elizabeth liked to enter the house from the back door so she could see which little strays were waiting for her in hopes of a snack. The crunch of her shoes walking on the gravel driveway was their signal that she was home. They made her feel like a hero as they turned their heads up at her and sang their chorus of meows. She would talk to them and their meows sounded just like they were carrying on a conversation with her. Flinging the door open, she stood aside as they pushed past each other to reach the food dish first.

Elizabeth was confident that she would find her mother in a sober state today. Helen had purposefully taken the day off to celebrate the end of year with her. Although this was a big deal, there were times Helen could make a production out of even St. Patrick's Day. She was touched by how her mother loved to make a celebration out of anything. She had never asked her mom if her parents had been kind in regards to her birthday as she was growing up. She thought she knew the answer already though. She was convinced that the reason her mom did make such a big deal out of Halloween, Valentine's Day etc. was because of the lack of them that she had during her childhood. It was like she was making up for lost time. Something Elizabeth could totally relate to.

"Where's my little Senior?" she heard the moment she walked in.

Smiling she responded, "Technically mom, I am still a junior until final report cards are released."

"Pish Posh, you know you passed."

"Pish Posh?" Elizabeth repeated. "Let me guess, you have been hanging around the new English neighbor that moved next door."

Their light banter continued for the next few minutes leaving them both feeling happy and content.

"Stay right here," Helen said, "I have a little something for you."

Another thing Helen seemed incapable of resisting was giving a gift for everything. They were usually small, cheap trinkets that Elizabeth rarely used but no matter what, she always found herself getting a tiny bit excited each time she heard the next line she knew her mother would say.

"Close your eyes and open your hands," Helen trilled from the next room.

Elizabeth obediently did both and felt a slight weight land on her two upturned palms.

"Open!"

When she opened her eyes, she saw a lovely nail polish kit with six different colors, all very trendy. Included was a nice emery board for filing and a small pair of nail clippers.

"This is so cool," she exclaimed. Kissing her mom on the cheek she said, "Thanks mom, I love it."

Helen was beaming at the fact that she nailed the gift perfectly. Hugging Elizabeth, they both enjoyed the rest of the day with nothing more than just hanging out together.

In the early evening hours, Elizabeth headed to the back alley with a bag of trash. The garbage truck would be picking up in the morning and she didn't want the shrimp shells from their dinner stinking up the kitchen.

Dropping the lid on the garbage can, Elizabeth caught movement out of the corner of her eye. Instinctively spinning around, she saw a man just turning the corner on the next block. There was no mistaking the build or hair on the person and after her initial shock at seeing Marcus, she returned indoors.

In the past, Marcus had been very possessive of Elizabeth but not as someone who cherished what they were trying to keep close. He had kept her in a vise like grip to keep her away from friends and family while at the same time neglecting her while she was with him. He was like a spoiled child who wouldn't share his toys even though he had no use for them himself.

From the moment they met, she could tell that she evoked feelings in him that he was not comfortable with. He had been just as drawn to her as she had been to him. He would hurt her with words and other times with his hands and then show such grief at her sadness in the aftermath of his behavior.

135

Having seen him show classic signs that certain things had not changed, Elizabeth resolved to end things with Marcus. For once in her life, she was not willing to give up the joy that she felt when things were going well with her and her mom. A sense of pride welled up in her as she thought of her family. In no way were they perfect and she was including herself in these thoughts, but in her heart, she knew that both her mother and brother would go to the ends of the earth to help her if she were in trouble.

Marcus gave her a thrill from the raw emotion he evoked, like the other day with Wayne, but it was dangerous and hurtful. She did love the power she had held in the car the last time they parted but she had no right to manipulate him in order to maintain that control. How could she do to someone what she so hated being done to her?

Grateful for the fact that they were meeting in a public place on Sunday, Elizabeth was not so fearful of what his reaction would be. For one thing, she knew that his arrogance would not believe that she would leave him and he would most likely let her go without too much of a fuss. She knew that he would try and sabotage the relationship that she and her mom were trying to strengthen. Causing a scene outside her home as well as numerous phone calls would ensue but as long as she didn't react in the same way that she had in the past, there would be a different outcome this time.

Reciting in her head, Elizabeth repeated: "The definition of insanity is doing the same things and expecting a different result. The definition of insanity is doing the same things and expecting a different result."

Throwing the serenity prayer in for good measure, Elizabeth returned to the house with a newfound confidence.

Saturday morning came in a flash and before Elizabeth knew it, she was giving hugs and kisses to Mary and her family. Waving until their car rounded the bend, Elizabeth set off for home. Enjoying the feel of the sun on her face, Elizabeth took her time. Other than attending the A.A. meeting with her mom in another hour, there were no demands on her time for that day. She usually dreaded time to herself but today she was excited at the prospect of going up to the attic and looking through old boxes. One particular corner of the attic had been reserved for her shoeboxes full of notes from Dunbar Middle School. What a great time in her life that was. She had been head of the drama team, winning numerous awards and loved seeing her name in print for articles she had written in the school paper. In the same token, she loved the mystery she held by being part of Dear Eagle, where her name was not shown due to her being the anonymous advice columnist.

Looking back, this had never held any appeal for Elizabeth; she always opted to chase the next thing whether it be the next high, concert, or just hanging with friends. Middle school was the only exception. She enjoyed most of the memories from that time and it was going to be great fun dusting off old yearbooks and reading through old notes.

Her mind wandered back to the day at hand and the meeting that she was both dreading and looking forward to. This would be the first time that Elizabeth and Helen had ever sat in a self-help group together, where it was for the both of them. Helen had joined Elizabeth in a couple of sessions at Helping Hands because it had been required. Elizabeth was sure that Helen would have preferred to have kept her head in the sand like an ostrich rather than hear all of the gory details of Elizabeth's escapades. Unfortunately, there was no other alternative if you wanted to advance in the game that was Helping Hands.

Helen called out that it was time to leave.

Climbing into the car, Elizabeth asked, "So where is this meeting?"

"It is over the bridge in some Veterans Hall. We will be there in two shakes of a lamb's tail."

Smiling, Elizabeth closed her door and buckled her seat belt. Glancing at her mom, she saw that Helen still refused to buckle up.

"Why are you so stubborn about wearing your seatbelt mom?"

"They are so constricting," replied Helen.

Laughing, Elizabeth said, "That's the point, so if you have to break really hard or hit someone else's car you won't go flying through the windshield."

Helen's retort was, "And what if you hit water and the damn thing decides not to unfasten, what then?"

It still amazed Elizabeth to hear her mother utter such fears when so often she would take her life into her own hands by drinking and driving. Helen feared what might be beyond her control but it would never cross her mind as to the danger she lived in when drinking. If there was any way that Elizabeth could steer today's meeting to this topic, maybe her mother would get it. Then it wouldn't be so obvious that is was targeted towards her. Elizabeth bet that most everyone she would meet that day had at one time or another, gotten behind the wheel after having too much to drink.

At the very least, they would have put themselves in a position to either be hurt in a fight or accident. The women risked being assaulted or raped. Then there was always the chance of blackouts and accidental overdose.

Annoyed at how morbid her thinking had become, Elizabeth did what she always did in this type of situation…she changed the subject.

Elizabeth counted eight cars as they pulled into the driveway, so unless more showed up in the next five minutes this would prove to be a small group. This would allow Elizabeth a chance to get a feel for things without feeling so overwhelmed by a lot of people. Holding the door open for her mother, they entered the hall.

They were met by a dimness that caused Elizabeth to squint in order to see properly. The smell of stale smoke and beer met her nostrils which almost caused her to recoil. Her senses were momentarily confused because this was not what one would expect to be assaulted with at an A.A. meeting. Well, the cigarettes were, but certainly, not the smell of alcohol.

She smacked herself playfully on the forehead as she remembered what type of hall she was in. She had only been to one other Veterans Hall because one of her old friends had a dad that spent most of his days in one. She and Carol would be called to fetch her dad whenever he had failed to return home by dinner time. They knew they would either find him leaning against the bar or in a hot debate over war stories. The bartender would kindly give both girls a drink called a Shirley Temple which was Sprite with cherry syrup in it. On average, it would take them a good half hour to convince Carol's dad to come home with them.

Nobody blamed him for not wanting to return home to his wife because she was a gargantuan woman with a mean spirit. Most weekends, Carol couldn't come out until all the laundry was done and the house was cleaned. During these cleaning spells, they would come across all of Carol's mom's hiding places for her candy and snack stash. They would giggle as they found boxes of moon pies and candy bars; sometimes keeping them for themselves and other times laughingly hiding them in different places to aggravate her mom.

There were times that Elizabeth did feel guilty because after all this woman was the mother of one of her best friends. One of those times was when she would be standing at the school bus stop and she and her friends would see her riding her bicycle to work. It was a comical scene to watch her balance her large frame on this bike with its little basket tied to the handle bars. Nicholas would usually do the background music from the Wizard of Oz while someone else cackled that she looked like the wicked witch of the west. In the moment, it was hysterical but then Elizabeth's loyalty to Carol would kick in and she would heave a sigh of relief that Carol was two grades higher than she was and wasn't there to witness her betrayal.

Coming back to the present, Elizabeth took in the rest of the room. Her eyes had adjusted and she saw that there were floor to ceiling windows covered with heavy draperies. A small slit of sunlight was trying to penetrate them to no avail.

All of the people present seemed to be gathered around one table in particular and as Elizabeth approached it, she could see a large coffee urn. Addicts were known to replace one vice with another and this group was no exception. They were practically elbowing one another to get their cups filled as well as grabbing multiple handfuls of sugar packets. *That should keep them going for the next hour,* thought Elizabeth.

Whispering to her mother she said, "Doesn't this seem like an odd place to have a meeting for recovering alcoholics?"

In response, Helen said," Well, for one thing, not too many places are keen to open their doors to a group of people who admittedly have problems with alcohol. Then maybe from a psychological standpoint, they are replacing the memory of a bar with drinking; whereas, here we are in recovery." Shrugging her shoulders, she added, "but what do I know?"

A voice announced that the meeting would be starting in another minute and asked everyone to be seated. A long table was set up with about 16 chairs around it and reminded Elizabeth of a picture she had seen of the last supper. Smiling, she took a seat and acknowledged the person to her right with a quick nod. There wasn't time to look at each and every person in the room which was probably good because Elizabeth was known to judge people on first appearance.

The person sitting at the head of the table introduced himself and thanked everyone for joining him that day. Elizabeth's hands sat in her lap where they were clasped together, not in prayer but in comfort. Giving her the strength she needed to face whatever was to come.

A sort of roll call of first names started at one end of the table and moved like a wave. "Hello, my name is _____ and I am an alcoholic," became almost a chant as each person introduced themselves. Helen's voice rang out in introduction without any embarrassment and Elizabeth, who seemed to gain strength from her mother's confidence, was able to say her name without her voice cracking; which would have been a dead giveaway of how nervous she really was.

The greetings were followed by an announcement congratulating a couple of people who had reached certain stages of their sobriety, reminding Elizabeth of Helping Hands. As this went on, it allowed Elizabeth a chance to catch a glimpse of everyone in the group. She appeared to be the youngest with the eldest being around the age of 60. Some of the people looked nothing like what Elizabeth would have pictured as an alcoholic. One lady was dressed beautifully with impeccable makeup. Others, however, looked so beaten down that Elizabeth felt such a pang in her heart for them. She began wondering to herself if they had struggled since childhood or if drinking had just snuck in later in life.

The topic that Elizabeth had hoped would come up did not but the meeting was fascinating nonetheless. It began as almost a pissing contest in Elizabeth's view with a lot of "Oh yeah, you think you're such a drunk, well listen to what I have done." Rolling her eyes, she grew impatient with this line of conversation. People's desire to be the best at something, no matter how stupid, just amazed her.

In the middle of these discussions, someone abruptly set their cup on the table and began accusing whoever had made the coffee of using decaf. This comment had an instantaneous effect on the group, causing them to each take quick sips to decipher if what had been said could possibly be true. Like a bunch of wine connoisseurs some swirled the liquid around in their mouths while others breathed in the coffee while closing their eyes as if by shutting off one sense it would heighten the other.

Elizabeth had heard the running joke about how seriously people in A.A. took their caffeine but actually witnessing it was beyond anything she would have imagined. Unable to keep her mirth in any longer, Elizabeth released a loud guffaw. Every head turned to peer at her and she merely shrugged her shoulders and said, "For crying out loud, has anyone thought to just look at the damn coffee can?"

Helen remained beside her, shaking with silent laughter. The effect of her sentence broke the tension and everyone seemed to realize how foolish they had appeared. It wound up being a great opportunity for the head of the table to offer a change of discussion.

He was a man of about 40-years-old with handsome features. There was a weariness to his voice, but a steely determined look in his eyes. "Look at all of us," he began. "Acting like a bunch of simpering fools over a cup of coffee. Does caffeine really have that much hold over you? I think it is time that we all exercise a bit more self-control." After a pause, he continued, "I commend all of you for the strength you have shown to give up alcohol but what I just witnessed shows that until the cause of obsessive natures is figured out, it will continue to rear its ugly head."

There was a lot of head nodding going on as he spoke and Elizabeth was surprised as he finished his dialogue with an apology.

"I am sorry to have taken our round table discussions hostage. A.A. is supposed to be a place that you can go and be treated like an equal, not a place with a designated leader or worse, dictator. I just didn't like what I was seeing and I consider you all my friends and I wish for your victory as much as mine." He looked down at the table as if he were almost ashamed at how much of his feelings he had shared but it had the desired effect. He had everyone's rapt attention.

Elizabeth could almost hear the wheels turning in the heads of everyone at the table. Self-analysis was evidently taking place and the lady with the beautiful make up slowly began to clap. Smiles broke out on a few faces and the applause continued to mount, reminding Elizabeth of the time she had received such a response at Helping Hands.

That is how the meeting adjourned and Elizabeth felt mentally exhausted from the experience but physically energized by the renewed hope for her future. She decided that when she got home, she would peruse the school notes she would retrieve from the attic and save any that may be dear to her heart and chuck the more superficial ones. She had grieved her past for too long and had to come to terms with the fact that she could not have a so called "do over." The best she could do was learn from her mistakes and forge ahead.

"Thanks for bringing me to your meeting mom. I like this place and think I would like to come back again." said Elizabeth.

Helen smiled and said, "Let me warn you though, they are never half as exciting as today was."

Laughing, Elizabeth added, "I will never look at my cup of coffee the same again."

Their ride home was filled with animated talk of moving around some living room furniture and sprucing up a few things around the house to give it a bit of a face lift. Elizabeth felt a sense of relaxation come over her. She thought to herself, that life didn't have to be so complicated. She was beginning to see the attraction of a simpler existence.

Chapter 44

Sitting in the attic amongst a myriad of discarded items, Elizabeth rummaged around for the few things she had stashed herself. A sparkle of color caught her eye as she was rearranging some boxes. Her beloved shoe box was retrieved and Elizabeth smiled as she turned it to view each side which were covered in different stickers. There were pictures of kitty cats, sunsets, and a few actors she had been in love with at the time. The last side of the box made her smile fade as she read stickers that said things like "support higher education" with the picture of a pot leaf plastered on it.

The sticker was an attempt to sully her memories of her middle school days which were pretty positive. She had begun to smoke pot in high school and one day while cleaning her room she had come across the shoe box and was revolted at the sight of what she deemed as childish stickers. She thought she was so cool by slapping the drug related stickers on it. She had even contemplated throwing the whole box away since by then she wasn't in touch with anyone who had written any of the letters but something inside of her convinced her to just stash it up in the attic. Drugs had made her believe she was indifferent to all things sentimental but there had obviously still been a rational part of her buried away that knew the box would be missed some day.

The smell of Love's Baby Soft perfume was released into the air as Elizabeth lifted the lid. She was immediately hit with nostalgia as she breathed in the scent. Every girl in middle school had worn it.

Running her fingers through all of the letters, Elizabeth had no trouble recognizing who each letter was from just from the type of folds that were made. Note writing during that time was almost an art form. Beautifully colored gel pens were the mark of a true letter writer as was the origami style of folding them. They each had a little pull tab that would unfold the letter and reveal all of the secrets inside.

The blue colored letters had been the trademark of her then best friend, June. Grabbing one of those first, Elizabeth felt almost giddy at the memory of their first meeting. They had clashed like oil and water. To this day, she couldn't remember why they had seemed to hate each other on sight. The only class they had together was art where they spent the entire period sending signals of dislike to one another. It ranged from rolling the eyes to doing a mock whisper to someone with every intention of the other hearing every word.

Then as if someone flicked on a switch, they became inseparable. Elizabeth thought she remembered how the ice had been broken. She had been in the middle of a story she was telling and she heard June laugh in appreciation of what she had just said. What the story was about had completely escaped her but she knew that from then on, Elizabeth began to give June a head nod of recognition in the hallway and then there they were…best friends.

141

Girls certainly were strange animals, thought Elizabeth. Minutes went by as she stared at the letter. Her hesitancy at opening it up surprised her.

"What in the world do you have to fear from reading an old letter from June?" She scolded herself. In her haste to open it without backing down, she tore the edge of the letter. Her hands were sparkling as she noticed loose bits of glitter escaping from the note. Taking a deep breath, she began to read.

"Dear Elizabeth, did you get the film developed yet from our cottage cheese fight? If not, do it soon, I have a terrible feeling my butt crack was showing and I want to destroy them before anyone gets a chance to see." Elizabeth was doubled over with laughter because she still had that picture somewhere and sure enough June's butt crack had been showing. They were wearing t-shirts and panties as pajamas that night and her bottoms must have slipped as they were flinging cottage cheese at each other as well as ducking in order to not get hit themselves. Wiping the tears from her eyes, Elizabeth continued to read.

"Does your brother have some weird sixth sense or something? He always seems to barge in with a camera at the most embarrassing times. What was the name of his friend that showed up that night? He was super cute…don't tell him I said that though, OK? Anyway, I have to go now because the teacher is starting to walk around the room. Talk to you later. June."

Laying it beside her Elizabeth grabbed another letter randomly. It was messy looking which meant a boy had written it. It wasn't uncommon in those days for a boy to write a line or two. It was usually gibberish but made you feel so grown up at the idea of a guy singling you out with a letter because nobody else knew that it was just junk inside. They could be imagining all sorts of things. Which is what she had hoped at the time.

Sweat had begun to bead on Elizabeth's forehead and it wasn't until a drop of it dampened the letter she was reading that she snapped out of her daze. She had no idea what time it was but if the stack of letters that filled her lap were any indication, it had been at least an hour. She didn't want to throw them back in without folding them again but also did not want to lose track of which ones she had read and which she hadn't. She opted to stack the unfolded sheets together and placed a vase that she found on top of them which served as a sort of paper weight.

Most of the letters were trivial in nature except for one. It was from her secret crush at the time. His name was Rick and he was what her mom would have described as the whole package. He had dark eyes and even darker hair that swept off to the side. Elizabeth thought she had overheard someone say that his mom was Hawaiian which would account for his perfect complexion. He was the perfect height and wore his jeans as tight as some of the girls. He was super popular but had no girlfriend that Elizabeth knew of. The note had been the one and only one that she had ever received from him.

All it had contained was a sentence or two stating that he had liked the article that she had written in the school newspaper. It ended with him sharing that he hoped that they would have more classes together the following semester. That was it but it was enough for a girl of 13 to cling to.

A sort of melancholy had begun to take hold of Elizabeth as she thought of Rick because it had not ended there. He would remain the guy that would wipe out the memory of any other guy Elizabeth had ever crushed on or even dated. The strangest part of it all was that nothing became of them as far as being a couple went. He was, to this day, the first guy that led her around like a puppy dog. He never made any promises or verbalized in any way that he was attracted to her. He had mastered being unattainable while at the same time not setting you free.

Her mind had fast forwarded to high school where she continued to have a note ready and waiting for him should he pass by her classroom that day. When he would see her, his eyes would light up for a split second before he slid right back into cool mode. He would give her the briefest of hugs while his jock friends would call to him to hurry up.

She knew she had not imagined the attraction that he had for her but they were in two totally different social classes. By then, there was talk of him dating this short (even shorter than Elizabeth) cheerleader, who Elizabeth knew from one of her classes. It had broken her heart when she heard the news and she felt so betrayed by him even though he had never led her to believe anything was between them.

The confusion did not end there because one night Elizabeth was staying the night with a friend when they heard about a neighborhood party. She and her friend had a few joints on them which gained them access to the party even though they had not been officially invited.

Not long after arriving, her heart was in her throat as she saw Rick enter the house carrying a six pack of beer. It gave them the perfect opportunity to talk more than they could at school even though the same people were around. It was like there was an unwritten rule that you could approach people outside of school from certain social circles even if you weren't in the same cliques at school.

They had shared a joint and enjoyed the close proximity that they were in. A few people had whispered to each other as they watched the two of them. It was obvious to others that there was some sort of attraction there. Feeling like an exhibit in the zoo, Elizabeth had excused herself from the table and walked out into the back yard. There was a detached pool cage and some of the other kids were jumping in while pulling others in with them. It sounded like they were having so much fun, which just added to the loneliness that Elizabeth was feeling.

She wished that people could see past the façade of her smiling face and witness what was really lurking beneath it all. She wished people would reach out with genuine friendship and help her demolish the vulnerability that plagued her.

The only other thing she remembered from that evening was waking up on one of the chairs in the living room and seeing a few girls sitting on their boyfriends' laps while they talked. She had tried to play it cool at the fact that she had obviously passed out and was now joining the world of the living again. One of the girls said, "Rick just left…but it was so cute how you fell asleep while sitting on his lap." She giggled after saying it.

What? thought Elizabeth, *I was sitting on Rick's lap and I don't even remember? Oh! If I could just remember, I would savor the memory forever.* It took all of her strength not to try and nonchalantly pry into what had occurred. Girls her age were not stupid and knew that the less interested you appeared about something meant you were dying to know inside.

She had found the friend she had arrived with and they headed back to her house. In the future, she was left with her pathetic attempts of recreating whatever it was she had missed. She would stroll the video arcade that was attached to the movie theater on weekends in hopes of catching a glimpse of Rick. She had fantasies of bumping into him and him asking her to sit down and talk.

Shaking her head as if to dislodge the memories from her brain for good, Elizabeth stood up, ready to leave the attic as well as the past. Now that she was almost 18 and technically an adult, she felt a bit humiliated at the desperateness that she had always worn so openly on her sleeve. She wished that she knew then what she knew now because she would have flat out walked up to Rick and said, "Do you like me or not? Are you embarrassed to hang out with me or do you want to meet up sometime?"

Knowing the truth about a situation from the get go would save people from so much bullshit, she thought. Her stomach began to grumble, letting her know it was lunch time. She descended the stairs and walked toward the piano. There was a strip of mirror along the top of it and Elizabeth stared at her reflection. Her eyes looked on the verge of tears. Elizabeth slowly shook her head "no" at her reflection.

Out loud, she said, "No more tears for the past, Elizabeth. You have already experienced every negative emotion there is to experience. You are a different person now…a better person." She forced herself to smile and held it in place for what seemed like an eternity. When she allowed the smile to drop, she tried it again. This time it fell into place naturally and her whole face changed. Her eyes were glistening but not from tears, her smile revealed her crooked teeth and all but Elizabeth didn't care. The self-pep talk had done the trick. She was ready to take on another day.

Opening the fridge, she began to pile up an array of food on the kitchen table. Today's revelation deserved a smorgasbord. She grabbed a platter from a shelf and created a feast fit for a king. She clicked on the TV and plopped herself on the couch. The Waltons were on and the good old fashioned values that the show portrayed was just what the doctor ordered. Elizabeth immersed herself into their world for the next hour and followed it with Little House on the Prairie. There was nobody there to mock her as she lost herself in these worlds where family was everything.

Later in the day, she was back in her room mentally preparing herself for the following morning when she would officially break things off with Marcus. With her goodbyes to Mary out of the way and her somewhat of a success with her A.A. meeting, she felt that she could focus all of her attention on the next step that would radically change the course her life would take.

She approached the situation like an actor. She recited her monologue as different scenarios popped into her head to the potential outcomes of this meeting. Elizabeth knew that she was only flattering herself with a few of them. One in particular had Marcus pleading for forgiveness for all of his past misdeeds followed by a litany of compliments that he showered on her.

Her goal was to get it over with as quickly as possible. She hoped he wouldn't do anything stupid to try and win her back. Picking at her fingernails in agitation, Elizabeth wondered aloud, "Why do men only want you when it is too late and they can't have you but the whole time you are with them, they show nothing but neglect and discard you like some unwanted trash?"

The room suddenly felt hot; crossing the room, Elizabeth opened the two windows letting in a gentle breeze. Sitting back on her bed, she admitted that she did not have the answer to the question she had just posed but she did know one thing…she was going to look like a million bucks when she handed Marcus his walking papers. She wanted his last glimpse of her to be the only one he remembered. She wanted to erase all images of her stumbling, slurring drunkenness that he might have stored.

Elizabeth also wanted to choose her words carefully. She wanted him to see the Elizabeth that had attracted him in the first place. The one he quickly tried to smother, leaving her in a state of constant uncertainty. Fearing that she would lose him the moment she denied any of his commands.

Rather than have all of these thoughts running rampant through her brain, she decided to log them in her journal. She wanted this to be the last entry that delved into her past. She had made up her mind that she wanted to start a fresh clean journal that only talked of her present and future. Elizabeth recognized the benefit of going over the past to recognize negative patterns and to help heal, but she felt that there was also a danger to revisiting it. She could see how she had softened certain altercations, skimming over injuries and blunting words that were hurled at different people. In an attempt to not re-live the pain, she had altered her memory which then made her think things may not have been so bad. This is what she believed caused her to be willing to meet up with Marcus again when he had first called the house.

Elizabeth had found an old purple gel pen in the bottom of the shoebox earlier. After several attempts at getting it to write she did the old trick of placing a lighter at the tip and letting the flame soften whatever ink was there. To her pleasant surprise, it began to work again. This was the pen she decided to use for this last journal entry.

Hello Dear Friend,

I am sure it will come as no surprise to you to hear me completely contradict everything I wrote to you in my last letter. I now know that agreeing to meet Marcus a couple of weeks ago was a big mistake. Wow, look at me…admitting my faults and not trying to blame others. Seriously though, he caught me in my moment of loneliness where I welcomed anything familiar even if it wasn't healthy for me. Within the first meeting, it was obvious that our cycle of dysfunction picked right back up where we had left it. In this case, dear journal, there is no doubt in my mind that if I were to continue to see him, history would most definitely repeat itself.

I have tried to rationalize things, even going as far as imagining Marcus cleaning up his act by giving up the drugs and getting a real job. If I spent all of my energy trying to save him, I would lose myself in the process. Life certainly is complicated.

Anyway, that bit is sorted but then there is the issue of my mom falling off the wagon. If I am going to be spending any energy on someone other than myself, I would rather it be my mom. I know in my heart that she did her very best in raising us. I couldn't imagine going through my party days while having two children and holding down a job. Through all of my mom's failures, I still commend her for getting up each day and trying again.

I would be lying if I said I wasn't scared about seeing Marcus in the morning. He will be so confused because the last time I saw him I pledged myself to him. I expect him to become angry about the mixed signals I will be giving him. That is precisely why I chose a public place to meet.

145

Wish me luck and the next time I write to you it will be with a beautiful pink gel pen and crisp new journal. Our future looks bright my dear journal.

Love
Elizabeth

Chapter 45

Sunday greeted Elizabeth warmly, literally. She had forgotten to close the windows the night before and the air in her room was muggy and stagnant. She flipped on the fan wondering if she was living in the only house without air conditioning. Turning the clock to face her, she saw that it was nearly nine, giving her three hours to get herself together as well as make the three-mile trek to Village Inn.

Peering into her mother's room she saw the bed was empty, which was a good sign. Helen was always up bright and early. It was a sure sign that she was sleeping it off if she were in bed past 7 a.m.

Finding a note on the kitchen table, Elizabeth recognized her mother's beautiful handwriting. The note said she was at the flea market, one of Helen's favorite places. Groaning aloud Elizabeth said, "Please don't buy any more junk mom." The house was already becoming an obstacle course with each new treasure that her mom brought home. Helen believed that every item she brought home was an antique and was potentially worth far more than she had paid. Elizabeth had tried to tell her that just because something was old it did not make it an antique. Knowing a lost cause when she saw it, Elizabeth just learned to let her mom have her fun and not try to spoil it for her.

Counting three cats already lined up in the kitchen waiting for what Elizabeth was sure would be their second breakfast, she opened the back door to allow any other stragglers in. Taking a can of cat food and tapping the lid with a spoon she instantly had their attention. Feeling like the pied piper, she marched through the house with them all trailing behind her. After sufficiently torturing them, she bent down and filled several bowls with food. "OK, mind if I eat now?" she asked them.

Sitting down to a quick bowl of cereal, Elizabeth figured out what she could wear that was cute but practical. Busses did not run on Sunday and she had nobody that she could ask for a ride, so walking was the only option to get her to where she needed to go.

Settling on a pair of red denim shorts, a white crop top and a pair of Keds, Elizabeth showered and got dressed. The majority of her time was spent blow drying her hair and carefully applying her makeup. Taking a final look in the mirror, Elizabeth was pleased with what she saw. She no longer looked like the naïve school kid that Marcus had first met. A young woman stared back at her. She practiced a few "Hello Marcus...thanks for meeting me," in the mirror before turning away and gathering her things.

She planned her route carefully, picking the shadiest streets and avoiding the main roads. It took her about 40 minutes and when the restaurant came into view, doubts began to creep in her head. She did not want to hurt Marcus or make him pay for any past hurts. She just wanted the two of them to be over.

147

As she walked past the front windows, she saw him sitting in the front waiting area. Once he saw her, he jumped up to open the door. Giving her a quick peck on the cheek he told the waitress they were ready to be seated.

Sliding into a booth and taking the menus that were handed to them by the waitress, they both ordered coffee. While Elizabeth felt awkward, Marcus seemed completely at ease. If things were to go her way, she knew she had to get it together. His appraising looks gave her the confidence she needed to start the conversation.

"So how was your week?" she began.

Flipping his hair back from his face he said, "Good, good. Congratulations on finishing your school year."

It was refreshing to hear him compliment her on her education. When she had originally quit, he was all for it, but it didn't take long for him to use it as a way of making her feel like a failure. Marcus had gotten as far as his first year of college and then quit, but he still acted superior to her in the area of education.

When the waitress returned to the table to take their order, Elizabeth asked for a bagel and cream cheese knowing full well she did not have the appetite for it. She was trying to act normal, but the thought of having to swallow seemed impossible.

She happily listened as Marcus rattled off what he had done the day before; allowing her a chance to wrack her brain for all of the intros she had practiced at home. They eluded her, so she decided to speak from the heart.

Marcus had stretched his arms across the table to show her the calluses on his hands from his guitar practicing. His palms were facing up and Elizabeth placed her hands-on top of them.

In a calm voice she said, "I have to share something with you." Looking into his eyes she knew they would betray her, but she guessed it was best to end things with honesty instead of deception.

Marcus sensed the change in mood and sat up a little straighter in his seat. He did not know if he should pull his hands back or not.

"After careful consideration Marcus, I have decided that it is best if we do not rekindle our relationship."

Marcus was fully aware of their environment and adjusted his intended reaction. Elizabeth noticed all of this in a millisecond. The flash in his eyes, the bristling of his shoulders, and the tightening of his lip were all too familiar signs to Elizabeth and she was so glad that she had the foresight to pick a public place to meet.

"Who are you?" he asked. "The last time I saw you, you were kissing me and giving me all of your new rules." Shaking his head in disbelief he continued, "and now…this?"

He drew his hands away from her and rather than draw attention to herself, she slowly brought her hands back to her lap. It was then that the waitress brought their food and Elizabeth slipped her smile into place and thanked her. Luckily this was a place where they left a pitcher of coffee on the table so Elizabeth was confident that they would not be interrupted again.

His head had dropped down like a child's and he just stared at the table. Elizabeth took a quick sip of coffee to help swallow the lump that appeared in her throat at the sight of him.

"Marcus, please look at me."

He finally tilted his head up and looked at her. It felt like an eternity before he blinked and then to her astonishment he picked up his fork and began to eat. It was then that she was brought back to the reality of the master manipulator that sat across from her.

He was treating her like some sort of toy that he wanted to possess, but there was no real affection there. She wasn't even sure if he was aware of the fact or if he believed his own garbage. One of the terms her mom liked to use popped into her head, "He's full of baloney," she could hear her mom say.

"You are absolutely right, Marcus." She knew that would be a great beginning because who doesn't like to be told they are right.

Thinking that this was an indication that things were going his way, Marcus allowed himself to smile at her.

"I have sent you such mixed signals, it is no wonder you are confused by what I am saying. The way I treated you the other day in the car was shameful. You are a human being and I acted as though I could manipulate you into what I wanted you to be."

Shaking his head in agreement, Marcus wiped his mouth with a napkin and responded. "I get it, Elizabeth. You were afraid I was going to slip back into my old ways so you laid down the law. I wanted you so bad that day when I was driving back to my place. You're the only one I ever loved and I know we can get back to where we used to be."

"That is the problem Marcus...we are trying to regain something we never had. Don't you see? Our relationship began with a betrayal. I cheated on my boyfriend who was also your best friend. It then caused me to lose another friend who was convinced you were coming back to Fort Myers to be with her. I lied to my mother about everything from your age to your occupation. How could we have ever thought a relationship that was built on lies could survive?"

There, she had said it. Elizabeth was out of breath as if she had just run a marathon.

Watching Marcus to try and gauge his reaction, Elizabeth could almost hear the wheels spinning in his head. It was obvious that, to Marcus, this was nothing more than a challenge, like a game that he wanted to win.

Taking a last sip of coffee, Elizabeth signaled to the waitress for the check.

"OK," he shrugged with a smile, "so we didn't start off on the right foot."

"Understatement of the year," she blurted before she could stop herself.

They both began to laugh and Marcus continued, "All I know is that the night I met you, I knew in an instant that I had to have you. I will not apologize for that. We have been through a lot but as long as we stick together nobody can tear us down. Not even your mom."

Elizabeth found herself still very protective about any criticism toward her mother. She chose not to respond to the way he portrayed Helen as the enemy but used his mention of her as a way to steer the conversation to its conclusion.

"Speaking of my mom, I told her that I have been in touch with you." Elizabeth hadn't wanted to lie but thought that this might prevent him from coming to her house and trying to sabotage the relationship that Elizabeth had worked so hard to mend.

149

"You what," he sputtered. Then he changed gears, "What does it matter anyway, you're almost 18 now, she can't tell you what to do anymore."

"That's just it Marcus, it isn't her telling me anything. This is my decision. There is no doubt in my mind that you have strong feelings for me and I have certainly had feelings for you that bordered on the fanatical. But together, we destroy each other and that is not what a healthy relationship is all about."

Marcus sighed and as the waitress placed the check on the table, they both pitched in their share of the bill. In Elizabeth's mind, she had accomplished what she had set out to do but looking at Marcus, she could tell, that to him, this was nothing more than round one.

As they walked out of the restaurant together, she turned to give him a hug goodbye. After the embrace had ended she had hoped they would walk in separate directions but Marcus appeared to want to share her return walk home. This added to Elizabeth's anxiety because she knew that her mother had no idea that she had been seeing Marcus and that is the way she wanted to keep things.

Even though Elizabeth had overlooked the fact that her mother had fallen off the wagon, she knew that Helen would not be as charitable if she were to find out that Elizabeth had been seeing Marcus. Yes, it was a double standard but Elizabeth had no doubt as to the wrath that would ensue, should her deception be found out.

Marcus tried holding her hand while continuing to plead his case. She gently pulled away, not wanting to send the wrong signal. The mental exhaustion of this day was taking its toll on Elizabeth. She finally asked to just stop and sit for a minute.

The rest only gave Marcus additional time to wear her down some more. He brought up memories she did not wish to remember. He romanticized their sexual escapades leaving out the fact that they were all chemically induced. She hadn't even remembered their first time together, she had been so drunk. The next day, he had asked what she remembered and she had said, "I remember us falling off the couch," which made him laugh and say, "we didn't fall off the couch." She had been too embarrassed to ask what he meant but was sure that he was insinuating that they had sex.

Marcus was insistent that nobody belonged together as much as they did and that people like her mother would never understand. He stated that all of the girls that had tried to destroy their relationship were just jealous of what they had and that the moment he fell prey to them, yes, he actually used the word 'prey', he regretted it.

Elizabeth couldn't handle another second of it. She quickly stood up and began to walk as fast as she could towards home. Within a minute, she was out of breath where Marcus was easily keeping stride with her.

Swinging around to face him she screamed, "Stop following me!"

"I'm not following you, I am escorting you home." He began to egg her on, visibly enjoying himself. His arm swept across her as if he were saying "after you."

Anger was mounting in Elizabeth. Anger at his smugness and superiority. How had she even thought for a minute that she would be a match against him? He was years older and though he had been her first serious boyfriend; she, by no means, was his first girlfriend. He had been right when he said that he had to have her. He would have spotted her vulnerability from across the room that night and his need to control others made her 16-year-old self a perfect target.

Looking at him again, she had conflicting emotions. The flash of anger ignited an electrical charge as well. It made her more aware of his physical features. She found her eyes traveling from his lips to his arms and at the same time hating herself for this weakness.

It was obvious he had no intentions of letting her walk on her own and recognizing defeat in the communication battle, she opted for the silent treatment. The quiet was nice and as her aggravation began to wane, she slowed her pace. Marcus was right beside her by now rather than behind her. To a passing stranger, they would look like two people enjoying a walk together. Nobody would suspect the turmoil that they were both feeling, and there was no doubt in Elizabeth's mind that Marcus was struggling in his own way.

As they walked a little further, Marcus attempted to take her hand again, and this time, Elizabeth did not resist. It wasn't as if she returned the grasp that he had on her, she just didn't pull away.

Sensing the end of her resolve, Marcus spoke soothingly to her. Words that Elizabeth had been longing to hear. Tears welled in her eyes because she wanted to believe in him so badly but knew in her heart she could not have both him and her mother.

The thought of her mother brought fresh tears, and she knew that if she did not escape him now, she never would. Pulling her hand free and not caring what she looked like, she began to run. Grateful for her Keds, she ran without looking back. She had heard him call her name once but that had seemed a century ago. Slowing down, she risked a look over her shoulder but Marcus was not there.

She was only about a mile away from home, and she wondered where her sense of relief was. *Wasn't leaving him the ultimate goal?* There was no joy of choosing her mother over him because there were just as many problems with that relationship as there had been with Marcus.

Where is my happy ending? she whispered.

She had made it to the downtown area, and with it being Sunday, none of the stores were open. She peered into the window of the clothing store where she had worked her first real job. Main Street was deserted. Walking across the street, she looked at the upcoming shows at the Arcade Theater.

She told herself that one more rest was all she needed before finishing the last leg of her walk home. Finding a bench in the shade, she was left to her thoughts. Mourning the loss of what could have been between her and Marcus, she cried fresh tears. Wondering how long her mom would be able to stay sober this time, she cried anew.

A rustling noise beside her made her look up. Shading her eyes with her hand, it took a moment for her eyes to adjust and realize that her new company was Marcus. Sitting beside her, he murmured that everything would be all right. In an attempt to be gallant, he removed his t-shirt and began to wipe her face with it. He brought her closer into a hug and pressed her against his bare chest.

The warmth of his hug made her feel cocooned and safe. His lips remained close to her ear as he repeated his consoling words. They slowly moved to her cheek where he left gentle kisses. His hands moved from her back and clasped her neck as he turned her face upward to meet his lips. As they began to kiss, Elizabeth made a half-

151

hearted attempt to push him away but his grip was too strong. She gave in, and her lips began to respond to his.

A rumble in the distance did nothing to stop them until it was so loud and so close they finally broke apart. A motorcycle had stopped in the middle of Main Street, and the rider removed his helmet. It was one of her brother's best friends, Bill. Bill had only met Marcus once but had hated him instantly. Elizabeth had chalked this up to what she knew was Bill's secret crush on her. He was a childhood friend so Elizabeth always overlooked the unflattering descriptions that he had given Marcus in her presence.

The look he was giving Marcus now was of the deepest loathing, which Marcus returned with a sneer. They had been caught in a very compromising position. One that Elizabeth would never be able to talk herself out of. When Bill's eyes rested on her, she saw disappointment. His final look seemed to encompass them both, and this time there was no misreading his intentions as he quickly put his helmet back on. As he raced away, Elizabeth knew where he was headed and knew there was no way that she would beat him home.

Bill wouldn't hesitate to tell her mother what he had just seen. In fact, when she had first intimated to him that they were no longer together, he had threatened that if he ever saw them together again, their friendship would be forever changed and that for her own good, he would narc her out.

For this past week, Elizabeth had stupidly thought that she was the one controlling everything. That she had the final say in where her life would lead, and who she would allow to be in it and not be in it.

The only way she would ever get her mother to grudgingly forgive her for this disloyalty would be to rub her mom's face in her own recent indiscretions, but where would that leave them? If she were to continue to run away from Marcus, she would be utterly alone again.

The thought of Mary appeared but just as quickly disappeared because Bill would get to her as soon as she returned home, and Mary would be angry at her weakness.

Through all of these thoughts, Marcus had just stared at her, waiting to see what was to come. Elizabeth couldn't find her voice. The words came out in whispers that caused Marcus to lean in closer in order to hear. "If I were to go home right now and pack a few things," she couldn't continue.

"Yes?" Marcus asked expectantly.

"Where would my new home be?" she finished.

"With me, of course."

She was grateful for his answer and for the fact that he hadn't hesitated for an instant.

"Let's go then," she said.

The victory in Marcus' voice rang triumphantly as he screamed toward the sky, "Woo-hoo!"

Elizabeth smiled at him and his apparent joy. She loved him and knew that things would be great for a short time. She had grown more emotionally than physically in the past year and was entering this with her eyes wide open.

The last mile home was spent in silence as she planned on what she should bring and what she would leave behind. Facing her mother would be hard enough but facing her journal was unbearable at the moment. It would be tucked away with the letters from middle school, and Elizabeth knew that there would be another day when she would climb those attic stairs and retrieve it.

That day would be when this relationship was finally good and dead, and she would come back to her dear diary with her tail between her legs, asking for forgiveness and understanding. She had started today's battle strong and considered round one to be hers. In the end, Marcus had won the final battle using all of the mental, verbal, and emotional artillery he possessed.

Yes, Elizabeth thought to herself. *I have lost the battle.* She squeezed Marcus' hand and he kissed her again. She would ride this pleasantness for as long as it lasted and like her mom, take one day at a time.

Breathing in deeply, she repeated to herself, *I have lost the battle...but not the war.*